'Mr Hartwell?' a voice called in a reproving tone. 'His Majesty awaits you!'

Francis flickered one eyelid at Mary in the ghost of a wink, said quietly, 'Don't disappear,' and went to make a most elegant bow to the King and to drop on one knee, proffering his arrow balanced across his upturned left hand.

The King, his melancholy face looking genuinely amused, reached to take the arrow with both hands, commenting, 'A most unusual rent, but I've heard the history of it!', and then his eyes fell on the palm of the hand which was offering it, and his amusement vanished. He looked sharply at Francis's face.

'Hartwell,' he said thoughtfully. 'Are you the same Francis Hartwell who sailed to the West Indies with my Cousin Rupert?'

'Yes, Sire, the same,' Francis replied quietly.

'Had I the power then that I have now, you would not have come by those,' Charles said, touching the scarred palm. 'I owe more than I can ever repay to men like you. Why have you never come to claim your reward?'

'I have no need,' Francis replied simply, letting his hand fall to his side. 'I lost nothing but a few years of my life and a little skin, and I learned a great deal.'

The King considered him with close interest, and then said, 'But there must be something you desire, something you lack, which is close to your heart?'

'Only one thing, Sire, and even you can't give me that,' he replied with a wry smile. Then he turned his head slightly and looked across at Mary . . .

Dinah Dean was born in Northamptonshire, but she has lived for most of her life in the Home Counties. She was a teacher until 1979, when she decided to give more time to her writing, and since then has fitted it in 'around local history studies, reading and conversation, well-seasoned with trips abroad, preferably to Scandinavia and Russia.' She lives in Waltham Abbey in Essex which, in some respects, bears a strong resemblance to the fictional Woodham, which also featured in her earlier novels, *The Country Gentleman, The Country Cousins* and *The Briar Rose*. Her six novels set in Russia at the time of Napoleon are *Flight From the Eagle, The Eagle's Fate, The Wheel of Fortune, The Ice King, Tatya's Story* and *The River of Time*. She has also written two Masquerade Historical Romances under the pen-name Marjorie May.

THE MAID OF HONOUR

BY

DINAH DEAN

MILLS & BOON LIMITED
15-16 BROOK'S MEWS
LONDON W1A 1DR

First published in Great Britain 1987
by Mills & Boon Limited

© Dinah Dean 1987

Australian copyright 1987
Philippine copyright 1987

ISBN 0 263 75786 2

Set in Monotype Times 10 on 10.5 pt.
04-0787-79740

Typeset in Great Britain by
Associated Publishing Services
Printed and bound in Great Britain by
Cox & Wyman Ltd, Reading

For Judith, Camilla and Helen

HISTORICAL NOTE

As USUAL, several real people have managed to insin-
uate themselves into this book. They include, besides
King Charles II and Queen Catherine of Braganza and
a number of small dogs; Lady Castlemaine; the Duke
of Albemarle and his physician, Dr Gumble; Lords
Craven and Shaftesbury; Harry Killigrew, Will Chiffinch;
Sir Charles Sedley; Butcher Bridges, who brought the
plague to 'Woodham'; the Reverend Thomas Reeve, his
long sermons, pulpit and hour-glass; the Reverend
Nathaniel Hatley; the refugees in the Forest; Thomas
Farriner, the baker of Pudding Lane; the absent Prince
Rupert and deceased Charles Berkeley, and (believe it
or not!) Polycarp Wharton and his wife Philadelphia,
who later had a daughter called Theophila! The other
characters are, on the whole, fictitious.

CHAPTER ONE

UNDER THE CONCEALMENT of her long, full skirts, Mary Hook delivered a sharp kick to the left ankle-bone of the fourth Earl of Sherford, and unobtrusively moved two or three yards away from him, her golden curls bouncing as she jerked her head in indignation. The noble earl's yelp of pain was lost, as Mary had calculated, in the ripple of relieved applause which greeted the end of the tediously long ode of his own composition that Sir Toby Ward had been declaiming for the edification of Queen Catherine and her attendants.

'Quite delightful, Sir Toby!' the Queen exclaimed with well-meant insincerity, the socially necessary lie troubling her conscience sufficiently to make her pretty Portuguese accent more apparent than usual. 'Now, dear Bellamy, will you sing for us?'

As her fellow maid of honour tuned her guitar with much artistic play of her elegant white hands, Mary moved as far as possible from the intrusive fingers of Lord Sherford and found a place by one of the long windows overlooking the river. It was open, but there was not a breath of air, and the sun beat down unmercifully on the water and burned the already scorched fields beyond Lambeth Palace on the far bank. Even the trees in the Archbishop's garden had a dusty look and Mary, looking longingly out at them, sighed and wished herself in the cool glades of the Forest above her home at Woodham, away from the stench and heat of London.

Presently Queen Catherine gave up her attempt to

prevent the thoughts of her Court from turning to the
troubles outside the Palace of Whitehall, defeated by
the lamentable lack of talent available to amuse them,
and settled to a game of basset with the Duke of
Albemarle and two of her older ladies, leaving the rest
to their own devices, or their private thoughts and fears.
The Duke of Buckingham embarked on the building of
a house of cards—an art for which he had a singular
talent—encouraged by a gaggle of chattering, giggling
females. Lord Sherford stood in a far corner, gazing
frowningly at Mary, who ignored him, and some of the
more serious-minded gentlemen drew together near
Mary's window to speculate about the significance of
the distant rumble of gunfire which had been heard
three days before, and, more important, the reason for
its cessation.

Mary half-listened to them, vaguely thinking how
pointless it was to give earnest opinions on what might
or might not have happened, when the only facts they
had to go on were that the Duke of York and Prince
Rupert had been refitting their fleet in Sole Bay when
Opdam had brought the Dutch fleet out of the Texel,
and Mr Pepys, that plump little busybody from the
Navy Office, had come running to Whitehall to tell the
King that a battle was imminent. Since then there had
been nothing but that faint rumble, more felt than
heard, which Mary was half-inclined to believe to have
been thunder, for there had been a deal of sheet-
ligthning the past few nights, and the heat was growing
more and more oppressive every day.

'Look here, damn it!' said a low, intense voice in her
ear, making her start in surprise and turn to find that
Lord Sherford had sidled over to her unobserved. 'You
can't hold me off for ever with your whims and fancies!
What do you want of me, for heaven's sake? I've offered
you jewels, a horse, a carriage, a house . . . What's
your price?'

'I have no price,' Mary replied coldly. 'There is

nothing you can offer which would tempt me to your bed, so have done, my lord! I am not to be bought!'

Lord Sherford regarded her broodingly, his dark, melancholy eyes and elaborate periwig giving him the look of a mournful spaniel. Mary felt a little sorry for him, for he was a serious-minded man, not one of the rakehell crew which disgraced the King's Court with their loose ways, and she had no doubt that his desire for her was real enough, and probably was causing him some unhappiness.

'And keep your hands to yourself!' she added, thinking that he might be about to repeat the trick he had tried earlier, which had earned him a bruised ankle-bone.

He gave an impatient sigh, and said abruptly, keeping his voice low enough not to be overheard by the amateur tacticians fighting their imaginary battle nearby, 'All right, then—if there's no other way, I'll marry you! Will that satisfy you?'

This, for Mary, was the final straw. Her homesickness, the nerve-fraying lack of news from the Fleet, the intolerable heat and the fear of plague which it brought with it, had all wrought on her nerves these past few days, and Lord Sherford's ill-timed persistence incurred the brunt of her temper.

'To my mind,' she said icily, 'an honourable man who professes to love a lady offers her marriage first, not as a last resort when he has failed to buy her body at any other price! Do you take me for a green girl, a country wench, to be flattered by your noble self-sacrifice? Your offer, particularly in its mode of expression, is an insult! I will not marry you, I will not bed with you, and I will probably never speak to you again, so pray go away and leave me be!'

She had tried not to raise her voice, despite her indignation, but the nearby group had broken off their discussion to listen, open-mouthed, and to Mary's embarrassment Harry Killigrew, one of the King's attendants, cried 'Bravo!' and clapped his hands.

Lord Sherford, with commendable dignity, gave Killigrew one withering look (which had no effect at all on that merry rogue), said quietly, 'As you wish, Miss Hook,' bowed to Mary, and walked away.

'How can such a golden-haired beauty be so hard on a man?' Killigrew said, wagging a finger in mock reproof. 'I declare he truly loves you, but his old dragon of a mother won't let him marry below an Earl's daughter, so he risks an almighty roasting in offering for you! Won't you have mercy on him?'

'I'm afraid not,' Mary replied firmly. 'I've no doubt that he's sincere, but I don't reciprocate his feelings, and it would be no kindness to give him any encouragement—that would only make his eventual disappointment all the worse.' Killigrew gave her a shrewd and, for once, entirely serious look, and said, 'Quite right, m'dear! You stand by that, and he'll recover in time! Have you heard any news out of the City today?'

'Only that the plague is widespread about Drury Lane and Covent Garden, but I've not heard of it in the City itself,' Mary replied soberly.

At that moment a pleasantly cool breeze suddenly stirred, moving the fringes on the heavy curtains on either side of the open window, bringing with it the sound of a distant church bell. Killigrew glanced across at the handsome skeleton clock, one of the King's collection of time-pieces, which stood on an ornate bracket in the corner of the room. He obviously thought that a tower-clock was chiming the hour, but it lacked ten minutes to eight, and the King's clocks were never wrong. Another bell joined the first, then a dozen or more, and, within minutes, all the bells of London and Westminster were ringing wildly.

'What is it?' asked the Queen, alarmed by the sound. 'Is it ze Dutch? Have zey landed?'

'I rather think, Majesty, that they've been defeated!' Lord Albemarle said, leaning back in his chair and beaming all over his ruddy-cheeked face. 'They'd be ringing backwards if . . .' He broke off abruptly and heaved himself to his feet as the door opened and the tall figure of King Charles strode swiftly into the room with a dozen small dogs at his heels.

There was a susurration of silk as the Queen and her ladies sank into deep curtsies, and the men bowed, their ringletted periwigs temporarily eclipsing their faces, giving them, Mary thought, the look of a group of larger versions of the King's constant canine companions.

'News at last!' Charles exclaimed. 'A note from my brother! The Dutch are beaten, and Opdam killed!'

Catherine clapped her hands, her plain little face lighting up in reflection of the pleasure in that of her adored husband. There was a barrage of exclamations of joy, relief, amazement, and a discreet request from Albemarle, who would dearly have liked to have been present at the battle, for more information.

'Nothing more as yet,' Charles replied, his saturnine face unusually animated with his own pleasure and that of his Court. 'James—the Duke of York—sent only a hurried note. He'll not have had time to write despatches yet!'

'When and where, then?' Albemarle persisted.

'Oh, last Saturday—three days ago!' Charles replied from the midst of a cluster of beautiful ladies, all crowding round him to offer their congratulations and perhaps to catch his notoriously roving eye. 'As for where . . . Somewhere between Sole Bay and the Texel!'

Mary, who had remained by the window, was laughing and clasping her hands together, but some cool little corner of her mind noted the artificial way the rest of the Queen's maids of honour were fawning on the King, and she shook her fair curls a little at the sight of Miss Hall on her knees, having gained possession of the King's left hand, kissing it with every appearance of rapture. Charles, suffering the attention with no more

emotion visible in his face than a deepening of the
grooves between nose and mouth and a slight twitch of
his lips, caught her eye across the room, and black eyes
held blue for a moment as one lazy eyelid drooped in a
wink, thereby sharing an opinion with one of the few
of his wife's ladies who did not choose to make a
spectacle of herself.

'There'll be great doings in the City tonight!' exclaimed
Harry Killigrew. 'Who's for going out to see?'

Several of the young gentlemen whose duties did not
tie them to Whitehall for the evening were enthusiastic
about going to join the Cits in their celebrating, and
departed as soon as the King had returned to his own
apartments. The Queen gave them leave with good
grace, and, when two of her ladies asked if, not being
on duty, they too might venture out, she said, 'As long
as you are masked, escorted, and keep togezzer, I see
no objection, but go to Westminster, not the City, if
you please! I shall ask two gentlemen to go wiz you.'

Mary hesitated, half-inclined to ask if she might go
as well, as the two who intended to make the foray
made their curtsies and hurried out, chattering. Catherine
looked across at her, and said encouragingly, 'Pray go
wiz zem, 'Ook! Zey need a sensible head wiz zem, I
zink!'

The two maids, Miss Bellamy and Miss Webster,
shared an attic room with Mary, and she found them
there, Miss Webster in the act of putting on a velvet
mask which belonged to Mary.

'I shall need that myself, Webster,' she said, with no
particular expression in her voice. 'I'm instructed to
come with you.'

Miss Webster flounced and pouted, as she usually did
when caught in some act of petty larceny or an indis-
cretion with a gentleman, and flung the mask down on
Mary's bed, saying sarcastically, 'Oh, Miss Goody Hook
is to chaperon us, is she? It's hardly worth going, in
that case! I wonder you agreed to come, for you despise

all the simple pleasures of us ordinary mortals, from the height of your superior intellect and morality!'

'Don't be silly, Webster!' Miss Bellamy said mildly. 'I'm glad Hook is coming with us to enjoy herself! You may borrow my other mask if you can't find your own.'

Miss Webster muttered peevishly that the offered mask was the wrong colour and clashed with her gown, but she wore it none the less, and also borrowed a light silk hooded cloak from the kindly Miss Bellamy to cover her fine gown, and the three young ladies, masked and hooded, went down to the door into the Privy Garden, where they found Mr Hyde and Sir Toby Ward waiting for them at the Queen's instruction.

The two gentlemen were an ill-assorted pair, Sir Toby being resplendent in purple silk with at least fifty bunches of green ribbons on his petticoat-breeches, an elaborate periwig and moustachios, while Mr Hyde wore sober black like a puritan, save for an equally extravagant distribution of ribbons, but these were also black. He wore his own lank hair, and had a sour expression on his clean-shaven face.

The little group hastened, in the glow of the descending sun, to the great gate by the Tennis Court, and out into King Street, towards Westminster, where they found New Palace Yard thronged with people, laughing, singing, dancing, with half a dozen bonfires already burning merrily, fuelled by broken furniture, the remains of last winter's faggots, old clothes, and anything else which came to hand. The several taverns were doing a roaring trade, and a butcher was roasting a great joint of beef over one of the fires, with most of the hungry urchins of the neighbourhood watching attentively.

The noise was incredible, for the bells of Westminster Abbey and little St Margaret's were ringing as fast as the ringers could pull them, and Great Tom was adding a regular sonorous boom in a measured fashion, shaking the wooden houses on either side of his tower, so that

anyone wishing to converse had to shout. It appeared
to Mary that everyone had a great deal to say, for all
those not singing seemed to be shouting at the tops of
their voices.

Sir Toby managed to shepherd his charges across to
the steps of Westminster Hall, where a number of
lawyers and clerks who were employed there and about
Parliament had gathered to watch the fun. It afforded
the ladies a good view, while keeping them a little apart
from the roistering commons, but, naturally enough,
the lawyers found it a fine and rare opportunity to flirt
with the Court ladies. They were, however, more
restrained and discreet than most of the Court gentlemen
would have been, and gave Mary and the two escorting
gentlemen little anxiety, save when Miss Webster uttered
her over-frequent and remarkably shrill little shrieks of
laughter at their witticisms.

Mary's attention was caught by the butcher's assistant,
who had hung up a row of cleavers and was attempting
to ring on them in imitation of the church bells, and,
once he got them in the right order, did it very well,
only to be drowned by the hearty strains of the waits,
who came marching smartly out of Broad Sanctuary
with pipes, trumpets, tabors and a couple of fiddles to
add to the cacophony. They took up position near
Mary and her companions and struck up 'Dargason',
soon having most of the revellers dancing between the
bonfires. Unfortunately, the tune lacked any clear
ending, but contained an inbuilt compulsion to continue,
like perpetual motion, and so it did until the musicians
and dancers were near to dropping with exhaustion,
and Sir Toby exclaimed, 'A God's name! Play something
else!' and flung a handful of small change before the
musicians' feet.

'Dargason' ended abruptly and somewhat raggedly
as the men scrambled for the coins, and then, when
they had touched their hats or tweaked their forelocks
in a proper show of thanks, they struck up 'Sellenger's

Round' and followed that with 'John, Come Kiss Me', with hardly a pause. Then, of course, there were cries for the King's favourite, 'Cuckolds All Awry', and after that the waits were felt to have earned their ale, and were allowed a rest.

The bellringers, too, were tiring, and the ringing from the many towers in Westminster and the City gradually died away, many of them ending by 'firing' their bells—repeatedly ringing them down the scale as fast as they could go, sounding, as Mary always thought when she heard it, like someone falling downstairs. The bonfires were dying down for lack of fuel, and the butcher had cut his beef into slices and finished them on a griddle before selling them off with thick trenchers of bread to anyone with the necessary copper. The revellers, mindful of a working day tomorrow, drifted away, and the little group from the Court bade farewell to their legal acquaintances and started back towards the Palace.

'It was hardly worth coming out for!' observed Miss Webster sulkily. 'There was nothing to see but some common people making fools of themselves!'

'What did you expect?' asked Sir Toby, who would probably have preferred going into the City with his cronies to bear-leading a trio of the Queen's protégées. 'Riots and fireworks? These people are poor—they entertain themselves as cheaply as they can, and enjoy it none the less for costing nothing!'

'And no one made you come!' added Mary. She was not really a prig, but there was something about Miss Webster and a few of the other maids which made her respond like one to their silliness.

'Well, I think the King might have given a ball, at least, to celebrate the victory!' Miss Webster replied in a pettish, opinionated tone.

'Oh, Webster! Even the King can't give a ball at a moment's notice!' Miss Bellamy said gently. 'Besides, we don't know any details of the battle yet, and if we hear tomorrow that someone—some people—have been killed, think how dreadfully we should feel if we'd been dancing at a ball tonight!'

'Bellamy, you do have the silliest thoughts!' Miss Webster replied scornfully. 'Nobody of any importance will have been killed! The common sailors do the fighting, and the gentlemen only direct them!'

'I pray God you may be right!' said Mr Hyde in a portentous tone. He was a somewhat austere man, and Mary wondered what he was doing at Whitehall, for he must have found such a profligate Court peculiarly uncongenial.

She was distracted, however, both from the thought and from the conversation, as they neared the gatehouse into King Street, for there was a row of poor houses built along the Palace wall, and the last flames of a dying bonfire nearby flared up, just as they approached, to illuminate the door of one of them. A crude red cross was daubed on it, and the words *Lord Have Mercy Upon Us*!

She caught her breath, and Miss Webster, also seeing the painted sign, gave a shriek and cried, 'The plague! Oh, heavens! Oh, why did I come out? The plague is in Westminster!'

'No doubt it will affect only the common folk,' said Sir Toby sarcastically, having obviously had his fill of addle-pated remarks from an empty-headed bird-wit. 'The gentry and nobility will stand apart and say "Oh, how sad!" and give alms to the survivors!'

'*As men, we are all equal in the presence of Death,*' said Mr Hyde in a very lugubrious voice.

'Oh, pray don't quote the Bible at me!' exclaimed Miss Webster, sounding a little hysterical. 'I cannot abide to have the Bible quoted at me!'

'The Bible!' Mr Hyde was shocked. 'That, madam, was a maxim of Publius Syrus. The Bible, indeed! Really!'

'Well, it sounded like the Bible, and every bit as

horrid and grim!' Miss Webster retorted. 'And I don't care for maxims—they're always very unpleasant!'

'Bow down thine ear, and hear the words of the wise, and apply thine heart unto my knowledge,' said Mr Hyde sententiously. 'Proverbs, 22:17. *That* was the Bible, and some people would do well to pay attention to it!' He spoke in an irritatingly calm and smug fashion, but Miss Webster chose to ignore the innuendo.

'I wonder if the King knows that the sickness is come so close to Whitehall,' Mary said anxiously.

'I doubt if there's much goes on anywhere in England but he gets to hear of it,' Sir Toby replied. 'But I'll mention it to him when I see him.'

'Within the hollow crown that rounds the temples of a king keeps death his court,' Mr Hyde offered even more lugubriously, and Miss Webster gave another scream of either anguish or irritation—it was difficult to tell which.

'It will come into the Palace, and we shall all die!' she announced shrilly.

'Very likely,' said Sir Toby grimly. 'But at least a tomb will be quiet, and free from screeching females!'

'The grave's a fine and private place, But none, I think, do there embrace!' Miss Bellamy said absent-mindedly. 'Oh, dear! I'm sorry—it just came into my mind!'

There was a sudden flash of lightning, which made them all jump. It illumined the statues in the Privy Garden so briefly that Mary felt she had hardly seen them, yet she was left with a vivid impression of a lithe Mercury, poised on the ball of one foot, which she did not recollect having noticed before. Miss Webster, naturally, shrieked, but the sound was almost drowned in a sharp crack of thunder, and the small party broke into a smart trot in order to reach shelter before the rain began.

It was a false alarm, however. No rain fell that night, but the thunder rumbled occasionally, and lightning flashed, seeming to time itself to wake Mary every time she managed to reach the brink of falling asleep, as the head of her bed faced the window of her shared room. She contemplated moving the bed, but there was no room to do more than push it a little way to one side or the other, and even that would entail waking the other two, who were fast asleep; Miss Webster snoring gently, and Miss Bellamy lying quite still and composed, with her sheet neatly tucked over her bosom and under her arms in a very proper manner.

Resigned to lying awake, Mary wondered why she remained at Court, for she could hardly claim to be happy there. After three years, she still longed for home, for the country, and particularly for the Forest, and, but for her obligation to her father to stay until she found a good husband, she would have fled back to Woodham long ago. She was fond of the little Queen, who was a most gentle, sweet-natured creature, and she had a grudging respect for King Charles, despite his faults. He appeared lazy, self-indulgent, easily swayed by any pretty face or neat ankle, and he seemed indifferent to the distress he caused his wife by his insistence on her receiving his various mistresses, although it must be obvious to him that the Queen adored him. He surrounded himself with profligate, degenerate fools and loose women, and did little to curb their outrageous behaviour or their extravagance, and yet, somehow, she could not help, however reluctantly, admitting that he was an extraordinarily intelligent and capable man, making his own decisions and carrying them out with an iron determination and remarkable patience which were almost entirely hidden by his easy manner.

She wondered why so few people realised that he was not the indolent, futile fool he chose to appear. Did it not occur to those who laughed or sneered at him behind his back that a lazy man does not rise at dawn to row himself two or three miles up-river to swim, and play a hard game of tennis for an hour or more when he returned? He might play with his dogs or chase a butterfly during Council meetings, but she knew that he was always aware afterwards of precisely what had been said and who had said it, and usually the meetings concluded by agreeing to follow the policy he had chosen.

She tried to think of anyone else at Court for whom she had any liking or admiration, and found one name and face after another slipping through her mind, dismissed. Of her fellow maids of honour, she had a mild liking for Miss Bellamy, but found the other four irritatingly sulky, empty-headed, and concerned only with getting as many admirers as possible, at more or less any cost, the price usually being what was euphemistically termed their 'favours', and eventually capturing a rich husband, intending, of course, to continue taking lovers thereafter.

They regarded her, she knew, as a puritanical prig, a freak, because, after three years at Court she was still a virgin, and steadily refused all offers and persuasions to change that condition. She supposed that her parents hoped she would marry before long, for that was why she was here, and preferably to someone of wealth and title, but there was no one she would wish to marry among all the men at Whitehall. The rakehells she dismissed out of hand—Lord Rochester, Sir Charles Sedley, Bab May and their like—and the ambitious place-seekers, who might honour their marriage vows (once they had taken them) but were aiming for something more in the way of a bride than the daughter of a mere baronet with a modest estate and two sons.

There was, of course, Lord Sherford, who was a half-hearted rakehell, more interested in politics and position, and who had actually offered her marriage before witnesses, but she could find no spark of interest in her heart for the idea of marrying him, only a leaden reluctance.

In fact, there was only one man in the whole Court, she decided, who she could contemplate marrying with any equanimity, and he was quite out of the question, being a Royal Prince, a confirmed bachelor, eccentric, as proud as Lucifer, in uncertain health, and twenty-six years her senior! Despite all that, Prince Rupert was undoubtedly the most interesting, most intelligent (save for the King), most honourable, reliable, courteous, chivalrous and handsome man at Court. If only she could find a man like him, but attainable, and country-loving, with no desire to spend his life at Whitehall!

The thunder rumbled again, further away, and no flash of lightning came for a long time after, and that was very faint. She thumped her pillows, rearranged the single sheet that was all the oppressive heat allowed for covering, and thought firmly of home, of the cool, green glades of the Forest, and the sweet scent of violets in the spring. She was still thinking of them when Miss Bellamy shook her awake in the morning.

It was still hot, and the leaden clouds had cleared, leaving a brilliant blue sky from which the sun beat down unmercifully. Queen Catherine chose to go riding that morning, and her Court set out, a colourful caval-cade fluttering with ribbons and laces, the ladies as well as the gentlemen wearing broad-brimmed hats a-drip with ostrich plumes of various hues. Their mounts, Mary thought privately, looked more healthy and better bred than some of the riders, being all of undoubted pedigree, glossy and bright-eyed with virtuous, healthy and well-regulated living.

A gallop in Hyde Park raised a little breeze for each rider, which was most welcome and refreshing, but the Queen was not a good or an enthusiastic rider and soon slowed to a walk, and so, of course, must everyone else. Mary observed to Miss Bellamy, who was riding somewhat nervously beside her, that a horse gives out a surprising amount of heat.

'I suppose that's why very poor people in the country still keep their animals in their hovels in the winter,' Miss Bellamy said thoughtfully. 'I hadn't realised that before, though I've often wondered how they could bear to sit in a room next door to one occupied by cows and pigs and things, for the smell is quite dreadful!'

Mary, whose remark had been light-hearted, wished that the girl were not always quite so earnest.

The day crawled along in the usual slow and futile manner. The King and Queen dined in state, as they did on most days, attended by their various ladies and gentlemen, who must stand about looking interested and attentive while the succeeding courses were ceremonially brought in, presented, tasted and served. Both Catherine and Charles ate sparingly, the former mostly in silence, for she had never grown used to being watched at close quarters by any member of the public who cared to come and see the King eat his dinner, which was considered one of the sights which every visitor to London must not miss at any price! The King made a little polite conversation with one or other of his gentlemen, entirely about nothing in particular, for the edification of all the world and his wife and children, who could then go home and boast to their neighbours that they had heard the King express this or that opinion about something of no great importance.

In the afternoon it was too hot to do anything but sit about in the Queen's drawing-room, talking quietly or playing interminable games of cards, while the Queen made conversation with a succession of her ladies and gentlemen. She was engaged in an edgy and acidulous exchange of pleasantries with Lady Castlemaine, still the King's *mâitresse-en-titre* (but no longer the only one), when the King himself entered unannounced in a wave of small dogs, and said abruptly, 'The despatches have arrived from the Fleet!'

Catherine rose to her feet, her great dark eyes on his face and an anxious frown furrowing her brow. Mary also gazed fixedly at Charles, and then glanced about her, amazed that everyone else was smiling broadly, exclaiming excitedly, and apparently quite oblivious of what was perfectly obvious to her. The King had been weeping.

'James?' whispered Catherine, her lips moving, but her voice so faint that it could hardly be heard.

'Is safe. And Rupert,' Charles replied swiftly.

'Zen . . .?' Catherine still looked anxious.

'Charles Berkeley . . .' The King's voice broke. 'Charles Berkeley is dead! He and Muskerry and Richard Boyle . . . killed by one shot! They were standing with James . . . By God! I'll not let James command at sea again! My immediate heir . . . Until we have a child of our own, that is!' he added swiftly, his quick wits catching the *faux pas* before his childless wife could be hurt by it.

'But we—James and Rupert—zey won?' Catherine asked, her voice stronger now that her worst fears were relieved.

'Yes, they beat the Dutch soundly! Sixteen of their sail sunk, and nine more captured! Opdam's flagship blew up, and he with it!'

'And our losses?' asked a quiet but carrying voice amid the hubbub of exultant courtiers. It was Lord Albemarle, who had come in behind the King.

'No ships lost. Some men, but far fewer than the butterboxes lost!' Charles replied, swinging round to face the newcomer, and setting up a surge amid the half-dozen little dogs remaining about his feet—the rest had gone exploring about the room.

'And how many got away?' Albemarle enquired, exercising the freedom Charles allowed him for bringing about the restoration of kingship five years before.

'Forty-three, the Lord High Admiral estimates!' Charles gave his brother James his official title now that he was no longer speaking to a member of the royal family. 'I have despatches from him, from Prince Rupert and the Earl of Sandwich, and they all agree in every major respect,' he added, for James, the Duke of York, was known to take an optimistic view of things in his reports.

'And Lord Falmouth is lost, you said?' Albemarle gave Charles Berkeley the title he had been granted only a few weeks before. 'A great loss. As fine and true a man as any I've known.'

A number of voices agreed with this sentiment, for several other members of the King's Court had arrived, alerted that more news of the battle was available. Mary heard several individual comments, among them the French accent of the Comte de Grammont exclaiming, 'Ze most disinterested, sincere and generous of souls! I shall 'ave Masses said for 'im!' Hardly a tactful remark in a Protestant court, but well-meant. Mr Hyde's lugubrious tones pronounced, '*In the midst of life we are in death! He was a very parfait, gentil knight! How are the mighty fallen in the midst of battle*!' and Mary wondered if he ever said anything in his own words.

There followed so many questions from the more intelligent gentlemen that the King thought it best to sit down (causing another tidal wave of little dogs) and read his brother's account of the battle aloud, occasionally pausing and obviously missing out some parts which might shock the delicate sensibilities of the ladies or cause offence to one or two of the gentlemen. It was an exciting story, beginning with the arrival of a yacht which had been keeping watch off the Texel and came flying into Sole Bay, where the English fleet lay at anchor, with the news that the Dutch had come out—sixty-eight sail—and were headed towards them. It continued with the first sighting off Lowestoft, and a blow-by-blow account of the fighting as each division of English ships came alongside its opposite Dutch division and the hammering began, ten thousand guns killing the wind and hurling their iron balls across the few yards of sea between the two lines. The account rose to a climax with the vast explosion which blew Opdam and his flagship to the darkening skies, and

tailed off with the battered remnant of the Dutch fleet
creeping back to the shelter of the Texel.

After the King's voice ceased to read, there was
silence for a few moments, and it was broken, to
everyone's amazement, by the staid and dignified Duke
of Albemarle, who leapt to his feet and fairly pranced
about with excitement, exclaiming, 'By God, I wish I'd
been there! Licked 'em! Licked the butterboxes to hell
and gone! Oh, I'd give my dukedom to have been there!'

'And next time, so you shall be!' the King said briskly.
'You and Rupert shall command the Fleet when they
come out again, as they surely will! Now, before I leave
you,' turning to the Queen, 'I must tell you that I wish
you and all your Court to prepare to leave here for
Hampton in two weeks' time. I've appointed the
twentieth of June for the day of Thanksgiving for our
victory—that's twelve days from now. I wish you to
leave Whitehall the following day. Can you be ready?'

'Yes, but why?' the Queen asked, amazed that there
had been no previous mention of the move.

'The plague is on the increase. I'd prefer you to be in
a safer place.'

'And you will come too?'

'I'll follow as soon as I may, but *Madame ma Mère*
departs for France that day, and I must go with her as
far as the Nore, and then I wish to go to Portsmouth
to visit the Channel Fleet. I hope to join you after that.
Now, if you will excuse me, Ma'am . . .' The King
went out, as he had come, with his dogs milling about
his feet, yet never, by some miracle, tripping him or
being trodden on by him.

Mary suddenly found herself walking across to where
the Queen sat looking slightly bemused, and heard
herself say, quite calmly, 'Ma'am—if you please—when
you go to Hampton, may I have leave to visit my home?
I've not seen my family for three years.'

Catherine looked at her, her expressive face filled with sympathy, and said, 'But of course, my dear 'Ook! And you may stay wiz zem until we return to White'all!'

CHAPTER TWO

ON THAT FATEFUL day in 1642 when Charles I raised
his standard at Nottingham, Charles Hook of Pinnacles
House at Woodham in Essex was struck by a gouty
rheum, and took to his bed. The King's standard was
blown down during the following night, as Mr Hook
moaned and groaned about the pain in his limbs. His
illness progressed as men took sides for King or Parliament, but, by the time the real fighting began, he was
sufficiently recovered to hobble about with two sticks,
and, on his good days, to drive himself round his land
in a little two-wheeled basketwork carriage drawn by a
steady horse.

As the Civil War progressed, so his illness fluctuated.
Sometimes he seemed fairly well, but at other times he
returned to his bed and suffered mustard plasters and
large doses of electuaries of mixed herbs in various foul-
tasting combinations, which smelt almost as bad as they
looked. At no time was he well enough to pay attention
to affairs beyond his immediate locality, but concen-
trated what energy he had (when he was more or less
up and about) on running his estate, attending to his
household, and reading.

His two sons were aged respectively five and two, and
Mary was not yet born, when he first fell ill. They grew
up accepting that their father was an invalid and must
not be troubled with anything which did not closely
concern the family or estate, but by the time Richard,
the elder, was fifteen, John twelve and Mary six, King
Charles had lost his head and the Prince of Wales had
failed to recover the kingdom and gone into exile, and

the children had observed that outside events nevertheless affected their father's well-being.

He was always worse when the news, from the Royalist point of view, was bad, and when matters came near home. For instance, when the Major-General appointed for the Eastern area proposed himself for a visit to Pinnacles, Mr Hook took to his bed, finding himself too ill to receive him, and Mrs Hook took to hers, declaring herself in danger of a miscarriage, so the visit did not take place, then or later. Once the danger was past, Mr Hook slowly recovered his normal level of poor health, and Mrs Hook airily announced that she had been mistaken in thinking herself with child. By then, Richard had come down from Cambridge, where he took a very good degree, and was enrolled at Lincoln's Inn, where he studied hard and abstained from political discussion, not wishing to cause his father any anxiety. John and Mary remained at home, and both were aware, although they never mentioned the fact, even to one another, that their father frequently rose in the night and left the house, and often shadowy figures slipped out of the Forest and came across the garden, to be admitted to Mr Hook's cabinet on the ground floor, where low voices could be heard talking until the early hours. After these visits, Mr Hook was usually poorly again the next day and stayed in bed, and there was never any sign of the visitors.

Of course, as national events were never discussed, all three young people assumed that Mr Hook was not in the least interested in them and was completely neutral on political matters, so, one day in the spring of 1660, when John was down from Cambridge recovering from the chickenpox, and Richard came out from London to announce with ill-concealed jubilation that General Monck had dismissed the Rump Parliament and was going to bring the King home from abroad, all three were startled by the effect of the news on their father. He leapt to his feet, danced vigorously round the room, snapping his fingers and singing 'Hey Boys, Up Go We!' at the top of his voice, and thereafter was as healthy and active as the next man!

They were even more surprised when Mr Hook was summoned to London by the new King in that merry Restoration summer, and offered an earldom for his services. Mr Hook modestly declined so high an honour but accepted a baronetcy, a pension, and the promise of a place among the Queen's maids of honour for his daughter when the King should take a wife.

Of course it did not take the young Hooks long to discover that their father, after his initial genuine rheum, had never really been ill at all, but had been one of the agents in their strongly Parliamentarian part of the country, first for the old King, and, after his death, for the members of the Sealed Knot, helping the exiled King's various supporters to enter and leave London, and passing on letters, money and information to assist King Charles during his exile.

As Mary prepared for her journey home from White-hall, she remembered all this, and wondered what sort of a welcome her father would give her: whether he might be angry that she had deserted her post, and send her back to join the Queen at Hampton Court.

Several times during the two weeks she had to wait before she could leave she came near to withdrawing her request, but her longing for the country prevented her from doing so. However much she told herself that Hampton was so much better, more countrified, than Whitehall, her heart denied that it could compare with Woodham and the Forest.

The day of the Thanksgiving arrived at last. By then the plague had increased in Westminster and the City Liberties, and was in the City itself, and the mortality bills were rising more sharply every week. Many people who had no duties to keep them at Court had already fled to safer places. The sweltering heat continued, and anyone who complained that it made them feel dizzy or

faint found that their companions backed away hastily
and offered no assistance, for everyone was waiting
nervously for the first case of plague to appear at Court.

The Queen, being a Catholic, attended a Mass and
Te Deum in her own chapel at St James on Thanksgiving Day, but Mary, with the other Protestant
members of her Household, was excused attendance
and went instead to service in the King's Chapel, where
Charles, for once, did not fall asleep during the sermon,
but followed its two-hour convolutions with apparent
close attention. Afterwards he took his wife and her
attendants for a sail on the river in one of his yachts,
although they made little progress, there being hardly
any wind. It was pleasant, though, to sit under the
awnings stretched over the deck and listen to the music
of the royal musicians and the singing of madrigals,
with water lapping against the sides of the small ship,
giving an illusion of coolness.

In the morning, the Queen's Household left for
Hampton, the King set out for the Nore with his
mother, and Mary slipped away with two stout, well-
armed grooms and her maid, to go home.

She chose to go on horseback, wearing a plain habit
and a hooded cloak, for it was too hot to be cooped up
in a hard-seated, springless wooden box of a coach,
jolting over the rutted roads, which were baked to iron
hardness by the long drought. The small valise that
contained her essential needs was strapped to the back
of the maid's horse, her great trunk having been
entrusted to a carrier, and there was no need to keep to
the dusty roads at all, which made for the possibility of
a more pleasant and direct journey.

It was, of course, advisable to avoid the City and the
suburbs between Whitehall and Ludgate, so the small
cavalcade turned left at Charing Cross and worked its
way circumspectly northwards, past Leicester Fields and
on towards Hampstead, where the riders turned more
westerly and rode by way of the villages of Highgate,

Hornsey and Tottenham to join the Cambridge road
well out in the country. They did not stop in any of
them, but rode on steadily, ignoring the fact that in
almost all the inhabited places they passed, people
withdrew indoors, or at least moved back from the
roadside, and eyed them with suspicion or even hostility.

Mary realised that the people who had already fled
from London must have spread the fear of plague in
the areas through which they had travelled, and she
soon saw that they had spread the sickness as well, for
in several places there were cottages shut up, their doors
and windows barred by pieces of rough timber, and the
ominous red cross daubed on their doors. She wondered
uneasily if the plague had yet reached Woodham, or
she herself might be bringing it, for no one knew how
it spread, or why it struck down some people yet missed
others, and gave no warning of its coming, save, as she
had heard, a sudden rise in the death-rate among rats.

At long last the little party reached the great ornate
stone cross, a memorial to a long-dead queen, and
turned off to cross the marshes and channels of the
River Lea on a long causeway, which the townsfolk of
Woodham believed had been built either by the Romans
or by the fairies (and most were not sure that there was
any difference). In the distance they could already see
the white stone tower at the west end of the church,
built to prop up the remnant of the great Abbey church
which was all the townsfolk had been allowed to keep
for their parish use after the Dissolution of the Abbey
in King Henry's time. The gilded weather-cock on its
top, new since Mary had last been here, gleamed in the
sun, facing the south, but it lied, for there was no wind
at all, not a breath of air to lessen the heat of the day.

Once across the marshes, the road passed Mr
Hudson's gunpowder-mill, which provided a great deal
of employment for the townsfolk, and then became
West Street, paved, and lined with a variety of houses,
inns and shops, all timber-framed and leaning at eccen-

tric angles. There seemed to be few people about, but, being a Wednesday, there was no market, and presumably most of the women would have gone shopping in the early morning, and would now be indoors or in their gardens, out of the sun.

One of the peculiarities of Woodham was its corn-mill stream, which served both a corn-mill and a pin-mill, both so close to the church that the latter almost obscured the new Rectory, and then flowed across the road, effectively cutting the town in two, with the only communication by a rickety wooden footbridge or the ford beside it. Mary automatically drew up the skirts of her habit and raised her feet from her footboard as her horse trotted through the water, but she need not have bothered, for the stream was barely an inch deep instead of the usual two feet or so.

'The miller must be having trouble,' observed one of the grooms, who were both local men. 'There's not enough water here to turn the wheel!'

'Maybe the sluice is down,' said the other, discreetly waving to a pretty girl of his acquaintance behind Mary's back.

West Street turned itself into Church Street at the ford, passed along the north edge of the market-place, and became East Street, which was, perhaps, the busiest street of the little town, for most of the shops were here. It had a curious dog-leg halfway along its length, and Mary wondered, as she always did when she passed it, how it came to be there.

At the far end of East Street the town came to an abrupt end at a T-junction with Straight Mile, which took a tortuous route northward to Nessing, and a more reasonable one southward towards Chingford and, ultimately, Stratford-by-Bow. Mary and her escort turned right, and then, almost immediately, left into the Forest lane. As its name implied, this much-travelled lane climbed the long slope to the Forest, where it vanished amid the trees to re-emerge on the top of the ridge at a cross-roads. Just before it plunged into the dark mass of oaks, beeches and hornbeams, there was a small lodge-house on the left, and a track leading to Pinnacles, Mary's home.

The house had originally been a farmhouse, perhaps a little better than most, with a stone chimney at one end of its galleried hall, but Mary's great-grandfather, having put some money at the disposal of one Francis Drake and sat safely at home while that madman went a-voyaging, collected a handsome profit on the sailor's return and promptly invested it, first in the new Muscovy Company, then the Levant Company, and finally (and most profitably) in the East India Company. As a result, Mary's grandfather had been able to afford to rebuild the modest farmhouse in the fashionable Jacobean style, with long windows, ornate brickwork, and four little turreted towers, one at each corner, each sporting an elaborate copper weather-vane. These never agreed, corrosion having impeded their movement, and the unsuspecting visitor received the alarming impression that the wind was blowing simultaneously from four different quarters. The turrets had given the house its name—Pinnacles—but Sir Charles sometimes referred to it as The House of Aeolus because of the vanes.

Mary's eager eyes picked out its eccentric silhouette almost as soon as she topped the first rise in the road out of town, but most people would have been unaware of its presence until they were much closer, for it was built at the very edge of the Forest, and its deep red brick and green copper-roofed turrets merged into the dark, brooding wall of trees behind it.

Her apprehension grew as she drew nearer to the house, and she wondered if she should have sent a messenger ahead to say she was coming. What if her parents were away, gone visiting her uncle in the Midlands, perhaps?

The front of the house faced the Forest across a formal garden, and the back looked over the valley, with the slope of the ground terraced down to the first field and the footpath which ran along the side of the ridge. The driveway from the road passed through a gated arch in the garden wall and opened out into a broad gravelled semicircle before the porched entrance, where Mary dismounted. As she did so, the house door opened and her father came out, dressed for riding, looking just as she remembered him, slim, brisk and handsome, his fair hair barely touched with grey.

'Why, it's Mary!' he exclaimed, not sounding particularly surprised, despite his words. 'I wondered if you'd be coming home for a spell! Has the Court left White-hall, then?'

'Only the Queen's Household. The King means to stay a while longer, I believe. How are you, Father?'

Sir Charles's mobile face broke into a mischievous smile, his dark blue eyes twinkling. 'It's little use to say, for nobody believes a word I say about my health!' he replied. 'I've no reason to feel anything but well at present! John is here—the Inns of Court have sent most of their young gentlemen home for the time being. I gather the plague is bad in London?'

'There are several houses shut up in the western Liberties, and in Westminster, and I heard yesterday that it's been in the City, about Fanchurch Street, these past ten days. People are very frightened, and leaving London and Westminster if they can.'

'You're well yourself?' Sir Charles studied Mary's face seriously, noting that the girl who had left home three years before was now a woman, and a beautiful one at that, but looked pale and tired.

'Very well, thank you,' she replied. 'How is Mama, and my brothers?'

'Richard is still abroad in Portugal, with the Ambassador—he sends a pipe of port wine from time to time! Your mother is well, as you may see for yourself—I believe she's in the stillroom. John, I fear, is sick of love, and spends most of his time pressing his suit!

Come inside. No need to exchange all our news on the doorstep when it's cooler in the house. I must say that it's good to have you safe at home while the sickness is about!'

Mary found nothing changed in the house, except that it seemed smaller and a little more old-fashioned than she remembered. Her own room was just as she had left it, and, by the time she had greeted her mother, changed her dress and supervised her maid's unpacking of her great trunk, which had arrived by the carrier a few minutes before her, she felt quite at home again. The maid, a silent young woman called Eleanor, seemed pleased to find that she had a little room to herself, next door to Mary's, which must have been a considerable improvement on the attic at Whitehall she had shared with ten other girls, for she was moved to say, 'Thank you for my pretty room, ma'am!'

'Did you notice the view?' Mary asked, and sensed, from the girl's blank expression, that, London-born, she had not thought to look out of the window. 'These rooms face west, and you can see right across the valley. It's a fine sight, especially at sunset!'

When Mary returned downstairs, she found her mother had emerged from the stillroom with a great jug of cool lemonade, with half a dozen expensive lemons floating in it, Sir Charles had changed out of his riding-clothes, and her younger brother had returned from his wooing.

John Hook seemed to her not to have altered much since she last saw him, but that was only three months before, as he sometimes walked across from Lincoln's Inn to Whitehall to visit her. He was in his mid-twenties now, but looked younger, and still had an air of hopeful eagerness, as if he expected something pleasant to happen at any moment. Poor fellow—it seldom did, for he had never been very lucky. Unlike his quick-witted elder brother, he was a plodder. Where Richard had left Cambridge with a double first, John had only managed

a respectable degree after an extra year of study, and
his progress at Lincoln's Inn had been hampered by his
first master's sudden death of an apoplexy (not, John
anxiously assured everyone, through any fault of his),
and then he had broken a leg during a visit home. This
had been slow to knit—indeed, he still limped a
little—and now he was home again, his vacation starting
early because of the plague. He had brought a great
pile of books, but had no one to explain the difficult
parts to him, and, he confessed to Mary over the
lemonade, he found much of the legal jargon hard to
follow.

'But I mean to succeed, because Jem wishes it!' he
assured her. 'You remember Jem, don't you?'

'Jem?' Mary was puzzled, unable to place the name.
'Oh—do you mean Jemima Hartwell?'

From the pink flush which suffused his cheeks and
the fatuous expression on his face at the sound of the
magical name, he did. Mary was amazed. She remembered Miss Hartwell as a shy little mouse of a girl, the
same age as herself but seeming younger, all eyes and
too thin, always with an anxious expression and a way
of listening for her grandfather's voice calling her to
run and do this or that, which he did constantly.

'Is she still at Mr Hartwell's beck and call?' she asked.

'Oh, the old gentleman died eighteen months past!
Francis Hartwell has Canons Grange now—Jem's
brother. I don't expect you remember him, though.'

Mary had a brief inward vision of a boy of about ten
or so, of an age with Richard and, to some extent, on
friendly terms with him, but silent, reserved, and with a
fierce restlessness, barely contained, like a hawk in the
mews.

'Did he not quarrel with his grandfather and run
away?' she asked, trying to remember.

'Yes, and when he came back, the old gentleman
wouldn't have him at Canons Grange. His name was
never mentioned at all, from the day he ran off, and

Jem was not told where he had gone or what happened to him. I suppose old Mr Hartwell must have relented in the end, though, for he sent for him just before he died, and they made some kind of a truce.'

'And where did he go?' Mary asked, smilingly accepting another glass of lemonade as her father offered the jug round.

'I don't know,' John admitted, looking a little sheepish. 'I've never liked to ask, and he never mentions anything about it. He doesn't say much about anything personal to himself.'

'He went to serve his King,' Sir Charles said quietly. 'The old gentleman was for Parliament. Francis went to sea with Prince Rupert. I believe he was a prisoner of the Spanish for some years, but no doubt he would rather forget about that!'

There was a short silence as they considered the probable dreadfulness of being in a Spanish prison, but their imaginings fell short of the true horror of such a situation, and then John said, 'Would you like to ride over to Canons Grange with me after supper and meet Jem again? I'm sure you'll be great friends!'

'John, dear!' Lady Hook said gently. 'You've been there most of the day. You must leave the poor girl a little time to herself, and not outstay your welcome. I'm sure Mr Hartwell must be growing tired of seeing you for ever about the place!'

'I don't think he notices much,' John replied, honestly but mistakenly. 'He's always busy. The old gentleman neglected the estate at bit, in the end, you know, and Francis has been putting it in order ever since he came back. If he's not about his fields and meadows, he's with the animals, or in his library with his books—and Oliver, of course!'

'Oliver?' asked Mary, wondering whom that could be.

'Oliver actually owns the house, you see, and everything and everyone in it!' John said with a grin. 'We'll go over in the morning and see if he approves of you. I warn you—if he takes a misliking to you, you'll never feel welcome there!'

'And does he approve of you?'

'I think he's reserving judgment, for the moment, to see how I turn out!' John replied cheerfully.

Mary rose early in the morning, while it was still fairly cool, and went out of the house while only the servants were downstairs, busy about their duties. It was another flawless morning, not a cloud in the sky, and as she passed through the garden, two of the gardeners were watering the parterres, hurrying to finish before the sun rose above the trees and baked the earth again.

The garden was surrounded by a high, deerproof wall, but a little iron gate provided a way through it, and a few yards beyond, the Forest began. Mary followed a familiar path between the great beech-trees, noting that the brambles and other plants were encroaching on what had been a wider path when last she came this way, and she supposed that it was not much used these days.

She had remembered the Forest, during the past three years, as a quiet, mysterious place, but in reality it was noisy. Every tree seemed to have its quota of birds, all singing at the tops of their voices before they settled down to the business of their day. The dry, coppery leaves beneath the trees were full of stealthy rustlings and creepings as small creatures fed on beechmast, and the oinking of pigs could be heard in the distance, where someone was exercising his ancient right to pannage for his animals. Once, a small sound behind her made her turn, just in time to catch a glimpse of a red hind and her fawn trotting across the path, to disappear among the trees. She was glad to see them, for so many of the deer had been killed by the Parliamentary soldiers and by poachers during the Commonwealth that it was feared that none were left.

Presently she came to an open area, where the trees drew back about a dark pool. It was only a dozen yards across, but it seemed strange and mysterious, for the water always looked dark, almost black, yet was quite clear, as she and John had once proved by filling a wineglass with it. A few clumps of sedge sparsely fringed its edges, but no water-plants floated on its surface, and no ripple ever seemed to disturb it, in Mary's recollection. Today, however, this had changed, for a pair of mallard and their gawky, half-grown brood were busy swimming about, up-ending in their endearingly comical fashion as they looked for food. The duck anxiously fussed around them all the time, but the drake pursued his own interests, and seemed a little bored with his family.

By the water was a rough seat, cut from a log by Richard and John long ago. It had a fine growth of moss on it now, and some ferns sprouted from one end, but Mary was wearing a dull green stuff gown, not her Court silks, and she sat down on the moss without a second thought, and relaxed contentedly, pleased to be at home in the cool of her beloved Forest after so long away.

Her home-coming had caused no surprise, and certainly no reproaches, both her parents assuming that she had come to take refuge from the plague, and thinking her wise to do so here, rather than at Hampton, with its constant to-ing and fro-ing of messengers from London while the Court was in residence. She was relieved that she did not have to admit to them how much she had come to dislike life at Court, and she thought fondly of her father, always good-humoured and unfashionably loving towards his children, and her mother, who was a quiet, gentle lady, but had a far stronger character than most people realised. She had brought up her three children to be responsible, sensible and high-principled, as Mary appreciated now that she had seen something of the world and met people who had few principles and even fewer morals. After a pleasant half-hour of idle thinking and watching the antics of the ducks, she returned to the house, finding the day to be already hot as she emerged from the trees, and likely to be hotter.

She was in good time for family prayers, which Sir Charles conducted briskly in the big square entrance hall of the house, standing with his back to the magnificent carved fireplace and overmantel, his wife on his right and John and Mary on his left, and the servants standing in a orderly double semicircle, juniors in front and seniors behind, facing him. After that, the family took a light breakfast in the parlour, during which John repeated his suggestion that Mary visit Canons Grange with him.

'Jem will be so pleased to see you, for she has hardly any friends. There's a dearth of young ladies about Woodham at present, and the old gentleman would never let her consort with anyone below her in rank!' he said. 'You're sure to like her, she's such a dear, sweet little thing.'

Mary thought wryly that she had had her fill of 'dear, sweet little things' at Court, for she had heard these, or similar, words applied to her fellow maids of honour, whom she knew to be, on the whole, first-class, empty-headed bitches (in every sense), apart from Miss Bellamy, who was well-meaning and still comparatively innocent.

'If you're sure the Hartwells won't mind my arriving unannounced,' she said. 'But I'll not walk—it's far too hot already, and likely to be hotter.'

'I always ride,' John assured her. 'It's just too far for a comfortable walk.' Mary was about to say that it was not above three miles, when she recalled John's slight limp and wondered if he still found walking painful.

'I doubt if my horse is fit, even for so short a distance,' she said. 'She had a long and trying ride yesterday, in the heat and dust.'

'You may ride Lucinda,' Lady Hook said between

sips of the new-fangled coffee which she preferred to ale for breakfast. 'She needs some exercise, for I don't ride as much as I was used to do.'

Despite the heat, it was a pleasant ride. They took the track which ran along the foot of the terraced garden and on to Cob End, a tiny hamlet beside a pretty little stream in the shelter of the Forest. On the way, it ran along the very edge of the Forest, and was consequently called the Selvedge. Sir Charles could remember when a deer fence marked the boundary, with the Forest on one side and the path on the other, but the fence had fallen into disrepair during the wars. Just before the path reached Cob End, another track turned off and ran along the top of a finger of a ridge which projected into the valley, and this they followed almost to the tip of the finger, and then dropped down the slope with it, through a paddock, and into the stable-yard of Canons Grange.

Unlike Pinnacles, Canons Grange had not been built all of a piece, but had grown over a period of centuries by a process of accretion. Its core was a stone-built hall-house which had been erected for the Austin Canons of Woodham Abbey to house the bailey of their grange. Timber-framed wings had been added, and then partially rebuilt in brick, the hall had been divided into two panelled rooms, with an upper floor of bedchambers made in its high roof. An entrance hall with a fine porch and a drawing-room with oriel windows had been built on at the side, giving the front of the house a curiously patchy appearance, fast mellowing into something pleasing in its irregularity. Like Pinnacles, it was built at the top of a steep slope, which had also been turned into a terraced garden, but at the front of the house instead of the back, for it faced the valley, whereas Pinnacles turned its back on it. The terracing here was informal and irregular, in the form of a meandering path going to and fro acorss the slope amid a prodigious number of rose-bushes and aromatic shrubs.

From the back, which was not the view Mary remembered, having, in the past, visited the house only occasionally, and then arriving formally at the front door, the buildings did not appear as odd and patchy as they did from the front, for a large brick kitchen had been built across the space between the two wings, and the stableyard behind it had been partly enclosed by two L-shaped brick blocks to house stables, tack-room, haystore and cart-house. From one of these, a groom emerged to take charge of their horses, greeting John with respectful friendliness. Then, to Mary's surprise, John led the way into the house through the kitchen.

'Surely we should go to the front?' Mary whispered, catching her brother by one of the bunches of ribbons at the waist of his breeches.

'I always come in this way,' he replied, grinning. 'We're on informal terms here!'

Mary felt he was carrying informality a little too far, but followed him in without further protest, having the natural curiosity of any woman about someone else's kitchen.

It was certainly worth seeing, for it was better planned than the gloomy equivalent at Pinnacles, being well lit by three wide windows with a long bench running along beneath them containing three large sinks with a small pump apiece let into its top. There was a good big cooking-hearth in a great brick chimney-piece, and no fewer than four ovens of various sizes, two in each side of the chimney-breast.

A stout woman in a clean cap and apron was kneading dough on a well-scrubbed and very large deal table, a younger, slimmer girl was rolling out pastry on a marble slab, a second girl was plucking a chicken at the far end of the table, and a little scrap of a scullery-maid was washing dishes in one of the sinks, and, to judge by the steam, using plenty of hot water for the job! There was a pleasant air of busyness, as if everyone knew what she had to do, how best to do it, and enjoyed her work.

Despite the hot weather, the fire and two glowing ovens, the open windows and door kept the room reasonably cool.

'Good morning, Mr Hook!' exclaimed the cook, smiling at the new arrivals, but without ceasing to wrestle with the dough, and a quiet chorus of supporters echoed her greeting.

'Good morning, Cook, Ellen, Molly, Sukey,' John replied affably. 'This is my sister, come home from Court on leave.'

The entire kitchen staff contrived to bob curtsies without stopping their work, and Mary replied with a courteous, 'Good morning! What a pleasant kitchen!' From the outbreak of pleased smiles on all their faces, the kitchen staff appeared to agree with and appreciate the comment.

'Miss Jemima's in the parlour,' Cook said to John, with a knowing look which contrived to be encouraging without being over-familiar.

'Thank you,' John replied, and passed on into the house, Mary following, still a little dubiously.

They traversed a passage with room doors, all closed, on the left, and long, low windows on the right, looking out on a courtyard which contained a well-head, an assortment of urns and boxes bright with flowers, and a sundial which Mary calculated could never actually stand in the sun in its present position. At the end of the passage, they tripped in turn down an unexpected step and emerged into a square, rather dark entrance hall, panelled in dark oak, floored with black and white marble, and dominated by a great oak staircase. John crossed it without pausing, opened a door on the left, and ushered Mary into the parlour.

It was a big, well-lit room, with the two great oriel windows which Mary remembered seeing from the front of the house, although she did not recall ever having entered this room before. Old Mr Hartwell had received his rare guests in his library, at the other end of the front of the house. There was a great arched fireplace, filled with flowers instead of a fire, and a deal of heavy dark furniture, brightened by a profusion of embroidered cushions.

A young lady was putting the finishing touches to a well-arranged bowl of roses on a small table between the windows. She swung round as they entered, and stood poised for a moment, a damask rose held in her uplifted left hand, and Mary thought what a charming portrait might be painted of her in just that pose.

She was a slight, small girl with big dark eyes in a heart-shaped face, which was made to look too broad across the cheeks by the outmoded bunches of ringlets which sprouted over her ears. Her dark grey gown was also out of date, and not improved by a narrow plain lawn collar at its high neckline. The colour was unbecoming, for she had a pale complexion, and the general impression was, in Mary's eyes, downright puritanical. She knew they were the same age, but Miss Hartwell looked much the younger.

She came forward to greet her visitors with a charming but shy smile, looking a little nervously at Mary, who had put on her man-tailored riding-habit and a broad-brimmed plumed hat for the visit, and consequently made, as she realised herself, a strikingly fashionable contrast to her hostess.

'My sister Mary!' John announced with a flourish. 'I found her come home when I returned there yesterday. The Queen's given her leave of absence while the Court's away from Whitehall.'

'I'm very happy to revive our acquaintance,' Miss Hartwell said, sounding a little like a well-schooled child repeating her lesson, and curtsying in much the same fashion.

'And I yours,' Mary replied. 'I'm surprised that you remember me. I used to come here occasionally, to visit your grandfather, but we never seemed to exchange more than a few words.'

'I was still in the schoolroom, and Grandfather didn't allow me to go into company.' She regarded Mary warily, and then ventured a hopeful smile. 'John's told me about you. I hope we may be friends.'

'Of course you will! Why, you'll be like sisters in no time at all!' John said heartily.

Mary noted with amusement that Miss Hartwell eyed him with the cautious expression of one faced by a very large, shaggy, well-meaning dog, and answered on her own behalf, 'I'll be very happy to have a friend in Woodham. There are very few ladies of our age, I think—at least, I don't recall any, but I've been away for three years.'

'Hardly anyone, except Lady Dallance and her daughters at the Manor House, but she's quite old, and the girls are hardly ever in residence,' Miss Hartwell said a little distractedly, for John had somehow possessed himself of the rose she had been holding and was stowing it away unashamedly in some inner pocket of his doublet. 'Do, pray, sit down, and may I offer you some refreshment? There's fresh lemonade, I think, or cider or ale, or perhaps some coffee . . .?' She sounded dubious about the last-named, so Mary said, 'A cup of ale or cider would be most welcome. It's very hot again today.'

Miss Hartwell went to the fireplace and carefully tugged the cord of the bell-pull, as if she thought it might bring down the coffered ceiling, but no such calamity occurred, so she sat down, very upright, on the edge of a chair which was much too large for her, gazed earnestly at Mary, and prepared to make conversation.

At that moment, the door opened and Francis Hartwell walked in.

CHAPTER THREE

ALTHOUGH SHE COULD barely remember him, Mary
had no doubt that this was the present owner of Canons
Grange, for he still bore a strong resemblance to that
reserved, intense boy. He was a tall man, lean in body
and face, dressed in a plain buff coat and breeches in
the unfashionable style of a well-to-do farmer, eminently
suitable for an active country life. His cravat sported a
little lace, but he wore his own hair, dark and curly, cut
just short of collar-length. There were a few white hairs
visible, although he could not yet have reached thirty.
He had deep-set dark eyes, a beaky nose, thin, firm lips
above a well-cut chin, and thin, mobile eyebrows, which
had risen a little at the sight of the visitors.

'Good morning,' he said, his voice pleasant, but oddly
unemotional. 'You're about early today, John.'

'I thought I'd call before the sun rose too high. It
promises to be a scorching day again. I don't suppose
you remember my sister Mary?'

'Yes, I remember her well—a determined little girl
who wished to ride a great horse, not a wooden hobby!
Welcome back to Canons Grange, Miss Hook. You've
changed somewhat, I think.' His voice was cool, despite
his pleasant words.

Mary made her curtsy, surprised that he had remembered her childish aversion to the poor hobby-horse,
which she had almost forgotten herself, and replied,
'You, too, are a little different, I believe.'

'Hardly the same person at all,' he said unsmilingly,
his eyes calmly considering her fashionable riding-habit
and the swirling plumes on her hat. 'You are a lady in

waiting to the Queen, I gather.'

'No, merely a maid of honour,' she replied, smiling
to show that his error was unimportant.

'Ay, yes—a maid of honour.' There was an odd,
acidic emphasis on *maid* and *honour* which caused
Mary's smile to vanish suddenly, but she said quite
smoothly, 'A lower form of life entirely! The Queen's
left Whitehall while the plague's in London, and given
me leave until she returns.'

Mr Hartwell looked at her, then at his sister, who
was watching Mary with admiration and a touch of
envy on her ingenuous face, and he frowned a little, but
said nothing more.

There was a slightly awkward silence, and then a
footman came in with a tray of bottles, glasses and a
plate of small cakes. He was accompanied by a large
spotted tabby cat, which sat down in the middle of the
room, looked firmly at each of the humans present,
then fixed Mary with a solemn, golden-eyed stare, which
seemed to look through rather than at her.

'This is Oliver,' Mr Hartwell said, looking at the
animal, and then at Mary, as if to judge her reaction to
the formal introduction of a cat.

Mary returned the cat's stare, then closed her eyes
very deliberately in a long, slow blink. When she opened
them, the cat pushed his whiskers forward and blinked
in reply, rubbed himself against her skirts in passing,
and walked purposefully across to a chair with a
cushioned seat, on which he arranged himself artisti-
cally, put his tail over his nose, and withdrew from the
world.

Mary looked at Mr Hartwell, and was pleased to see
that he appeared surprised. 'A friendly cat is a pleasant
change from an army of small dogs,' she remarked.

'Has the King very many now? I thought it was only
half a dozen.' Mr Hartwell was clearly no country
bumpkin, but was acquainted with some aspects of life
at Court.

'Fourteen, I believe, at the last count, but they move about very rapidly, and appear like a regiment!'

'Obviously trained by Prince Rupert. He was ever a believer in brisk movement by the cavalry!' Mr Hartwell suddenly smiled, and his face was transformed. Mary realised, with surprise, that he was handsome, and probably worth getting to know better, not, after all, the dull, sour puritan she had thought him to be at first.

'Will you take a glass of cider, Miss Hook?' Miss Hartwell asked shyly.

'Oh, pray call me Mary!' she replied, turning a warm smile on the girl. 'And I shall call you Jem, if I may. Cider will be most welcome, thank you.'

'Perhaps you'd prefer wine?' Mr Hartwell put in, returning to his former slightly frosty tone. 'We have sack, or canary . . .'

'So early in the day?' Mary opened her blue eyes wide and turned them on him in a shocked manner. 'You mustn't believe that everyone at Court exists in a drunken stupor, Mr Hartwell! I shall be very happy with cider.'

He made her a little bow, his lips twitching at one corner, although whether from annoyance or amusement she could not tell, poured her a glass of cider and handed it himself, dismissing the footman with a slight gesture of one hand. Mary noted that the hand was long-fingered and graceful, but the palm was calloused and scarred to a far greater extent than one would expect in the hand of a gentleman, however hard he might choose to work on his own land.

'Ale, John?' he asked.

'Please, Francis. How is your pregnant mare?'

'She foaled at two o'clock this morning. Not a convenient hour, but she dropped a fine little colt with no trouble at all, despite the fuss she'd been making!'

'And there speaks the man!' Mary said, pulling a face at Jem. 'I dare say he wouldn't call it a fuss if he had to carry a new creature in his body, and expel it into the world!' She was pleased to see that Jem smiled, and did not appear shocked, but Mr Hartwell frowned again and gave her a hard, considering look, then silently offered her the plate of cakes.

As she took one with a polite word of thanks, Oliver suddenly materialised before her, staring fixedly at her hand. She broke off a piece of the cake and offered it to him, and he took it daintily, ate it with the air of a connoisseur considering a work of art, and then washed his whiskers.

'Why Oliver?' Mary asked. 'I thought you were a Royalist.'

'He has a harsh voice, spots on his nose and a dictatorial manner,' Mr Hartwell replied. 'Also, he has ways of arranging things to accord with his wishes. He believes himself to be the owner of the house, but allows his friends to live with him, provided they don't inconvenience him. He once demolished some rump steak intended for our dinner!' Mary laughed, and he smiled faintly in response.

John had meanwhile engaged Jem in a low-voiced conversation, and, after a few moments, her brother said, 'Jem, perhaps you would like to take John to see the new colt, and I'll show Miss Hook the rest of the house, if she would like to see it.'

From the expression on Jem's face, it was clear that she approved the proposal, and John went off with her in a jaunty fashion. Mary put down her glass, and said, 'It's so long since I was here, I've forgotten what the house is like. Not that I ever saw anything but the hall and the library, for your grandfather seemed to have no great liking for young people!'

'I've made some alterations, in any case,' Mr Hartwell replied, ushering her out into the hall in an unhurried manner. Oliver followed, no doubt to make sure that his property was shown off in a suitable manner by his man.

The dining-room was opposite, across the hall, and

they went there first, Mr Hartwell commenting, 'My great-great-grandfather, Matthew Hartwell, was given this house by King Henry when the Abbey was dissolved. This was part of the great hall, but he divided that into two to make this room and the library, and put another floor into the roof. The panelling was his work, and the furniture, but my grandfather cleared it all out and had only a flimsy little table and a couple of chairs. I found the old things in a barn, and brought them back.' He seemed to lose some of his reserve in talking about the house, and his expression already seemed more lively.

The room was dominated by a great oak table, long enough to seat a score of people, with high-backed chairs ranged round it, and two grand court-cupboards stood one on each side of the big arched fireplace. They were set with a display of silver which made Mary raise her eyebrows slightly, and revise her assumption that the family was not very wealthy.

'It's impressive, but a little dark,' she ventured, hoping he would not think her rude.

'Glass was expensive in those days, so the windows were made too small. I've debated whether to alter them, but that would spoil the ornamental work round them on the outside, so I've left them. It looks better with a good fire and plenty of candles.'

He crossed to one of the court-cupboards and picked up a pretty chased silver goblet, which he handed to Mary, who had followed him.

'Old Matthew's wife bought that at the sale of some of the Abbey's less important possessions,' he said. 'It was a chalice, of course, and she disliked the thought of its being used for secular purposes, so we never use it. She was the daughter of the last bailey of the grange.'

'Is that how her husband came to own the house?'

'No. He already had it before he married her. It was a gift from the King for saving his life. I'll explain that later, if you're interested.'

Mary said that she was, and looked at the little

chalice, wondering what had happened to all the treasures which the Abbey must once have held, for she did not know of anything in use in the parish church which had come from the Abbey. The present chalices had been a gift from one of the Lords of the Manor after the Dissolution. She put the one she was holding carefully back in its place, and went with Mr Hartwell out into the hall and round the corner, into the wide passage which led towards the library. She remembered it from her few visits to the old Mr Hartwell, but had never seen the row of portraits which now hung along the right-hand wall.

'These are our ancestors,' Mr Hartwell said. 'Grandfather kept them in one of the attics. My father . . .' He paused before the portrait of a young man with a milder version of his own face, and appearing much the same age. 'He died of the plague, together with my mother, my elder brother and two sisters. Jem and I survived.'

'You recovered from the plague?' Mary asked incredulously, for she thought that the sickness was usually fatal.

'Yes. Sturdy children often do, and a few adults, but only about one in four, at best. Jem had a poorer chance than I, being only a baby, but she must be stronger than she looks. This next is my mother. She's much like Jem, I think.'

There was, indeed, a marked resemblance, and Mary said, 'I can see where Jem got her pretty face!'

'She considers herself plain. Perhaps you can convince her otherwise, if you really think her pretty.'

'Of course.'

'Grandfather. I expect you remember him?'

Mary studied the stern, elderly, painted face and thought that the original had looked fiercer and more ill-tempered, but she said only, 'A good likeness. Is there no portrait of his wife?'

'No. She died after only a year of marriage, and he

never took another. The next is my great-grandfather. He was a great friend of your great-grandfather, and prospered with him through the India trade. His wife was a lady in waiting to Queen Elizabeth, who disapproved of the match, so they eloped. She was forgiven, eventually!'

Mary studied the two faces, so typical of their time, for the eyes were watchful, secretive, and both looked as if there was not a single spark of romance in them.

'How odd the ruffs look!' she commented. 'As if their heads have been cut off and put on plates!'

'A good many were, in those days!' he returned wryly. 'This is old Matthew and his dear Kate.'

Mary found the portrait of Matthew Hartwell quite startling, it looked so lifelike compared with the others, as if the man's vital personality had overcome the artistic conventions of his time. A pair of bright, enquiring dark eyes seemed to be looking at her with interest, and the lips were parted and seemed to be on the brink of a smile. He bore some likeness to the man standing beside her, particularly about the nose and chin, but looked a great deal more lively.

'Why is he holding an arrow?' she asked, noticing that this unlikely object was held nonchalantly in the sitter's left hand.

'He went hunting with the King and the Court in the Forest, and a local fellow with a grudge tried to shoot the King with a longbow. Matthew caught the arrow in mid-flight, through the palm of his left hand, and the King gave him Canons Grange and the estate as a reward, at a peppercorn rent of one arrow every seventh year!'

Mr Hartwell seemed to catch some of his ancestor's vitality as he spoke, for he smiled, his eyes gleamed, and he sounded far more warm, human and likeable than before.

'What a pleasant story to have about an ancestor!' Mary exclaimed. 'Was he a courtier, then?'

'No. He was the younger son of a West Country
knight, and went into Law to make his own way in the
world. He entered the King's service in the office set up
to administer the property of the dissolved monasteries,
and came here on that business, when Woodham
Abbey's time came. His Kate disliked him at first,
because of that, but changed her mind when she knew
him better! Later, his brother died, and left him the
West Country property as well, and we still have it.
This is his Kate, who was a wisewoman.'

The last portrait showed a brown-eyed, comely face,
framed becomingly by a french hood which showed a
little rich brown hair. Mary thought Kate looked a
pleasant, sensible female, but her mind had registered
that Mr Hartwell had said *wisewoman* as one word, and
she exclaimed, 'You don't mean she was a witch, surely?'

'No, of course not!' he replied sharply. 'A wisewoman
is skilled in healing and the use of herbs. Witch, indeed!
Both Jem and I have inherited some of her gift, I think,
and are very glad of it.'

'I'm sorry,' Mary said a trifle edgily, thinking he had
been a little too scornful about a perfectly natural
mistake. 'Some country folk say "wisewoman" when
they're afraid to say "witch", and I wasn't sure . . .'

He seemed mollified by her explanation, and said,
'She was actually accused of being a witch once, but
there was no truth in it, and Matthew soon put her
accuser to scorn.'

'He saved her life, then?'

'No. In those days, a witch was executed only if she'd
encompassed someone's death, like any murderer. I
don't think those in authority believed in witchcraft
then. The great fuss about it didn't arise until King
James came to England, and was stirred up during the
wars by bigots and charlatans like Hopkins.'

Mary was a little startled to hear the Witchfinder-
General of England so contemptuously dismissed, for
he had been a great power in Essex in his time, but she

agreed with the sentiment, even if she would have been less ready to express it.

'So she married him,' she said. 'Did they have only the one son?'

'No. There were two more, who both entered the church, and four daughters, one of whom married your great-grandfather. Did you not know we're related in the fourth degree?'

Mary counted on her fingers, and exclaimed, 'Why, so we are! Cousin!' and she curtsied, to which he responded with a bow.

'May I ask a favour of you?' he asked abruptly as they entered the library.

'Oh, but this is changed too! There are far more books, and those globes were not here . . .!' she exclaimed, swinging round to look all about her. 'I'm sorry—you were saying . . .? A favour? What may I do for you?'

He stood looking at the floor with bent head for a few moments, and then said harshly, 'I've been trying to find a way of expressing this more tactfully, but I'm forced to the conclusion that I must risk offending the daughter of an old friend in order to make sure that I'm understood. My sister has led a sheltered life here, meeting few people and having few friends. I'd be glad to think that she might make a friend of you, were you simply Miss Hook of Pinnacles, but you're not. You're Miss Hook, maid of honour to the Queen, and you've lived at Court these past three years. I know there's a degree of exaggeration in the tales that pass about concerning the Court, but undeniably it's as dissolute and immoral a collection of empty-headed hedonists as ever disgraced a king, and I will not have my young, innocent sister . . .' He broke off, biting his lip.

'Corrupted?' Mary supplied. She was angry, but her anger showed only in the coldness of her voice. 'You think I shall teach her Whitehall ways? I judged from your tone when you repeated the title of my office that you think me a typical Court *miss*, but you don't know me! I shall not corrupt your sister, if only for my brother's sake, for I believe he hopes to marry her, and I'd not play him such a trick! Nor shall I encourage her in foolish extravagance or careless ways, but you must decide whether or not you choose to believe me.' With that, she clamped her lips together and glared at him.

He could not have looked more taken aback if she had bitten him, and she had to bite her lip to stop herself laughing at his expression, some of her anger evaporating, although she was still piqued by his assumptions about her character.

'Thank you,' he said.

She waited to see if he meant to add anything, but he remained silent and did not look at her, so she resumed, 'As I was saying . . . There seem to be a great many more books here than in your grandfather's time.'

'Yes. I found some of the ancient manuscripts of the Abbey locked in a coffer in the cellar. They're mostly in Latin, apart from half a dozen in Greek, and two Bibles in what I think must be Old English, although I can make little of it. The other books, apart from my grandfather's, I brought back with me from Paris, and have added to since.' He began stiffly, but again became more easy as he spoke of things dear to his heart.

'Paris? But I thought you ran away to sea!'

There was what seemed a long silence, during which he looked at her, his face quite expressionless, and then he turned his gaze towards the windows and said reluctantly, 'I joined Prince Rupert on his voyage to the West Indies.'

'You must have been very young!'

'I was thirteen, but I looked older. I served as a cabin-boy at first, but the voyage lasted nearly five years in all, and I was a junior officer by the end of it.'

'And you returned to France with the Prince in '53, then?'

'No. I went overboard off the coast of Spain on the way back, and was picked up by a Spanish fishing-boat. The Spanish decided I was a prisoner of war.'

'My father said that he thought you'd been in a Spanish prison for a time. I'm very sorry. It must have been a horrible experience!'

'I wasn't in prison.' He was still avoiding looking at Mary, and he seemed almost to be talking to himself. 'They sent me to the galleys. I escaped from there, eventually.'

'The galleys? But were you not chained to an oar? How did you escape?'

He sighed, and looked reluctantly at her face. His expression was that of a man with painful thoughts, and she felt sorry that she had pressed him, having done so at first out of pique, determined to take a kind of revenge for his assumptions about her by making him talk about something which he seemed to wish to avoid.

'It's a long story,' he said. 'Suffice it to say that I did escape, and was picked up by a Portuguese caravel, which took me to Lisbon. From there I made my way to Paris, and, having nothing else to do, studied at the Sorbonne and took my degree, having missed the opportunity of doing so in England. Prince Rupert and Prince Maurice had taught me a great deal while we were at sea.'

'Prince Rupert is a remarkably talented man!' Mary exclaimed. 'Soldier, sailor, chemist, artist, inventor and, now, schoolmaster!'

He gave her a hard look, as if he thought she might be mocking the Prince, but then realised that she was serious. 'I owe him and Prince Maurice a great deal. They taught me French and German, and improved my Latin and mathematics. I think it deplorable that he has received so little recognition for his abilities!'

'Indeed,' Mary agreed warmly. 'I think he's by far the best man at Court, but only the King pays him any attention! How did you live in Paris? Surely it must be costly to attend the Sorbonne?' She was still perversely determined to make him talk about himself, and felt less guilty about it now the subject appeared less painful to him.

'No. The University of Paris is well endowed, and it costs very little for a good worker to study there. I earned my food and lodging and a little money by translating, and writing letters for poor folk who couldn't write—whatever came to hand. Occasionally I received a purse of English gold, which I think may have come from my grandfather, but . . . You know that we quarrelled?'

'Yes.' She now found that she was seeing this austere man in a more favourable light. He had obviously had a hard life, yet he said little about the hardships, giving only the bare outlines of his tale. He now stopped altogether and stood in silence, as if at a loss.

'And you gained your degree?' she prompted.

'Yes. Hence the books.'

'And you returned to England at the Restoration?'

'Yes, but not to Woodham. Grandfather wouldn't have me here. He allowed me to live on the Somerset estate.' He gave a twisted little smile. 'History repeating itself! He'd quarrelled with my father in '44 and sent us all there, out of his sight. The result was that my father went into Bristol on business, and brought the plague home with him . . . It was very bad in Bristol that year.'

He stopped again, then very firmly changed the subject by asking Mary if she had ever seen such a pair of globes before as were in the alcoves on either side of the doorway. She went to look more closely at them, for they were large and very fine, the one on the left being terrestrial, and the other celestial. Oliver was sitting by the latter, looking inscrutable.

'The King has a pair very like them, but not quite as fine, I believe!'

At that moment, the door opened and a footman made a silent entrance, coughed discreetly, and intoned, 'The Reverend Mr Reeve, sir!' then retired, leaving the Rector of Woodham standing in the doorway. Oliver turned his head to look at him, then retired behind Mary's full skirts and peered at him from that safe vantage.

Woodham considered itself lucky, in some respects, to have Thomas Reeve for its Rector, for he was a notable preacher and a good pastor, but less lucky in that his sermons were usually at least two hours long, and the seats of the pews in the parish church were very hard. When he first came to Woodham, his reputation had preceded him, and the Churchwardens collected the money to buy a fine new pulpit to do him justice. The following year, the Lord of the Manor died, and Mr Reeve preached for four hours at his funeral, so the Churchwardens expended a further shilling on an hourglass as a gentle hint. He was a short, spare man, serious in aspect and severe in expression, but genuinely interested in and concerned about the welfare of the people in this large and not well-endowed parish.

'Good morning, Mr Hartwell. I trust I'm not *interrupting* . . . I see you already have a visitor . . . Why, it's Miss Hook, it is not? My dear young lady! I trust you're well? Your father will be happy to have you at home in this dangerous time, and your *mother* as well, of course. How are they? Well, I trust?'

Mary smiled, but made no attempt to answer the flow of questions, save by nodding where appropriate. She recalled with inward amusement that her father usually referred to the Rector as Thomas the Trusting, because his enquiries almost always assumed a favourable answer by means of the iterated 'I trust'.

'Quite well, thank you,' she said when he ceased. She was about to enquire after Mrs Reeve, but recollected in time that the Rector was a bachelor, and substituted, 'And is Mr Hatley still your curate?'

'Yes, thanks be! And I trust will so continue for many years—an *invaluable* man! His poor wife died in March, but his children have sustained him, I'm glad to say . . . Mr Hartwell, may I trespass on your good nature yet again? It appears that Gabriel is *cracked* . . .'

'Gabriel?' queried Mr Hartwell, looking bemused.

'The tenor bell,' Mary informed him in an aside.

'Quite,' Mr Reeve continued, ' . . . and needs to be recast. Thomas Plomer—the Captain of the Tower —says that it will save a deal of *expense* if the bell is got down from the tower and carried to Watford by the parish, rather than bring the bell-founder and his men to fetch it. The ringers say they can get the bell *down*, and Mr Wharton has promised to lend a cart . . .'

'What, George Wharton?' interrupted Mr Hartwell. 'I thought he was still in London.'

'No, no—the younger Mr Wharton, Mr *Polycarp* Wharton . . . He can lend a cart of sufficient dimension, but can't spare the horses, they being needed for hay-carting, it appears—not his, but Lady Dallance's.'

'What does this Gabriel weigh?' asked Mr Hartwell, ruthlessly cutting through the undergrowth.

'Ah!' exclaimed Mr Reeve, patting himself industriously until he located a small notebook in his coat pocket. He consulted it and announced, 'Thomas Plomer said that information might be sought. Here it is—*nineteen hundredweights*! Goodness, that seems a very large amount! Almost a ton!'

Mr Hartwell appeared unimpressed. 'My hay's almost all in. You may have a pair of horses and my tranter next Tuesday, if that will suit.'

'How kind—how *very* kind!' Mr Reeve exclaimed. 'I trust your generosity won't cause you any inconvenience?'

'Is that all you wanted? If it is, you could have sent your lad with a note, and saved yourself a walk in this heat,' Mr Hartwell said abruptly. 'You'd better come and sit down for a while and take a cup of ale before you go home.'

'Most kind, most welcome!' Mr Reeve murmured, allowing himself to be conducted back along the passage and into the parlour. Mary and Oliver followed, the former assuming that the tour of the house had been abandoned.

'In fact,' Mr Reeve resumed when he was installed in a comfortable chair with a tankard of cool ale in his hand, 'there was another matter . . .' He looked nervously at Oliver, who was sniffing at his shoes in a manner which suggested that he might have trodden in something unpleasant. 'Such a very large cat! Quite a *tiger*, I do declare! Or perhaps I should say a *leopard*, he being spotted!' Oliver gave a deep sigh and walked across to Mary, who held out her hand and was allowed to rub him behind his ears.

'Another matter,' prompted Mr Hartwell, who was standing before the flower-filled hearth looking a trifle impatient.

'Yes, and I thought I should consult you about it, and Sir Richard as well, he being a *Justice of the Peace* . . . It appears that a group of poor folk from London have set up camp in the Forest. Two of them were in Horsing yesterday, seeking to buy food.'

'How many?' Mr Hartwell asked.

'About a dozen, I understand. The Horsing folk would have nothing to do with them, fearing they might bring the infection into the town, although they swore they had no sickness among them! The Vicar of Horsing pitied them, and sent to let me know, for it seems that their camp is within our parish. I think we should try to do something for them, if only to sell them food, for it seems they wish to pay their way, not beg. I trust it may be true that they have no infection . . .'

'We could arrange something, I should think,' Mr Hartwell said thoughtfully. 'Provided it can be managed without setting the Woodham folk in a panic of fear that they might bring the plague here.'

'We already have visited sick in Woodham,' Mr
Reeve said almost apologetically. 'George Bridges the
butcher died yesterday, with all the *signs* on him. We
buried him last night.'

Mr Hartwell took an uneven couple of breaths and
closed his eyes momentarily. 'Lord, have mercy on us
all!' he murmured.

'Amen,' responded Mr Reeve gravely. 'The poor
fellow had been taking beasts to London every ten days
or so, as was his custom, and is supposed to have taken
the infection there. He felt unwell a few days ago. The
house is shut up, and the constable has set a guard on
it. He leaves a wife and three children, and there are
two servants . . . The Churchwardens have arranged
for food to be supplied to them. Of course, there will
be more, I don't doubt, for his shop was popular, and
there are folk fleeing from London into the country
hereabouts. They say it's *rumoured* that the Government
means to place bars on all the roads to prevent people
leaving London, so that many are fleeing before it can
be done . . .'

He looked pointedly at Mary, and she said defensively, 'The Queen and her Household are gone to
Hampton, and I was granted leave to come home, for
I've not seen my family or home these three years. The
sickness was only about St Giles and Westminster two
days since, and hardly in the City at all. I've heard
nothing of any attempt to prevent people leaving the
City.'

'No one whose presence in a stricken city is unnecessary can be blamed for leaving it,' Mr Hartwell remarked
in his coolest and most dispassionate manner. 'Best to
leave before they're visited, rather than after . . . Less
danger of carrying the infection with them. Even a
Government decree won't keep folk in a place where
they can expect an unpleasant death, for fear drives
harder than any Government! How did you come up
from the town? On foot?'

'Indeed,' Mr Reeve replied, absent-mindedly tugging at his plain cravat and clerical bands.

'If you mean to go on to Pinnacles, you'd best borrow a horse. This heat is enough to bring on an apoplexy, toiling up the hill. I'll see about it.'

With that abrupt statement, Mr Hartwell went out of the room, ignoring Mr Reeve's conscientious, 'Oh, but—I'd not trouble you . . . Oh! Most kind, most kind!'

There followed a brief and awkward silence, and then he said to Mary, 'I hope I gave you no offence—I didn't mean to imply—I meant only to enquire if you had heard anything of any *decree*, coming so recently from the Seat of Government . . .'

'Nothing at all,' Mary replied. 'I think it most unlikely. The King has the sense to know what's possible and what is not. Besides, as Mr Hartwell says, it's better for the non-essential folk to leave Town before the sickness grows too widespread, otherwise we may finish with London quite depopulated!'

'I trust not! Too dreadful to *contemplate*!' Mr Reeve closed his eyes and raised his hands, apparently in prayer, and remained so until Jem and John entered the room together a few moments later, looking self-conscious.

'Why, Mr Reeve!' Jem exclaimed. 'You've not walked out from the town in all this heat to call on us? Has Francis given you any refreshment? Where is he? Has he abandoned you both? Really, it's too bad of him!'

'I came on business,' Mr Reeve replied, making a clutch at a small table which he had almost sent flying as he rose to his feet at Jem's entrance. 'Indeed, I'm well refreshed, and I believe he is about to have a *horse* prepared for my use. Most kind, most kind!'

Mr Hartwell re-entered the room, looked at Jem and John with a singular lack of expression, and resumed his stance before the hearth. Everyone turned to him, but he seemed quite oblivious that they were expecting him to say something.

'Er—she's a very fine little foal,' John said at length.

'Yes. *He* is,' Mr Hartwell replied.

'Oh, yes—of course—he. The mare looks well, too,' John offered.

'As well as can be expected, considering. No doubt she's glad to have the business over and be rid of the extra weight.' Mr Hartwell looked at Mary, who thought she detected a slight twitch of amusement at the corner of his firm lips. 'If you're riding home to dinner, perhaps you'll take Mr Reeve with you. He wishes to see your father.'

'Yes, of course.' John nodded and smiled at the Rector as if to reassure him. Oliver walked across and rubbed affectionately against his legs, then returned to Mary, paid her the same compliment, and retired to his chair, no doubt exhausted by his social exertions.

'Did Francis show you all the house?' Jem asked Mary, sounding puzzled. 'I thought it would have taken more time, but perhaps we were in the stable longer than I realised . . .'

'We only progressed as far as the library,' Mr Hartwell said before Mary could reply. 'Perhaps we can continue during Miss Hook's next visit.'

'I do hope you'll come again soon,' Jem said shyly, turning again to Mary. 'I should like very much to talk to you, and—and perhaps ask your advice—if you wouldn't mind, that is . . .'

'I shall be happy to talk to you, and to advise you, if you think my advice would be of help,' Mary replied with a warm smile. She allowed her eyes to flick briefly to Jem's hair, and then to her dress, and saw that Jem had understood and welcomed the unspoken message. Then she glanced sidelong at Mr Hartwell, and noted his bleak expression with a tinge of annoyance.

'Well, I suppose we should be on our way home,' John said, looking vaguely about him. 'Father likes to dine sharp at noon. If you're ready, Mary, Mr Reeve?'

There was a general rising and movement towards the door by everyone except Oliver, who merely raised his head to see what was happening. Mary went back to stroke his head and bid him goodbye, and found, when she turned again, that everyone had gone out but Mr Hartwell, who stood by the door waiting for her.

'I'm sorry . . .' he began slowly, apparently having difficulty in finding the words he wanted. 'I seem to have talked inordinately about my own . . . misfortunes . . . this morning. I'm not given to doing so, and I can't imagine why I should have—er—inflicted so boring a tale on you.'

'It wasn't in the least boring!' Mary assured him truthfully. 'I should like to hear more of it, unless it distresses you to speak of unhappy memories, that is.'

She waited for some response, but he seemed to be studying the floorboards before his feet, and said nothing.

'I know that some people love to talk of their adventures,' she went on, feeling that she probably sounded as empty-headed as he apparently assumed her to be. 'The King does—he often tells of his escape after Worcester, and makes a very good tale of it—but others seem to prefer not to say anything about what has happened to them . . . Prince Rupert, for example. He must have a fund of interesting and exciting stories to recount, but he never tells them, even when he's asked. You remind me of him, you know!'

Mr Hartwell looked her straight in the face, and seemed surprised. Then he gave a wry smile and said, 'Proud as Lucifer, ill-tempered, short-spoken and acid-tongued? A fair description of both of us these days, I fear! I'd have been most flattered to be likened to him in his younger days, however! I'll take your comment as a compliment!' He made her a small bow, then gestured for her to pass through the door before him. She felt as if he had, in some obscure way, given her a set-down.

They went back through the house after the others, and Mary tripped up the small step from the hall to the passage to the kitchen, but was saved from falling by Mr Hartwell, who seized her arm just in time, so sharply that she was swung round by her own momentum to face him, and, being off-balance, fell against him. He caught hold of both her shoulders and held her while she recovered.

'That damned step!' he said. 'I sometimes think it was put there a-purpose to trip people! I'm sorry. Are you hurt?'

'I think not, if you will only hold me a little less tightly!' Mary said tartly, for his fingers had a steely grip on her upper arms.

'I'm sorry.' He released her and stood silently for a moment while she adjusted her hat, which had tipped to one side when she tripped. 'I forget my own strength,' he added belatedly, and rather lamely.

'I doubt there's anything to be done about the step, without taking up the floor of the whole passage, which would leave you with an equally awkward step up into every room, and increased chances of tripping!' Mary said briskly, going on her way. 'You could, perhaps, have a ramp . . .'

He made no reply to that, but followed her in silence until they rejoined the others in the stableyard, where John and a groom were getting Mr Reeve up on a placid-looking piebald. The Rector was clearly no cavalier, and made heavy weather of mounting, held his reins incorrectly and very wide apart, and looked far from confident.

'That's a very quiet horse,' Mr Hartwell said reassuringly. 'If he does decide to throw you, he'll do it gently! Keep your feet in the stirrups, don't saw on the reins, and don't raise your voice, and you'll have a pleasant, steady amble to Pinnacles.'

'Most kind, *most* kind,' Mr Reeve murmured in a hushed voice. 'I trust you may be right!' he added despondently.

CHAPTER FOUR

MR HARTWELL was right, and Mr Reeve did arrive in reasonable order at his destination, having conversed in a whisper while progressing at a slow amble, lost his round clerical hat twice and had it retrieved and cursorily brushed by John, and gone round in two successive slow circles every time they stopped for John to open a gate. Mary was ready to swear that the very quiet horse was consumed with suppressed laughter under his placid exterior, for his lower lip trembled and his ears twitched increasingly as they advanced, but he had his lashes demurely lowered over his eyes, and it is never easy to judge a horse's expression.

John conversed brightly of this and that most of the way, but eventually could contain himself no longer, and said to his sister, 'What did you think of Jem?'

Mary thought it hardly proper to discuss John's beloved in front of the Rector, so she confined herself to saying only, 'She's a pretty thing, and could be more so, with a little help. Sweet-natured too, I believe.'

'Not *paint*, I trust!' Mr Reeve whispered anxiously, 'I should not like to think of any young lady using artifice!'

'Oh, nothing like that!' Mary assured him comfortingly. 'Just a different arrangement of the hair, and a more flattering colour of gown, that's all.'

At that moment John's horse set up a hare, and he uttered a bellow of 'So-ho!' and spurred after it. Mr Reeve dropped his reins, took a good grip of his mount's mane, closed his eyes, and waited for disaster. The horse stopped and turned his head back as far as he could, as if trying to see what his rider was about.

'All's well!' Mary said reassuringly. 'Let me give you your reins—that's it. Now, hold them so, just before you, and loosely. Lean forward when you wish to go forward, and back when you wish to stop. If you wish to turn right or left, lean a little towards that side and pull gently on the rein at that side as well.'

Mr Reeve obediently put his weight forward, and the horse lurched on in the curious gait of his kind, picking up the feet on one side, then those on the other, giving the rider a smooth and comfortable ride.

'Ah, I see! I must *signal* to the worthy beast what I require of him!' Mr Reeve commented more cheerfully. 'But he doesn't seem to progress in the same *fashion* as your horse!'

'No,' Mary agreed. 'He has a different gait. It's a matter of inclination and training. One discovers how a horse prefers to go, and then trains him to do it better.' She felt a strong desire to laugh at him, which was unfair, for he was a very good, sensible man, and he could not help being an inexperienced rider.

They arrived at Pinnacles just as Sir Charles and Lady Hook were considering sitting down to dinner without waiting any longer for their missing offspring. Mary and John made their apologies, and explained the presence of the Rector, who was still putting himself to rights after dismounting in a most unorthodox fashion, face out and on the wrong side of the horse, which made the horse turn his head to look at him again, as if he could hardly believe what was happening. Mr Reeve was, of course, invited to dine, and was obviously only too pleased to accept, despite his protests of not wishing to be a *burden*. Lady Hook exchanged a meaning glance with her daughter, by which it was conveyed that both ladies assumed that the Rector's housekeeper was not a good cook, and the Rectory larder no doubt sparsely furnished. The poor man's stipend was, admittedly, a hundred a year, but he gave a large part of that to his curate, who had four children.

There had been a difference of opinion about the menu for dinner, which Cook had settled by providing both the roast mutton, pigeon pie and currant pudding desired by Sir Charles, and the sallet, cold cuts, raspberries and cream and junket preferred by Lady Hook. The choice overwhelmed Mr Reeve, who ended up with something of everything, and then the gentlemen retired to Sir Charles's cabinet to discuss the problem of the refugees encamped in the Forest. Mary went with her mother to the stillroom to hang bunches of fresh-cut herbs and mix pot-pourri, and, of course, to indulge in a little gossip.

'And what did you think of Francis Hartwell?' Lady Hook enquired when they had finished discussing Jem's pleasant nature and the desirability of improving her appearance.

'I hardly know,' Mary replied thoughtfully. 'On the whole, I found him cold, critical—even censorious—and very reserved, but he did relax a little for a few minutes, and then I thought him modest and sensible . . . I had the impression, once or twice, that he had a pleasantly quirky touch of humour about him, but that may have been unintentional.'

'No, I think not,' her mother replied. 'I've noticed it too, but he always keeps such a straight face that I've often not realised until afterwards that some of his remarks were really witty. I feel sorry for the pair of them, to tell truth! To lose one's parents, brother and sisters, all within a few days, and so horribly—it was plague, you know. Of course, Jemima was a mere babe in arms, but Francis was old enough to know and remember. Poor Jemima was brought up by old Mr Hartwell, and an ill-tempered old curmudgeon he was! One shouldn't speak ill of a neighbour, especially when he's dead, but nevertheless . . . And poor Francis, of course! Cast out, a mere boy, for disagreeing with the old tyrant, and then to have suffered so dreadfully. You saw his poor hands?'

'Yes,' Mary replied soberly. 'He said the Spaniards sent him to the galleys.'

'It could have been worse, I suppose, though I'm not sure if they still burn Protestants there or not! Jemima told me that he claimed to be a Catholic, just in case, and who can blame him? All for trying to do someone a good turn!'

Mary gave her mother a surprised look, and said, 'Oh? He didn't mention that.'

'Of course not—he wouldn't! It took me a great deal of effort and shameless prodding to get the story of his adventures out of him, and then only when he was laid up with a feverish rheum last winter, and I had him at my mercy, Jemima having begged my help in dosing him. It would have been easier to pull out all his teeth, I do declare! He was keeping watch, whatever that means, on his ship in the night, and a sailor fell off into the sea . . .'

'Overboard,' Mary supplied, having heard a deal of nautical talk at Court since the war with the Dutch began.

'Quite. So Francis dived in to save him, but the ship went on, for it appears that one cannot stop a ship as one can a carriage, and then the others in the ship couldn't find him, and he couldn't find the poor sailor in the dark, so presently the ship went on, and he was left, until some Spanish fishermen found him in the morning.'

Mary was silent for a time, pounding lavender buds to make a paste, while her mother prattled on, passing from the Hartwells to all the other local doings and scandals of recent months. She half-listened, but at the same time she was weighing the various aspects of the character of Francis Hartwell against one another, and eventually concluded that his own self-deprecating description was probably near the truth—proud, ill-tempered, short-spoken and acid-tongued, like Prince

Rupert! And modest, also like the Prince. Not, on the face of it, at all a person one would wish to encounter more often than necessary, yet . . . Only a short time ago, had she not decided that the Prince was the only man at Court worthy of respect and affection?

Later that day, a message was sent to Canons Grange inviting the Hartwells to dine and spend the next afternoon at Pinnacles, so that the men might discuss the problem of the refugees in the Forest. Mr Reeve was, of course, included. He had been seen safely home by the groom who carried the message, who was able to convey the borrowed horse back at the same time.

Mr Hartwell and Jem arrived on horseback half an hour before the noon of yet another hot, cloudless day, Jem in a well-cut but old-fashioned riding-habit, and a passable imitation of Mary's dashing cavalier hat, made (she confided to Lady Hook) from a hat of her grandfather's and the remains of an old ostrich-feather fan. Mr Hartwell, to Mary's surprise, was as well dressed as any gentleman at Court might have been when dining quietly with friends in the country, in a camlet coat and petticoat breeches of a pleasant dark blue shade, plentifully trimmed with crimson ribbons and set off by a lace cravat. The only thing lacking was a periwig, but that hardly mattered as his own hair was so thick and curly. He was even wearing knitted silk hose, which seemed a rash proceeding for even a short journey on horseback.

'Your brother is very fashionable!' Mary remarked to Jem as she took her up to her own room to remove her hat and tidy herself.

'Yes. You didn't see him to advantage yesterday, for he'd been up half the night with the mare, and then out in the meadows to see if the last of the hay was ready for carting, and looking like a farmer. He's always teasing me to have new clothes made, but I hardly know what to choose, and what would suit me . . .' She looked hopefully at Mary.

'He doesn't object to your spending money on clothes, then?' Mary said, and wished at once that she had worded the question more tactfully, for it revealed her suspicion that perhaps Mr Hartwell was a little mean, or, at least, careful, with his money.

'Oh, no! Far from it! It's only that I'm so nervous of wasting it on the wrong things. Grandfather gave me only a small allowance, and I find the habit of frugality isn't easy to lose.'

Of course, Mary offered to help her choose a new wardrobe, and they went downstairs to dinner comfortably aware that each was in the process of making a good friend. Mr Hartwell also seemed to be aware of it, for he looked at his sister's smiling face in a thoughtful manner, then caught Mary's eye and quirked his eyebrows enquiringly.

To Mary's surprise, she found that she apparently comprehended his meaning, for she gave him a little nod, to which he responded with another and gave her his brief, charming smile before turning to answer a query from Sir Charles about the haysel.

'An excellent crop,' he replied, 'and we seem likely to live on rabbit pie for the next month! I'll be glad when Joel Warrener has the coney-fences mended, for the furry monsters are all over the valley now.'

'My fault, I fear,' Sir Charles admitted ruefully. 'I'd not realised how Joel's old father had neglected his work in the warren, but I'm sure Joel will soon have it all to rights, now he's in charge and the old fellow in his grave, God rest him.'

'I suppose his name is Warrener because he is a warrener,' Jem observed, 'and all his ancestors before him.'

'As Thomas Plomer's name comes from lead-smithing, although the family has had the blacksmith's forge as well for generations,' Sir Charles agreed. 'And so with Fletcher, Baker, Brewer . . . John Graygoose claims that one of his forebears fought at Agincourt, you know, so perhaps we can guess how he flighted his arrows!'

The interesting discussion was interrupted by the arrival of Mr Reeve, who came in style in the chariot which Sir Charles had kindly sent to down to fetch him, and entered full of exclamations, trusting he found everyone well, and even remembering to enquire after the health of the horse he had borrowed from Mr Hartwell.

'Quite well, I thank you,' that gentleman replied in his most expressionless manner, 'as also is the new colt, and the redoubtable Oliver, whom I left supervising the education of his latest clutch of kittens.'

'Kittens?' Mary exclaimed. 'I thought him a tom—I mean—his name and appearance . . .'

'He is,' Mr Hartwell assured her, with the twitch at one corner of his mouth which she was beginning to recognise. 'He takes an interest in his offspring, however, like any Christian gentleman, and boxes their ears when necessary. I suppose he finds it easy to recognise his own, as they're generally spotted like the pard!'

Mary had an inward vision of a vast horde of spotted kittens being drilled by Oliver like his namesake with the New Model Army, and laughed aloud, at which Mr Hartwell raised his eyebrows enquiringly. She told him what she had imagined, and succeeded in raising that rare smile again, so broadly that she was able to see that he had a good set of white, even teeth.

'Was that not Archimedes that you lent the Rector?' Sir Charles asked Mr Hartwell as they sat down to dinner.

Mr Hartwell merely replied 'Yes', but Mr Reeve exclaimed, 'Archimedes? What a strange name for a horse!'

'I bred him,' Sir Charles said with a reminiscent smile. 'The first time he was taken to be washed, he leapt out of the water and ran away.'

'Crying *Eureka*?' asked Jem eagerly.

'Something like it, but in Horse Greek, of course! I sold him to your grandfather,' Sir Charles replied.

'More like *You be damned*!' said Mr Hartwell. 'He's a horse of principle and strong mind. He has but one gait, and that a slow amble. I tried to make him trot once, but he stopped dead and rolled. I was hard put to it to get clear.' Seeing that Mr Reeve was evincing some alarm at this, he added reassuringly, 'Let him go his own gait, and he's as amenable as you please.'

Dinner was another attempt by Cook to cater for the tastes of both the traditional eaters and for those who preferred something light and cool in such hot weather. There was pottage, rabbit pie, roast beef, boiled worts, gooseberry pie and custard for the one and sallet, cold veal pie, ham, love-apples, small new potatoes, strawberries and cream and flummery for the others.

After the meal, the men were joined by the Church-wardens and retired to the library for their discussion, while the ladies went upstairs, Lady Hook to lie down with a book of sermons, which she usually read with her eyes shut, and the two young ladies to Mary's room, so that Jem could see the fashionable garments Mary had brought home with her, and decide what style and colours would be suitable for her own projected new wardrobe.

'I have the fabrics, for Francis often brings me a length of silk or satin when he goes to London, but I've never been sure how best to have them made up,' she explained. 'We have a good sewing-woman, and my maid is quite an expert with her needle as well.'

Mary suggested that the maid and sewing-woman might consult with her own maid Eleanor about the cut and construction of the gowns whose style suited Jem—not that there was much choice, for fashion decreed a stiff-fronted bodice cut to a point below the waist in front, a full skirt, much gathered at the waist, over two or three petticoats, and very full sleeves, which fell to just below the elbow and were finished with a

deep lace frill. Bodices were decorated with lace or
braid, and the neckline was either cut to leave the
shoulders bare, or close-fitting at the throat. Mary
advised Eleanor to see that Jem's gowns were either in
the latter style, or had a filling of lace, bearing in mind
Mr Hartwell's wishes concerning his sister's morals, and
Jem's slight figure, for the low neckline required a
shapely bosom to look well.

Jem's hair was soon rearranged by Eleanor, who
brushed out the bunches of curls, drew her hair back
from the forehead and swept up the back into a flat,
oval bun, then coaxed the sides into loose ringlets. It
suited her far better than the old bunches of corkscrews,
and caused John to gaze admiringly at her when he saw
her later in the afternoon. Mr Hartwell viewed the
transformation with a slight frown, but said agreeably
that Jem looked very well when she asked his opinion.

It had been decided by the gentlemen that arrangements should be made to supply the refugees in the
Forest with necessities at cost, with a provision put in
by the Churchwardens, not out of miserliness but in
defence of Woodham's own poor folk, that any costs
were to be borne by charitable contributions, and not
the church offertory, alms-boxes or Poor Rate money.
Mr Reeve undertook to collect what he could from the
more well-to-do parishoners, and all those present started
off the giving by putting what money they could into a
jug which the Rector borrowed and passed round.

The next day being Sunday, Mary went with her
parents and John to Mattins, summoned by the church
bells—apart from poor cracked Gabriel. The ringing
sounded odd, each run down the scale ending without
the usual sonorous final note of the tenor. Mr Reeve
preached (at considerable length) on charity, and
announced that Sir Charles would be happy to receive
contributions towards food for the poor refugees, and
thereby raised the princely sum of £6 8s. 3d. for the
fund, apart from the normal church offerings.

Sir Charles had decided to go down on Tuesday and watch the lowering of the tenor bell, so Mary, curious to catch a rare glimpse of one of the bells, went with him in his chariot. On the way down, she said, 'I suppose the bells came from the old Abbey?'

'Unfortunately, no,' Sir Charles replied. 'The Church-wardens did manage to buy some of the bells after the Dissolution, and kept the tower at the east end of the present church in which they were hung, but the tower was struck by lightning in Edward's reign and had to be taken down. They put the bells in a cage in the churchyard and began to collect money to rebuild the tower, but before they had enough, the church began to lurch to the west, and they had to use all the stone and money they had to build the present tower against the west front and prop the church up! There wasn't enough, so they sold the bells to pay for the rest. Our old Rector, during the War, used to say that Woodham changed from having bells but no tower to having a tower but no bells, but we've gradually managed to buy a new ring over the past fifty years. The first one was the treble, bought by the bachelors and maidens of the parish. Your grandfather gave a pound for each of his children, and so did some of the other gentry.'

'What a charming idea!' commented Mary.

Most of the people of Woodham were at work, in the fields, the shops, the workshops or the gunpowder-mill, but the bellringers were at the church with their burly Captain, Thomas Plomer the blacksmith, Mr Reeve, and Mr Hatley (a gaunt, sad-looking man at the best of times, but all the more so since the death of his wife). A few idlers or unemployed men had come to watch and perhaps earn a copper by lending a hand, and some of the gentry had come to 'see the fun', as Mr Polycarp Wharton put it.

He was a languid, foppish-looking gentleman, who affected the latest fashions in dress and manners, yet managed his father's estate in a most business-like way.

He spotted Mary as soon as she arrived, and wandered over, a gorgeous sight in pink satin with silver ribbons, a blond periwig, and a high-crowned hat with pink plumes, one hand uplifted in an elegant attitude to show off a lace handkerchief, and his pink-velvet-shod feet set in the fashionable turned-out position.

'Ged, Sir Cherles!!' he exclaimed in a most excruciatingly affected version of the modish drawl which transformed most *a*s to *e*s and *vice versa*. 'Cen this be thet same Miss Hook who laft us three yares ego? Ai declare, quaite the grend leddy, end so beautiful! Mai hert fairly swoons with delaight to see you!'

Mary made a polite but noncommittal response, and turned to watch the arrival, not of the expected Wharton wagon, but of a particularly well-built haycart from Canons Grange, lined with bales of straw and drawn by a pair of great horses which arched their necks, raised and lowered their great feathered feet and flourished their ribboned tails with all the pride of their warhorse ancestry.

'What a marvellous pair of horses!' Mary exclaimed.

'Hertwall's, of course,' Mr Wharton replied, sounding a little sad and envious. 'Ai wish Ai hed such a pair!'

Mr Hartwell's tranter was driving, a small, nondescript terrier by his side, and his master was sitting on one of the bales of straw in his shirtsleeves, bare-headed and obviously come to assist rather than watch. He spoke briefly to Sir Charles, nodded in a friendly manner to Mr Wharton and anyone else who caught his eye, and made Mary a slight bow which seemed so much an afterthought that she wondered he had bothered.

There was no room in the base of the tower, which formed the church porch, for any spectators, but the double doors from the street were open, as were the matching pair into the interior of the church, and Mary and her father, by going inside and standing on the back pew (at the invitation of one of the Churchwardens), had a good view of the proceedings.

There was a hatch or trapdoor in the ceiling of the porch, which was open wide, and Thomas Plomer, after some consultation with his helpers, went with two of them, carrying a deal of rope and a very large pulley-block between them, up to the bell-chamber, apparently opening more hatches in the two intervening floors as they went. There was much anxious gazing upwards and enquiring cries from those left below, and presently a muffled bellow from above conveyed news which, to judge from the nods and grins, appeared to be good. There was some bumping and banging and a loud clang, followed by an anguished yelp from the heights, which caused some more anxious upward gazing, always done, Mary noted, with open mouth, as if this assisted in some way. The muffled voice announced that 'yon gawk Isaiah' had cracked his shin on the tenor, but done the bell no more damage, and then there was a cry of 'Heads below!' and the end of the long, heavy rope came snaking down through the hatch and coiled many yards of itself serpentinely on the floor.

It was promptly seized by the rest of the ringers and Mr Hartwell, who spaced themselves along it, spitting on their hands and taking a good grip, and then, after some more calling to and fro, the men on the ground braced themselves to take a heavy weight, called out 'Ready!', each in turn. They were answered by a curious variation of the traditional bellringers' starting cry of 'Tenor's going—she's gone', and then were almost jerked off their feet as the weight of the bell came on the rope.

Slowly, painfully slowly, they paid out the rope, a foot or so at a time, sometimes hanging on grimly in response to an urgent shout from above, and waiting for the word to go on lowering. Occasionally one or the other would remove a hand from the rope, rub it against his breeches and spit on it before renewing his grip, and Mary thought sympathetically that even their work-hardened palms must be suffering from the rough hemp, and she remembered Mr Hartwell's scarred hands, and

craned her neck a little in an effort to see his face. Apart
from a slightly anxious look upwards, for the rope had
just jerked unexpectedly, he appeared unmoved.

Eventually the great circle of the mouth of the bell
appeared in the hatchway, and the men on the rope
tightened their grip, dug in their heels, and hung on
grimly as Mr Hartwell called to his tranter, and the
haycart was backed slowly through the open doors, the
horses stamping and tossing their heads as they pushed
backwards on their harness. When it was halfway in, it
had to stop while there was a certain amount of careful
manoeuvring by the men to make room for it, for they
dared not loosen their grip on the rope, yet had to
move, or the cart could not get under the bell.

It was managed in the end by Mr Hartwell, still
hanging on to the rope, turning himself about and
directing the men, one by one, until sufficient space had
been made, and the cart came back the extra few feet
necessary, the lowering continued, and the bell came to
rest fair and square in the middle of the cart. The rope
was untied from it and, in response to another shout,
slid slowly up until it was above the hatch. Presently
Thomas Plomer reappeared to supervise the securing of
the bell, the rope-haulers employing their time while
they waited in gazing ruefully at their sore hands, flexing
them and comparing burns and blisters. Mr Hartwell
took no part in this socialising, but busied himself
sorting the lengths of rope with which the bell was to
be tied down.

With the arrival of the Captain, the securing was
soon done, the bell covered with a tarpaulin, and the
cart was driven out of the porch, the horses stamping
harder than ever to get a purchase on the flagstones to
start off, but seeming quite unsurprised that the weight
of the vehicle had suddenly increased by almost a ton.
Thomas Plomer made himself comfortable in the cart,
the tranter flourished his whip, the terrier barked, and
the cart rumbled off through the ford on its way to the

bell-foundry at Watford.

'What about the trapdoor?' asked one of the Church-wardens.

'What about what about it?' asked Thomas Plomer's deputy, gaping up at it.

'Aren't you going to close it?'

The ringer scratched his nose while he thought about it, then said reluctantly that he 'sposed it might be closed, and went stumping off up the stairs in the north-west corner of the nave to see about it, his progress being marked by another outbreak of bumping and banging. When he returned, the ringers retired to the Boar's Head across the road for bread, cheese and ale at the Churchwardens' expense, and everyone else went home, the entertainment being over for the day.

In due course Gabriel returned, recast, perfect, and half a hundredweight heavier, and was hauled up in much the same way that he had descended. The ringers celebrated by ringing a touch for an hour or so, and then treated themselves to supper at a whole shilling a head at the Wyvern. Mary did not go to see the bell's return, being busy with a quantity of raspberry conserve, but she heard the bells ringing, and was glad that all had gone well.

During Gabriel's absence, more refugees had joined the original group in the Forest, and Mr Reeve and Mr Hartwell continued to go weekly with a cartload of provisions for them, meeting their spokesman near their camp, which, Mr Reeve reported, was an orderly place, with shelters made of coppice-poles, tarpaulins and bracken. They paid what they could for the food, and sent things they had made, such as clothes-pegs, wooden toys and spoons, to be sold at the market to help make up the difference and eke out what Sir Charles managed to collect from the charitable. Their leader always reported them still free from plague, but no one was allowed near enough to the camp to see if this were true or not, for they were very reluctant to allow any contact between themselves and outsiders.

In addition to these, there were other people from
London, many of the well-to-do folk who had a country
house in or near Woodham or had relations living in
the town. It was impossible to refuse these entry, but
others were turned back before they entered the town
by a group of volunteer guards organised by the Town
Constable.

Little news came out of London, and that little was
entirely bad. The plague increased daily, and there were
soon copies of the bills of mortality circulating which
reported more than three thousand a week dying of the
sickness, apart from the other, more usual, causes such
as consumption, spotted fever and plain fever, which
together claimed another seven hundred or so a week.
Sir Charles observed that even these figures were higher
than normal, and he wondered if the excess might really
be plague deaths wrongly reported.

Mary received a letter from Miss Bellamy at the end
of July, which, amid much vapid and ill-spelled gossip
about various love-affairs and quarrels, contained
mention that the Duke of Albemarle and Lord Craven
had elected to remain at Whitehall to govern London
on the King's behalf, and that the King had been to
Portsmouth, Greenwich and the Isle of Wight, and was
soon to go to Salisbury, where the Queen would join
him, plague having appeared in Hampton. Mary was
relieved that there was no message of recall from the
Queen, but only a postscript that Her Majesty had sent
her best remembrances.

With the passing of Midsummer Day, the hot weather
had moderated, following a couple of thunderstorms,
and July was passed in the pleasant country pursuits
that Mary had missed so much at Court. She rode or
walked in the Forest, often with Jem and John for
company, helped her mother with a little gentle
gardening or the concocting of herbal brews and
perfumes in the stillroom, stitched her embroidery and

visited the various families in the neighbourhood. Once
or twice a week she went down into the town to call on
acquaintances or to shop in the market (which dwindled
week by week as fewer people dared to come into the
town for fear of the sickness), and she attended church
on Sundays. She found Mr Reeve's sermons interesting
but long, and Mr Hatley's shorter but very dull. A
national fast day was proclaimed for the second of
August, and observed meticulously in Woodham, with
a long service in the church and one of Mr Reeve's
more impassioned sermons on repentance.

Despite a very nervous atmosphere of expectation
and dread in the town, and the news that there were
now more than ten thousand a week dying of plague in
London, no further visitations occurred in Woodham
during July, and the bereaved members of the Bridges
family were eventually allowed out of their incarceration
and reopened their shop. But, in the second week in
August, Mr Reeve again toiled up the long hill to
Pinnacles to report to Sir Charles that the normal figure
of three or four burials a week had suddenly increased
to ten, and he was sure six of those had died of plague.
One of them was Mary Jones, who had come from
Holborn the previous week to stay with her aunt.

Two of the deceased had been father and son, so five
houses were shut up, and Mary found, when she accompanied Cook to market the next week, that three of
them were next door to each other in East Street, and
everyone crossed the street to pass by on the other side,
as far as possible from the boarded-up windows and
barred doors with their sinister painted crosses and
appeals to the Lord to have mercy.

'God ha' mercy on us all!' said Cook fervently,
surreptitiously crossing herself—a wickedly Popish
practice. 'Mr Hartwell's cook's auntie is poorly, they
say, but she's a great one for feeling unwell when there's
any sickness about, so I doubt it's aught but a desire to
get a bit of attention!'

Mary remembered this item of information a couple of days later, when she went with John to sup and spend the evening at Canons Grange, and asked one of the footmen waiting at table if he knew how Cook's aunt did.

The man, who was serving her from a great dish of juicy new peas at the time, cast an anxious glance at his master, who expected the servants to remain unnoticeable during meals, and confided in a hoarse whisper, 'The old lady's always claiming she's ill, Cook says, and she'll go see her later this week and tell her not to be such a goose-cap.'

Since her return home, Mary had spent a good many hours at Canons Grange with Jem, who now had a small wardrobe of becoming gowns and was rapidly learning how to make the best of herself under her new friend's tuition.

The two young ladies were the best of friends, but Mary still found Mr Hartwell an uneasy person to be near. He was usually somewhere about when she was there, and did not avoid her, nor did she avoid him, but he said little to her and seemed, if anything, more cool and reserved than ever, as if to make up for his uncharacteristic unbending on their first meeting. He gave Mary the impression that he did not approve of her, but would not prevent her friendship with his sister as long as she had no bad influence on Jem. Naturally, not being the woman he seemed to assume that she must be, she resented his coolness, but, as there was nothing actually said and there was nothing she could do about it, even if she had wished to do so, she shrugged it aside and treated him equally coolly, never addressing him by his Christian name, as the rest of her family did, and he always called her 'Miss Hook' with the same formality.

There were four deaths in the town the next week, but three of them were of sickly infants and only the fourth of plague, and, again, the victim was someone recently come from London, from Allhallows by the Wall, near Moorfields. The constable urged his volunteers to increase their vigilance, and the townsfolk went about their business in a sober manner, avoiding close contact with one another, waiting to see what would happen the next week, when the deaths went up to thirteen, which, as everyone seemed impelled to mention, was a notoriously unlucky number, although only two were certainly of plague. The month of August ended with another thunderstorm, which interrupted the harvesting, and the total number of deaths from all causes for the month reached thirty, more than four times the average for August. An air of gloom as heavy as a thundercloud settled over the little town as the people eyed one another, and waited.

CHAPTER FIVE

ON THE FIRST day of September, Mary went early to Canons Grange, and alone, for John had undertaken to help to bring in the last of Polycarp Wharton's harvest, and both Mary and Jem proposed to be very busy all day about what he chose to dismiss as 'women's business', although, as Jem remarked slyly, he would be ready enough to eat the results, for they meant to make a deal of blackberry conserve.

The fruit had ripened early with the hot summer and was very plentiful, so, Mr Hartwell's corn being got in already, he had sent half a dozen of the women in his employ out the previous day to pick a great basketful apiece from his hedgerows.

Fortunately they had completed their task before the storm broke, and Mary found the two kitchen-maids in the kitchen, picking over great juicy, dry berries, removing stalks, spiders, thistledown and any other extraneous matter, while Cook weighed it, five pounds at a time, on her big iron scales, and Jem marshalled and washed the gallipots.

Mary helped Sukey, the scullery-maid, to pound the loaf-sugar to a rough, granular consistency, and then started to cut out circles of paper and muslin, which would be used to cover the pots after they had been sealed with wax.

Despite the storm, the weather was still hot, and the door to the stableyard had been set wide open to let a little air into the kitchen, where the fire was burning merrily and both bread-ovens had been heated to dry the gallipots. Through the opening, Mary could see another hive of activity, for one groom was helping the tranter to groom the two great horses, and another was curry-combing Mr Hartwell's black mare. A dozen hens were extremely busy foraging in the manner of their kind, interrupted from time to time by a young sheepdog, which seemed to be getting his paw in by herding them about, with a great deal of creeping on his belly and making short, silent rushes after any independent-minded hen which left the group to go after a choice morsel among the cobblestones.

All this business was being supervised by Oliver, who sat on a mounting-block in the sun, watching in a tolerant fashion as everyone else worked, although he did bestir himself once to stalk across to a corner where three spotted kittens were playing, and cuff them about the ears for some obscure breach of feline etiquette. From time to time a muffled barking came from the stables, where the tranter's terrier was hunting in the hayloft, with no apparent success.

The fruit was washed and heaped into three large pans, which were hung over the fire, and the younger kitchen-maid, Molly, was instructed to watch over them and see they did not burn while the others took a little refreshment in the form of cider and crusty new bread, spread with fresh butter and the last of the previous year's conserve.

'We shall live well this winter,' Jem confided to Mary. 'We've used an extraordinary amount of sugar—Francis says we must mean to bankrupt him in order to get a monopoly of sugar-loaves! There's been more good fruit than we could eat, so we've made pots of apricot paste, and conserved raspberries, gooseberries, strawberries —more than I've ever seen before, I think! Now the apples are ripening, and Francis is scouring the cider-vats in the cellar.'

When the fruit was cooked and the sugar added, Molly having turned faint with the heat, everyone took a turn at stirring the boiling mixture for a few minutes at a time, so that no one suffered too much from standing over the fire, and then there came the careful filling of rank after rank of gallipots, with the usual crop of burnt and sticky fingers. Cook, red-faced and irritable by now, was trying, in the midst of all this, to get dinner for everyone, for the men expected their meat, regardless of the busyness of the women.

Eventually all the pots were filled and sealed with melted tallow, and the women sat down to their own dinner round a table scrubbed clean of sticky patches of spilled conserve. Jem suggested that she and Mary might have their dinner in the kitchen, too, which Mary agreed to, although with some surprise, for she had never in her life eaten a meal with the servants. However, Cook made sure that there would be no awkwardness by bringing out a small table from the scullery and telling Sukey to put a cloth on it and set places for the ladies over by the door, where it would be cooler for them.

'Will your brother not wonder where we are?' Mary asked Jem as they sat down to veal cutlets, worts and potatoes, and a large bramble pie with cream.

'I expect he'll guess,' Jem replied, obviously not much concerned.

They could not help overhearing the conversation at the big table, which soon took quite a morbid turn, with the maids discussing the various methods they had heard for either averting or curing the plague, although they always added that they had only heard from someone else that this or that was a sure specific.

'My old granny always had a bit of rowan over her door in sickly times,' said Ellen, the older kitchen-maid. 'She swore it kept all sickness away!'

'No, that's for witches,' objected Molly. 'Rowan keeps witches away, but it kills all your parsley—that's what my Mam taught me!'

'I heerd tell,' Sukey offered humbly, 'that you can always tell when plague's about, in cause of all the rats start to die!'

'There's no rats here,' Cook said irritably. It was understandable that she should have been red-faced and sweating profusely earlier, when the fire was burning up, the conserve and vegetables boiling and the meat and pies cooking in the ovens, but the kitchen was quite cool now and no one else looked at all heated. 'That Oliver may think himself the Lord Mayor's Fool, but I'll say this for him, he don't let no rats or no mices live long about this house! He brings me a dead 'un every now and agen, just to remind me that he earns his keep, I reckon.'

She mopped her face with the skirt of her apron, and shifted uneasily on her stool, poking at her food but hardly eating anything. 'I wish I could get my old auntie to hev one o' the kits,' she said plaintively. 'Dirty ol' besom, she is. Lets the varmin run about the house like they owns it!' She mopped her face again, then plucked at the sleeve of her frock, pulling it away from her armpit as if it irked her. 'I was down to see her the end of last se'ennight, and there was a gurt dead rat lying on the floor in her back-piece, the biggest I ever saw! Not long dead, neether, for its fleas were still on it! Some of them must a got on me whiles I was throwing it out, for its taken ever since to be rid of 'em, and they bit me sorely in the night after I come back. Filthy creatures!'

She shuddered and picked at her food again, then pushed her plate away, almost as full as when she started.

'Lost your appetite, Cook?' asked Ellen, looking concerned.

'Can't seem to fancy it,' the woman mumbled wearily. 'I thought it were the thunder yesterday give me such a bad head, but it's no better today, and I feel . . . I feel . . .'

She got to her feet and started to go towards the door, muttering, 'So hot . . . I'm afire . . . Must get . . .' then staggered, and fell with a crash on the tiled floor.

There was a stunned silence, from which Mary was the first to recover. She rose from her place and went to kneel by the woman, rolling her over on her back, which required a considerable effort, although she was not an unduly fat woman, for a cook. She lay quite limp, breathing in a strange, gasping fashion, her face still suffused and two bright spots burning on her cheeks. Even as Mary looked at her, she began to shiver spasmodically.

'She's sick!' Mary said, her voice sounding very odd in her own ears. 'Sukey, I think you should fetch your master!'

Sukey, a thin little scrap of a girl with big, apprehensive eyes, gave a frightened sob and ran from the room. The other two maids got up and shrank away towards the far corner, but Jem came round the small table to join Mary, who said, 'Best keep away, I think.'

'I've had plague,' Jem said in a matter-of-fact voice. 'Hardly anyone ever has it twice. That's what it is, isn't it?'

Mary nodded, and whispered, 'I think so.' A shudder ran through her, an icy feeling developed suddenly deep within her, and she thought, It's the plague, and I've touched her! I've been with her all morning! I suppose I shall get it now.

She was surprised to find that a numb calmness descended on her then, and when Mr Hartwell came in and said anxiously, 'What's wrong? I can't make sense of what Sukey says—something about Cook saying she's on fire?' It was Mary who replied, 'She's burning with fever. We think she has the plague.'

'Let me see.' Mr Hartwell knelt beside her, felt Cook's forehead, then ripped the sleeves out of her frock, one after the other, and lifted her arms, looking in the armpits.

'Yes, I'm afraid so,' he said. 'There's a bubo forming

there already . . . You see? The red lump. Jem—call all the servants together, and tell them no one—no one—is to leave the immediate surroundings of the house, and no one is to enter it! You understand?' Jem nodded as he looked up into her anxious face. 'Mary,' he continued, using her Christian name for the first time, although neither of them noticed the fact, 'will you help me?'

'What must I do?' Mary asked, after swallowing hard to stop herself babbling nonsense about not being able to do anything.

'I'll carry her to her bed. I'll need you to help me to get her into it and make her comfortable.'

'Sir,' Ellen said timidly, coming forward a few steps, 'seeing as we're all going to get it, and like as not I'll be glad of someone to do as much for me when I'm dying, I'll come too and—and sit with her, if you'll tell me what to do.'

'That's a good, brave girl!' Mr Hartwell said encouragingly. 'But don't assume that you're all going to die! I didn't when I had it, and neither did Miss Jemima, for all she was only a baby! You have to make up your mind to fight back, not give in and let it kill you. You must tell yourself, even when you're sick, that you're not going to die. Hold on to that—you're not going to give in and let it kill you. You understand me?'

He spoke so vehemently that both Molly and Ellen looked deeply impressed and nodded gravely, saying, 'I'm not going to die', in nervous, uncertain voices, but at least looking as if they saw a tiny glimmer of hope, and Sukey, who had been sobbing quietly by the door, gave a hiccough, wiped her eyes on the back of her hand, and whispered, 'Whatever you say, sir!'

Mary wondered how Mr Hartwell proposed to get Cook up to her room, but he made no great ado about it at all, and simply picked her up, propped her against one of the sinks for a moment while he got a better purchase, and then carried her up three flights of stairs

to her bright, clean attic room and laid her gently on
her bed, where she lay, gasping and moaning faintly,
her head rolling slowly from side to side.

Mr Hartwell seemed a little out of breath, and flexed
his arms and shoulders as he turned to Mary and Ellen,
who had followed him and were standing in the doorway.
'Get her clothes off and the covers over her,' he said.
'Best open the window, for she'll start to stink before
long, and fresh air can do her no harm. She'll need
plenty of water to drink—get as much into her as she'll
swallow, for she'll sweat it all out again and dry out
otherwise. Try to keep her quiet. When she's settled,
you stay with her, Ellen, and M—Miss Hook come
downstairs again, if you will. Bring her clothes—they
must be burned on the bonfire beyond the stableyard.'
With that, he brushed past them, and could be heard
running lightly down the stairs.

He had spoken briskly, and was obviously in too
much of a hurry to mince his words, but Mary, aware
of all this and of the hundred other things he must have
to think of at this moment, noted the added courtesy
of the 'if you will'. It was clearly an afterthought, but
he had at least made the effort, and she appreciated it.

Ellen set about stripping the sick woman after a slight
hesitation, and needed very little help from Mary, who
bundled the discarded clothes together, noting that there
were still a few fleas in them, which she crushed fastid-
iously, having no wish to harbour any herself, but was
bitten by one in the process. Then she helped Ellen to
put the covers over Cook, finding that even the servants
had good linen sheets in this household.

'You'll be all right here with her, Ellen?' she asked,
hesitating before she left the room. Ellen nodded doubtfully. 'Well, if you need any help, call from the window!'
She had noticed that it looked out from the end of the
wing on to the stableyard.

'Yes, ma'am,' Ellen replied dutifully, and sat down

on a little stool, as far from the bed as the room would allow.

Mary returned to the kitchen, and carried the bundled clothes outside, for she had noticed the place just beyond the stables where household rubbish was burned. Mr Hartwell was out there, waiting for the stragglers of the household to join those already assembled in an uneasy group in the yard. He took the bundle from her and carried it to where the fire smouldered, stirred it into life and spread the garments on it, waiting until they were well alight before returning. Mary stood beside Jem, just outside the kitchen door, and managed to respond to her little smile.

'What will you do, Mary?' she asked very quietly. 'Francis will tell the servants that the house has to be shut up. At least, everyone will have to remain within the immediate area, and no one will be allowed to cross the boundary which he means to mark out, either going out or coming in, but he can't force you to stay here, if you wish to go home. I mean—it's not as if we were in the town, where the constable would come and nail up the doors and windows.'

'How can I go home?' Mary replied equally quietly. 'I was with her all morning, and I've touched her, helped her to bed . . . I'd carry the sickness home with me if I went there. Besides, how can your brother make the servants stay if he allows me to go? I shall have to stay here until—until it's over, one way or the other!'

Mr Hartwell came to join them, and looked at Jem enquiringly, but said nothing.

'Mary will stay,' she said.

He nodded, gave Mary a quick, bleak glance, but said only, 'I think everyone is assembled now.'

The three of them walked together to where the servants were waiting, and Mr Hartwell quickly explained what had happened, clearly, baldly, and without emotion.

'There's no doubt but Cook is visited by the plague,'

he went on. 'She has the signs on her already, which
mean she's had it for some days. I mean to mark a
boundary about the house and garden and the yard,
and no one within it may go out, and no one from
outside it may come in. All of you have been in contact
with Cook in the past few days, so you may or may not
have the infection already. If you go out from here,
you'll take it with you and be the means of killing other
people.'

He looked round at the frightened faces, and went
on, 'I've already stopped one of the farm workers who
came with a message, and sent him down to Woodham
to tell Mr Reeve, and he'll see that your friends and
families are told, if you have any in the town, and he'll
keep in touch by sending someone each day to the
boundary, across the paddock there, where we can shout
messages to him. Mr Palmer, the steward, will also
come to that point each day, and we can ask him for
anything we need to be left at the fence, so we'll not
starve or go short, and those of you who take or send
part of your wages to your families may trust him to
see that this continues. Some of you will fall sick, but
don't assume that you'll die! I know a good deal about
plague, for I survived it myself, as did my sister, and
I've tried to find out as much as possible about it. I've
talked at length with a learned man, a physician, who
had dealings with it in other places, and I assure you
that not all who are visited die. Those who do are
usually dirty, very poor, and underfed, and none of you
is any of those things, so be of good heart, and we'll
fight this together. Any questions?'

'Where'll we go when—if—we get sick?' asked one of
the footmen. 'All us indoor servants sleep in the attics,
and us men share one room. Will the sick be there with
the whole?'

'No,' Mr Hartwell assured him. 'That would be
foolish, and, in any case, those who are well must nurse
the sick, and there'll be your usual work still to do. It

would be easier if all the sick were together, on the ground floor. We'll clear the two big store-rooms in the north wing, and put the beds in there to make a hospital.'

The footman looked at his two colleagues, then said, 'If it's agreeable to you, sir, me and John and William'll go and clear the store-rooms now.'

'Very well. Thank you.'

The two grooms exchanged a few whispered words, and then one said, 'Me and Moses'll make some cots, sir. There's wood left from the new paddock fence, and a bolt of pauling in the loft.'

'A good idea. See to it.'

The men went off, apparently relieved to have some definite occupation which would help in the emergency, and Mr Hartwell said to the tranter, 'The great horses are already gone to pasture, are they not? Mr Palmer will need them, and I'm afraid young Josh will have to have charge of them.'

The tranter nodded and shrugged, and said, 'What yer going ter use fer markers? Them flinders o' the little ole cart'd do, and I've some red paint left from tiddy-vating the wagon . . .'

'You're right,' Mr Hartwell replied. 'We'll go now and set them up, and paint a warning cross on each.' He looked at his valet and the female staff, the kitchen-maids, the housemaids, Jem's maid, and the sewing-woman, who were all standing about, looking forlorn, and then turned to Jem and raised his eyebrows again. She nodded, and he went off at once into the cart-shed with Obadiah, the tranter, leaving his sister to send the others back to their normal work.

'I'll go up to Cook,' she said when they had gone. 'Ellen will be needed in the kitchen, for there'll be supper to cook for everyone, and I doubt Molly and Sukey can manage.'

'I can help in the kitchen, perhaps,' Mary said tenta-tively. Jem gave her a quick, grateful smile before she went indoors, and Mary was about to follow when Mr Hartwell came out of the cart-shed with a mallet in his hand, and crossed the yard towards her, looking at her with a frown and a watchful expression, as he so often did.

'Is something amiss?' she asked him, a faintly aggressive tone creeping into her voice and her blue eyes hardening.

'No. I'm surprised that you elected to stay. I can't compel you to,' he replied abruptly.

'It's a matter of common sense,' she said, equally abruptly.

'What do you mean to do?'

'When?'

'Now.'

'Help in the kitchen.'

His eyebrows rose. 'I'd not thought the culinary arts to be among the usual accomplishments of a maid of honour!'

'My mother taught me how to manage a household long before I went to Court,' she said coldly. 'And that included being able to do myself some of the practical things I could expect a well-trained servant to undertake. I can pluck a chicken as well as a guitar, and cook a plain meal as well as execute fine embroidery!'

His expression, which had been austere and what she considered critical, changed subtly to something more troubled, and he said stiffly, 'I'm sorry. I don't mean to quarrel with you. We face a difficult time, and I appreciate your willingness to give what help you can. It troubles me that you should have been caught up in this crisis in my household. If there's anything I can do to make your enforced stay here less difficult, please tell me of it.'

'Well,' said Mary briskly, 'if you have any means of communication with my family, I should be glad of some clothing. I shall need at least some changes of linen and some gowns, if I'm to stay here for six weeks or more!'

'Of course.'

'And, if I may make a practical suggestion . . . If Mr Reeve is to be expected to take on the responsibility of organising some of our contacts with the outside world, his task would be easier if he had a horse. I believe I saw Archimedes in the paddock when I arrived this morning. Perhaps you could spare him for the Rector's use, as you'll have no need of him here for some time?'

Mr Hartwell looked surprised, as if he had not expected so sensible a suggestion from her. 'An excellent idea!' he said. 'I'll tell Palmer, when he comes to consult me, to arrange for Archimedes to be lodged at the Rectory, together with a man to see after him and the necessary fodder. Thank you for thinking of it!'

Mary's antagonistic attitude towards him suddenly crumbled as she had an inward qualm of fear about her situation, and she said, in quite a different tone, nervously biting her lip to stop it trembling, 'Do you really know very much about the plague? Do you truly believe that anything can be done for the visited?'

'Yes, I do,' he replied with patent sincerity. 'I was old enough when I had the infection to wonder why Jem and I survived when the rest of the family . . .' He made a little gesture with one hand, as if to ward off the actual mention of dying when Death might already be in the room with the opened window, so near where they were standing. 'I sought out all the books I could hear of that discussed the disease, and had the good fortune to share an oar in my galley with a physician who'd worked in the Levant and Turkey, and knew much of the Arab methods of treating the visited—which, by his account, are more successful than those practised in Europe.'

'A physician in the galleys?' Mary exclaimed. 'How did he come to be there?'

'He had the temerity to compare Arab and Spanish medical practice, to the detriment of the latter,' he replied wryly. 'The Spanish will admit no good in the Saracen—hence his condemnation!'

'You say they are more successful . . . How much more?'

'A little more. I don't claim that I can cure it. If I did, I'd be in London, not here, shut up in my own home. It's a question of bringing the buboes to a natural breaking, so that the poison may be drained, but it's not easy. Our physicians use harsh means, caustic substances, or lancing, often before the buboes are ripe. It does no good, but more likely hastens the end. The—The pain can be—very bad . . . Extremely bad . . .'

Mary looked him straight in the eyes, and his, so dark, locked on the clear blue of her own. They exchanged a long, silent look, he reading the fear hidden under her apparent calmness, and she seeing something of his determination to save those he could, knowing that he might not succeed. A certain unwilling mutual respect entered their relationship, and was recognised by both of them.

'There's enough here to make a start, sir!' called Obadiah, emerging from the cart-shed, trundling a loaded barrow.

Mary started, realising that she had been keeping Mr Hartwell in conversation when he had so much to do. 'I must look to the kitchen fire,' she said abruptly, defensively implying that he had been keeping her from her chosen task. 'It may well be out by now.'

'If it is, you'd best give me a call. I'll not be far away,' he replied, already turning away to join Obadiah.

'I do know how to light a fire!' she replied tartly, and went into the kitchen with a distinct flounce of her long skirts.

The fire was burning low, watched carefully by Oliver from a convenient stool, but it took only a little attention to bring it to a proper brightness. Molly and Sukey were washing the dinner platters at the sinks, and presently Ellen came down, looking pale but resolute, and started to put the gallipots of blackberry conserve away in the pantry.

'How is Cook?' Mary asked, helping her.

'She'm sweating hard, and very restless,' Ellen replied. 'It don't smell like good, healthy sweat at all, but a dretful rotten stink, like summat gone putrid. It fair turned my stummick! I'm sorry you got catched up in our troubles, Miss Hook. It's a poor return for all your kindness, helping of us with the brambleberries!'

'It can't be helped,' Mary said resignedly. 'Can I help you with supper?'

'There's not much to do,' Ellen replied, looking about the kitchen to see that all was tidy. 'It's only veal and ham pie and cold cuts and apple pie, it being such warm weather. There's the taters, but Sukey'll do 'em, and Molly can wash the sallet. P'raps you'd carry up some water to Cook's room, if'n you wouldn't mind? Miss Jemima said as she'd be needing more, and a cloth to wash her . . .'

Mary took two jugs of water, a couple of wash-cloths and some towels, and thought, toiling up the stairs with them, how sensible had been the suggestion that the visited should be put on the ground floor, for the climb up three flights of stairs to the attics involved a deal of wasted energy, especially with a burden, and she recalled how often the housemaids must have to do it in the course of an ordinary day's work.

Jem was sitting by Cook's bed, her hands clasped together and her eyes closed, presumably in prayer, and the sick woman lay on her back, her head moving fitfully from side to side. She moaned and muttered incessantly, and Mary, looking at her, would hardly have recognised her, for her face seemed to have fallen in, and her hair, normally smoothed back under her neat cap, straggled over the pillow like wet seaweed.

The smell in the room was, as Ellen had said, putrid, and the open window did little to improve matters.

'Thank you,' Jem said as she opened her eyes and saw what Mary had brought. 'She's in such a high fever, and sweating so much that she'll dry out. I thought it might cool her a little if I washed her. What do you think?'

'Dr Gumble advised sponging down to reduce the fever when the Queen was ill,' Mary said doubtfully. 'He's Lord Albemarle's physician. Dr Hodges, one of the King's doctors, thought it inadvisable, and insisted that the stomach should be covered by a plaister and salty water given to drink . . . Her own doctors gave her Jesuit's bark.'

'I haven't any of that,' Jem said. 'I've a receipt which is *said* to be good for plague.' She was carefully dribbling water into Cook's half-open mouth from a cup with a spout. 'It's compounded of sage, rue, buttercup-root, angelica-root, snake-root and meadow-saffron, and infused in wine. I don't know if it will help, or make her worse. What do you think? I had a little Jesuit's bark, but I gave it to Mr Reeve for his ague. He contracted that when he was at Cambridge. I suppose Francis could ask for some to be obtained for us . . .'

'I've never heard of its being used against plague,' Mary said, thinking of her mother's instruction in herbal lore. 'It does reduce fever, though. Let me see—sage helps a sore throat and assuages boils, so it might help the buboes . . . Rue eases pain and cleanses suppuration. Angelica-root, you said? That's for plague and all infections, for sure, and so is snake-root; but meadow-saffron? Well, it's good for ague, but it's very poisonous, and I'd not like to try it, for fear of using too much! I don't know about buttercup-root . . . It's very acid, but I suppose it could do no harm, and we must try whatever remedies we have. Shall I sit with her while you make up the mixture?'

'I'd be grateful,' Jem replied with her sweet smile.

'But first I think I'll sponge her.'

She drew back the sheet which covered the sick woman, wrung out a wash-cloth in the second jug of water, and began to wash away the sweat which bathed Cook's body and had already soaked the sheet beneath her. Mary took another cloth and set to work from the other side of the bed.

It was a foul job, for the smell was nauseating, and Cook was sweating so profusely that the sponging seemed to make no difference. There were small scarlet patches in several places on her body now, and angry swellings under both armpits and in her groin.

Jem went to the window when they had finished, and leant out for a few moments, breathing in clean air from outside, then turned back towards the bed.

'It doesn't seem to have done any good,' she said. 'The plague doctors in the towns wear masks when they examine people, I believe. Have you ever seen them?'

'Not in the flesh, but I saw a broadsheet not long ago about the plague in Holland, and there was a woodcut of a doctor in it. He wore something like a great bird's beak, stuffed with spices, I believe.'

'I must see if I can make something,' Jem said thoughtfully, wringing out the wash-cloths and laying them on the window-sill to dry. 'I can't manage a beak, but a simple mask with cloves in it—they say oil of cloves is specific against infection. I'll go and make the compound, if you don't mind staying. I'll not be long.'

She was gone about half an hour, but it seemed much longer to Mary, sitting in the small, stinking room, feeling cut off from the rest of the household, along with the sick woman, who tossed more restlessly, muttered, sobbed and moaned, and kept raising first one arm and then the other, as if to ease the pain of the growing buboes.

Outside, there was a muffled sound of hammering and sawing from one of the buildings round the stable-yard. Mary looked out to see if she could catch a glimpse of anyone, and saw Mr Hartwell and Obadiah, working their way along the middle of the paddock, banging in stakes at intervals and daubing each with red paint before they moved on to the next. Mr Palmer, the steward, was visible by the fence on the far side of the paddock, trying to persuade a reluctant horse to stand and be harnessed, but the animal was skittish and danced away, until Mr Hartwell looked up from his task and called to it, when it stood primly, as if it had never misbehaved in its life. Judging by its piebald appearance, Mary thought it must be Archimedes.

Jem returned with a stone bottle of her mixture and some salt, which she stirred into the drinking-water, and, between them, she and Mary managed to get a dose of the medicine and some more water into Cook, who presently grew quieter and seemed to be sleeping. The two young ladies remained with her, talking quietly and keeping watch.

When Mr Hartwell had finished marking his boundary, he came upstairs and said that one of the store-rooms had been cleared and a cot made ready, and he proposed to move Cook downstairs, if Jem thought it would do no harm. She replied that it seemed the best thing, and so Cook was cocooned in sheets and a blanket so that she could not thrash about, as she was again becoming restless, and Mr Hartwell carried her downstairs as he had brought her up, Jem and Mary following with water-jugs and the herbal concoction.

The newly-cleared store-room was in the north wing of the house, with windows opening on the central courtyard on one side, and a shrubby garden at the side of the house on the other. This was an old part of the house, and the rooms opened one from the next, without a passage. The room was light and airy, but shaded from the sun, and so quite cool. Everything in the way of household stores had been removed from it, its tiled floor had been scrubbed, and a couple of sturdy wooden cots stood ready, simple frames and trestles, each with a length of pauling nailed across to make a firm surface for the patient to lie on. One of the grooms was there, who said his mate was already making another couple, and there was wood enough for more, should they be needed.

'Is that the same as tarpauling?' Mary asked him as he demonstrated the stoutness of the beds by bouncing a little on one.

'It will be when the tar's bin put on, ma'am,' he said. 'We has it in bolts, and cuts it and daubs Stockholm tar on it, or pitch, fer to make it waterproof and kip orf the rain from what's in the wagons, or whatever. My brother, what works down Deptford in the King's dockyard, says thet the sailors calls a orficer a tarpauling if he's bin bred to the sea, and not jest some gentleman what's bin appointed to it.'

'Like Sir Christopher Myngs,' Mary said, recalling one of the interminable Whitehall conversations about nautical matters, and was rewarded with a pleased grin from the groom.

'The buboes under her arms are growing,' Mr Hartwell remarked. He had put Cook down gently on the other bed and made a brief examination, keeping well within the bounds of decency, however, so that Jem was obliged to tell him that the poor woman had another swelling forming in her groin.

He looked grave at the news, and said, 'I mislike that. One we might manage to bring to a head and break, and two at a pinch, but I fear the pain might be too much for the poor soul with three! It can drive even a strong man mad.'

His expression as he stood looking down at Cook was very bleak, and Mary thought to herself that he knew very well what he was talking about. He must have suffered that pain himself when he had the sickness, and what more since, in the galleys?

She shuddered, and turned away to rearrange the jugs, bottle and cup on the table which had been stood ready for them against the wall.

CHAPTER SIX

AFTER THE GENERAL upset of the day, which, in a curiously petty way, had been symbolised by Mary and Jem dining in the kitchen, there was a certain relief in the equally petty normality of their taking supper with proper formality in the dining-room, waited on by the usual footmen. Of course, that was as far as the normality went, for everything else was decidedly abnormal, even in relatively unimportant matters. The potatoes were not as thoroughly cooked as they might have been, the lettuce in the sallet was rather wet, and there would have been no apple pie if Mary had not turned to and made the pastry, for she had returned from the new sick-room to the kitchen to find Sukey in tears having had a fit of hysterics, the pot boiled over and half the fire out, and Ellen near to panic from trying to do everything at once.

In the dining-room, it was impossible to behave normally. Mary felt uncomfortable, for her gown was crumpled and had traces of flour on it which had not responded to brushing, Jem started every time the door opened, clearly worried that her maid, who was sitting with Cook, would not be able to cope, and Mr Hartwell, after essaying one or two rather stilted attempts at conversation, lapsed into silence and seemed absorbed in his own thoughts.

When the apple pie had been brought in and served after a very long silence, Mary made up her mind that it was useless to avoid the subject which filled all their minds, and enquired of Mr Hartwell, 'Did your friend have any theory about how the plague passes from one person to another?'

He started, a spoonful of fruit poised halfway to his mouth, put the spoon down, and replied, 'No, apart from expressing the opinion that some agency of which we know nothing carries it from one to another, and it does not result from smells or miasmas. He had, however, a peculiar theory that one kind of animal may also suffer from the same disease. It seems that in eastern countries, an increased number of dead rats is regarded as a forewarning of plague.'

'Why, Cook said . . .' Mary exclaimed. 'Do you recall, Jem? She said something about rats at her aunt's home, in the town? That there was a rat lying dead on the kitchen floor when she was there a few days ago, and did Sukey not say that she'd heard that rats start to die when there's plague about?'

'Are you sure Cook said that—about a dead rat at her aunt's?' Mr Hartwell asked, looking keenly at Mary.

'Yes, quite sure.'

'So am I,' Jem confirmed. 'She remarked how dirty her aunt is become about the house, and she wished the old lady would have one of Oliver's kits for the rats and mice!'

Mr Hartwell let out a sighing breath, and relaxed. 'That's a relief to me,' he said. 'I've been puzzling and worrying about how the sickness had come to the house, not realising that Cook had been to her aunt's so recently. If she took the infection at her aunt's house . . . I've been afraid that it might be something here, in the house—the water, perhaps, or the soil . . . We've no rats or mice here, thanks to Oliver and his wives, and Obadiah's dog.'

'But it's almost a week since Cook went to the town,' Jem objected. 'I don't believe she's been away from the house since.'

'That's one of the great puzzles,' her brother replied. 'More often than not, one person is visited in a house and, a week or so after, another takes sick, and then, even as much as a month later, another will suddenly be stricken. It's as if whatever causes it has to—to ripen after it's entered the body, and takes longer in some than in others. I wonder if anyone will ever learn exactly what happens.'

'Perhaps, if they do, they'll also learn how to cure it,' Mary said soberly, 'or even to prevent it. What a great gift that would be to the world!'

Her remark was answered by a heartfelt 'Indeed!' from Jem, and one of his frowning, searching looks from Mr Hartwell, but any comment he might have made was interrupted by the entry of Henry, one of the footmen.

'Beg pardon for interrupting, sir,' he said. 'But there's Mr Reeve and some other gentlemen by the paddock, calling out to see you and the ladies.'

'Who are the other gentlemen?' asked Mr Hartwell as the ladies hurriedly put down their spoons in their half-eaten pie and rose to their feet, looking concerned.

'Sir Charles and Mr John Hook, and Mr Wharton, and two—three grooms,' the footman replied. 'Mr Reeve telt them all not to enter the paddock, very firm like, so they'm all lined up along of the far fence.'

Mr Hartwell caught Mary's eye, and held it with a direct look. 'No doubt your father is anxious for you to return home,' he said. He closed his lips firmly at the end of the sentence, but his eyes conveyed the rest of his message quite clearly, and Mary nodded in reply.

'I think he'll realise that it would hardly be sensible,' she said.

It was a grim-faced line of people who stood along the paddock fence. Mr Reeve was astride Archimedes, but Sir Charles and John had dismounted and were staring anxiously towards the house, and started forward a couple of paces when Mary and Jem appeared, then stopped, having come up against the fence. Polycarp Wharton was actually perched on the top rail of it, and doffed his hat with a flourish as soon as he saw Mary, nearly falling off as he did so. The grooms hung back, curbing their restless horses in an automatic fashion born of long practice, and looking as if they would rather be elsewhere.

There was also a small cart, loaded with Mary's large trunk, the driver looking very dubiously at the approaching group. As they entered the paddock, he got down and went to stand some distance away, leaving his horse to its own devices. Fortunately, it chose to droop quietly where it stood, a picture of equine dejection.

Mr Hartwell advanced as far as his line of markers, then stopped, and Mary and Jem followed, to stand on either side of him.

'I'm much obliged to you for coming,' he called to Mr Reeve. 'I know how great an extra burden of work you have, with all the sickness in the town!'

'But so much easier to manage with a *horse*,' Mr Reeve replied in his most carrying pulpit voice. 'So kind, so very kind! I trust all is well here? Er . . .' He stammered for a moment, realising that his choice of words was infelicitous. 'I mean, as well as may be *expected*, in the circumstances?'

'You had my message that my cook is visited?' Mr Hartwell asked. 'She's very sick, but everyone else appears well, so far. I've marked a boundary, as you see, and we're all agreed that no one shall pass it, in or out. My steward will come for orders each day and see we have whatever we need, and he'll carry news to and fro as well.'

'Excellent!' Mr Reeve nodded approvingly. 'I suggest that all messages and enquiries be channelled through him, for it will be better if people do not approach, even to this distance. We do not know how far the poisonous *exhalation* of the sickness may be carried in the ambient air.'

'Indeed.' Mr Hartwell looked at Archimedes, who appeared to be asleep. 'Is that horse behaving himself?'

'Indeed, yes! We are great friends, I assure you,' the Rector said earnestly. 'He stands quite still to allow me to climb up on him, and to descend, and goes and stops as I request.'

'Requast? Grecious heavens!' Polycarp Wharton exclaimed. 'Miss Hook, how do you do? Air you quaite wall, dear leddy?'

Mary suppressed a slightly hysterical inclination to laugh, for he looked so incongruous in this rural setting in crimson silk and Cambridge blue ribbons, and his affected mode of speech was so out of tune with the genuine concern on his face and in his voice that she wondered that he kept it up, unless it had already become his normal way of speaking.

'I'm quite well, thank you, Mr Wharton,' she said gravely. 'I trust you are in good health yourself?'

'Oh—er—yas, middling fair, thenk you.'

'I gather that you intend to remain here, Mary?' Sir Charles interrupted impatiently.

'I think it would be the wisest course, Father,' she replied, wishing that this conversation did not have to be held across twenty feet or so of space and before an audience. 'I know you and Mama will be worried, but I can be of use here, and I mustn't carry the infection to other people.'

Sir Charles nodded abruptly, and gestured to the driver of the cart to unload the trunk, but he shook his head violently and backed away even further, so John and Polycarp lifted it from the cart and set it down inside the paddock gate.

'Your mother packed some things for you,' Sir Charles said. 'I suppose you'll be here for—for six weeks, at least . . . If you need anything else, you can tell me, for I'll come and—and wave to you from here, every day. If Francis has no objection, that is?'

'I think, if you're agreeable, Sir Charles, that you should come at a set time and stay at a greater distance. Miss Hook can signal to you to approach to the fence if she wishes to say something, but otherwise, if you see her standing here, you'll know she's well,' Mr Hartwell said firmly. 'You'll understand that it's hardly fair to allow you to come and talk to your daughter, yet deny my servants a similar chance to converse with members of their families who live in the town.'

Sir Charles looked a little taken aback, for it had probably never occurred to him that there might be occasions when the gentry should not claim privileges denied to those beneath them, but he replied agreeably, 'I accept your point, Francis. I'll come to the top of the ridge when the 'prentice bell rings each evening, and if Mary comes out here, I'll see her and know she's well. We'll be thinking of you all, and praying for you of course.'

'I, too, shall come each evening at that time, and pronounce a blessing,' Mr Reeve said. 'I trust it may be of comfort to you all to know you're remembered. There's to be another day of fasting and prayer on Wednesday, and we shall pray for all by name in church, as for the members of every visited family in the parish.'

'I'm sure we shall find your blessing a great help,' Mr Hartwell said. 'But you mustn't feel obliged to come every evening, much though we should appreciate seeing you. Will it not add too much to your burden?'

'One doesn't enter into Holy Orders to be comfortable and live at ease! I go to every visited house in the town and pray loudly outside it, every day, so that the poor souls within may know they are not forsaken. It's not much more than a mile to here from the town, and my equine friend can compass the distance in very little time, at no cost of fatigue to myself. To tell truth, I am beginning to enjoy riding upon him, and being able to look about me at the countryside without fear of tripping over some obstacle!' the Rector said earnestly, and Mary felt very ashamed to recall how often she had thought him a little ridiculous.

"Perhaps you had better bring the groom with you,

then,' Mr Hartwell said doubtfully. 'I'll tell Palmer to
see that he has a mount. Archimedes can be difficult at
times, and you may need help with him.'

'He won't be difficult when he's about the Lord's
business,' Mr Reeve said confidently. 'He's a beast of
high principles, and would not so demean himself! Oh
dear! I seem to have made a *jest*! Principles
—Archimedes—oh, my goodness! Quite unintentional,
I assure you!'

He was obviously concerned that no one should think
that he would purposely make jokes to anyone in such
grave circumstances as were Mr Hartwell and his
companions, but Polycarp Wharton said kindly, 'It's es
good a jast es if you'd thought it out a purpose! Ai vow
that if Ai've heard a better this se'enight, mai name's
not Polycerp Wherton!'

At this, Mary could not help but let out a gasp of
laughter, due more to nerves strained by fear and
anxiety than actual amusement.

Wharton nodded encouragingly and said, 'Thar you
air! You've chared the leddies' spirits with it, sir! Miss
Hook takes the point!'

'Oh? Oh well, in that case, perhaps it was all to the
good,' Mr Reeve said, comforted. 'No doubt you good
people have all much to do, and we've assured ourselves
that all is well as—er—may be expected, so I shall give
you my blessing . . .'

Mr Hartwell turned and waved forward the members
of his household who had been watching and listening
from the stableyard. Not suprisingly, considering that
they were all anxious to know what was going on, they
were all there, apart from poor Cook and Jem's maid.
Mr Reeve spread his arms, dropping his reins on
Archimedes' neck, but the horse did not move a muscle
as the Blessing was pronounced in sonorous and author-
itative tones, the final *Amen* being echoed in a heartfelt
manner by everyone present.

Slowly, reluctantly, the visitors rode away, looking

back over their shoulders as they went, and the beleaguered garrison of Canons Grange watched them out of sight. It was only then that Mary realised that her brother had not spoken a single word the whole time, but only stood by the fence, staring at Jem.

'I'm sorry I had to discourage your father from coming to talk to you,' Mr Hartwell said to her.

'I quite understand,' she replied coolly. 'May I trouble you to have my trunk brought in? I'm sorry it's so large—I can't imagine what my mother has put in it.'

It took two men to carry the trunk up to the bedroom next to Jem's, which had been prepared for Mary's use, and there she unpacked it with Jem's help, and found that, beside toilet articles, an array of personal linen, half a dozen gowns suitable for day wear and a couple of more formal silks for the evening, there were some of her favourite books, her Bible and Prayer-book, two bottles of perfume and a quantity of Hungary water, a warm cloak, some jars of dried herbs (including Jesuit's bark) and some bottles of concoctions.

'How kind of her to think of those!' Jem exclaimed. 'I was worried that we might not have enough of some things. I've very little angelica-root, and I see she's sent a jar of it. Have you everything else you need?'

'I think so,' Mary replied, fishing her hairbrush, comb and a small mirror out of a bottom corner of the trunk. 'She's even included things I wouldn't have thought of.'

'Is that perfume?' Jem asked curiously, looking at the silver-stoppered bottles of pretty coloured glass.

'Yes, although I think the Hungary water would have been enough. These are hardly suitable for country wear.' Mary opened one and handed it to Jem, who sniffed cautiously.

'It's a little, well, suffocating,' she said. 'I mean, it's cloying, and doesn't smell at all like flowers.'

'It's not, in fact, a scent I ever use, to tell truth. It was given to me last New Year by a friend, and I sent it to Mama, thinking she might like to have the pretty bottle. Try the Hungary water—you'll like that better, I'm sure.'

Jem did, for it was a light toilet water with a pleasant lemony tang. She daringly dabbed a little on her wrists at Mary's bidding, and was persuaded to accept a bottle for her own use, although she added to her thanks, 'I don't know what Francis will say!'

'He can't object to that!' Mary exclaimed 'Why, it's perfectly respectable. My mother always uses it! She did not add that at one time it had been considered capable of making men mad with desire, for that had been quite two centuries before. 'If he says anything, tell him that even *Mrs Crumwell* used it.'

'What, Oliver's wife? Oh, but that would be no recommendation to Francis. He's never been at all of the Roundhead persuasion!'

'But a little puritanical,' Mary replied, not altogether jokingly.

'Perhaps—in a way. It's not that he's inclined to Presbyterianism, but more that he thinks a great deal about duty and . . . Oh, heavens! How can I be sitting here, talking as if we had all the time in the world, and I've not been to see poor Cook since before supper!'

'I'll go with you,' Mary said at once, and they went down together to the sick-room

It was quiet there. Two branches of candles had been brought in and stood on the table, far enough from the invalid for their light not to worry her, if she were even conscious of them. Jem's maid rose as they entered, and reported in a whisper that Cook had been less restless for the past half-hour or so, and Jem thanked her and gave her leave to go.

'What shall we do about the windows, do you think?' Jem asked Mary. 'It will grow chilly during the night, but the smell will be so dreadful if they're shut.'

'Leave one open, and whoever is here can sit by it, with a blanket or a cloak. If Cook has blankets over her, she'll not get chilled, and the cooler air may help to bring down her fever.'

'You don't think the night air might be dangerous?'

'No more than the same air by day.'

Mr Hartwell came in as Mary was speaking, and said, 'I quite agree. How is she?' He gave Mary another of his searching, frowning glances.

She went over to the bed and felt Cook's forehead and cheeks. 'Still burning, and her face is . . . it may be only a shadow. Will you bring the candles?'

Mr Hartwell brought a branch of candles over to the bed and held it so that Cook's face was fully illumined. There was a black patch on her cheek, another on her neck, and a third on one arm, which was lying over the sheet.

'Whatever are they?' Mary whispered.

'Plague spots. She has it badly, I'm afraid.' Mr Hartwell gently raised the arm that was outside the sheet, and looked at the swelling in the armpit, which had grown considerably. The sick woman gave a moaning cry of protest and shrank from the movement, as if she could not bear it.

Mr Hartwell carefully laid the arm down, and said, 'I've made out a roster of people to sit with her during the night. No one to be here for longer than two hours, and then to wake the next on the list. In that way, nobody will have to lose too much sleep. If there's any change, the person on watch will call me.'

'Where do Jem and I appear on your roster?' Mary asked, anxious not to appear reluctant to take her share of the work.

'I think it best if you both have the nights free, for the burden will fall on you during the day. So off to bed with you, and try to sleep. You'll do no good by lying awake and worrying.'

'And you? Will you not have more than enough to do during the day?' Jem demanded.

'I'll take the first watch, and then go to bed,' he replied. 'Don't worry, m'dear, I'll not try to do everything myself—I've more sense than that!' He put an arm about his sister's shoulders, hugged her to him and kissed her cheek, surprising Mary, who had thought him too austere for such gestures of affection.

'I must make those masks before I go up,' Jem said as she and Mary left the sick-room. 'Would you mind helping? It will halve the time it takes.'

'Of course. What had you in mind?'

Jem's idea was to make a simple mask of two layers of fine muslin, put in it coarsely-ground cloves and cinnamon, which would at least help to disguise the smell in the sick-room, and sew tapes to the corners so that it could be tied over the nose and mouth. She found muslin in the sewing-room, and, after a little experimenting, she and Mary made half a dozen masks and filled them, and then Jem took them in to her brother while Mary went up to bed.

It was a long time since she had undressed without the help of a maid, and she found herself involved in some awkward contortions to unlace the back of her stiffly-boned bodice, but managed it at last. She laid out clean linen and a fresh gown and petticoat for the next day, put on a nightshift, and laid her nightrobe to hand, in case she should need it, and then looked about the room in a distracted manner. She was tired, and the day seemed to have been incredibly long, yet she did not feel that she could sleep yet.

The room was pleasant, the end one of a range of family bedrooms along the front of the house, opening from a corridor which ran from one side of the building to the other and was lit by a large window in each end wall. The bed was old-fashioned, with a heavy, carved oak frame, curtained in crimson velvet with a tester and canopy to match, and the presses and chests had obviously been made to go with it, all being of oak and decorated with a wealth of carved foliage. The walls were panelled, and the general effect was dark, particularly by candle-light, but the windows, which were both wide and casemented, lightened the impression considerably during the day. She drew back the heavy velvet curtains from one window, opened a casement, perched on the broad sill, and looked out at the night.

It was fine, and the moon near to full, lighting the wide gravelled area before the house, and showing the winding path which terraced the slope down to the road from the town to Nessing, further up the valley. Beyond the road, the ground still sloped away, but less steeply. There was a copse, and the house was high enough above its level for her to be able to see over the trees to the fields and meadows beyond, where the seven streams of the river meandered between willows and alders, the water gleaming here and there in the moonlight. A little to her left, the white tower of the church shone, the gilded cock and the black wooden cross which crowned it edged with a faint silvery line, rising above the dark roofs of the town crouched about it like chicks around the mother hen. The church clock chimed faintly, and Gabriel struck the hour. It was already ten o'clock, late by country standards.

She sighed, and let her thoughts roam back over the events of the day, marvelling at how quickly everything had changed. Only that short space of time ago, she had been enjoying her unexpected vacation at home in the country, conscious that it had been granted her because of the plague, but the disease itself no more than a distant black cloud in the background, something to be thought of only when she said her prayers and included the general intercession for the poor visited sick . . . And now? Now it was all about her, as if the cloud had come sweeping, like a storm, up from the horizon to the zenith, to cover the whole sky and darken everything. Now she had touched a plague-stricken body . . . She shivered, but discovered on examining her feelings that she was not yet afraid for herself—that would come later, no doubt, and she would have to guard against thinking every physical sensation might be a symptom of the disease, remembering how Miss Webster had once had a spot on her chin, and a slightly sore throat at the same time, and had taken to her bed, convinced she had the smallpox!

What would Mr Hartwell make of that, she wondered. It would confirm his opinion of the stupidity of Court ladies, no doubt, and he would probably think it more likely that one of them would be suffering from the other kind of pox—the variety which followed indulgence in the pleasures of the bedroom.

'Oh, the devil take the man!' she exclaimed aloud. 'Why should I care what he thinks of me? If his blind prejudice makes him believe that every female at Court is a whore, well, a—a fig for him! If he persists, though, in treating me as if I had not a sensible thought in my head, I swear I'll lose my temper with him before long!'

She gave another shiver, from coldness this time, for a little breeze had sprung up and was breathing a slight chill on her bare arms, so she shut the window, leaving the curtain pulled back, knelt by the bed to say her prayers, remembering Cook in particular. She wished she knew the woman's name, for it seemed odd to ask God to bless Mr Hartwell's cook, but she had never heard her called anything else. Then she climbed into bed, settled into the feather mattress, and hoped she would not lie awake too long, for that was the time when troubled thoughts grew worse. She closed her eyes, sighed, and thought how tired she felt.

When she opened them, it was daylight, the birds were singing in the garden, and a handbell was ringing somewhere not far away—at the head of the stairs, in all probability. She got up and dressed, wrestling with the back-lacing of her bodice, but beginning to get the knack of pulling the laces tight from the top downwards.

As in most homes, the day at Canons Grange began with the household assembling for prayers and a Bible reading. This was normally in the entrance hall, which was spacious and uncluttered with any furniture, apart

from a table, but Mr Hartwell decided to adjourn to
the central courtyard, as it was fine and warm again.
This enabled the housemaid who was sitting with Cook
to join in from the open window of the sick-room, and
Cook to hear, if she was capable of doing so.

Mr Hartwell chose to read the ninety-first Psalm,
with its verse concerning *the pestilence that walketh in
darkness*, and Mary found it comforting and encouraging, for he read it expressively and with great feeling,
so that the promises it contained were impressed on the
minds of his hearers. They seemed to look a little less
anxious and unhappy after it.

After a hurried breakfast, Mary and Jem went to the
sick-room, releasing the housemaid to her own breakfast and her normal work, and conferred over Cook.
She was obviously worse, much more restless, crying
out at intervals from the pain of the buboes, which were
now huge and almost black. The poor woman looked
shrunken and weak, and was still sweating copiously. It
was impossible to wash her or change her sheets, for
any attempt to move her resulted in her writhing and
screaming, as if she thought they meant to hurt her.
Getting her to drink more of Jem's concoction, or even
plain water, proved difficult, she became so violent. In
the end, they got a small spoonful of the mixture into
her, and about the same amount of water, but the rest
of the jugful of the latter was spilled in the process, so
Mary went to the kitchen to refill it.

She found that Ellen had organised matters better
now, and preparation of dinner was under way. Ellen
was beating eggs and Molly was mixing something in a
bowl, and Obadiah, unable to do his normal work, had
been conscripted to tend the fire, keep the spit-jack
turning the roast meat, and prepare vegetables. He was
scraping some carrots, and cabbage, potatoes and peas
awaited his attention. He looked a little surprised to
find himself doing it, but made no objection, except to
remark to his shadow, the small black and tan terrier,

'This do fairly beat all, don't it, Dog?' The dog accepted a sliver of carrot and chewed it philosophically, wagging the tip of his tail.

Mary crossed the kitchen towards one of the pumps, saying 'Good morning. How is everyone today?' in a bright and friendly tone, and received a chorus of 'Good morning', and 'Fair to middling', and 'Not so bad, thankee ma'am', as she filled her jug. She was just turning away from the sink when Oliver walked in with a very small mouse dangling nonchalantly from the corner of his mouth at the end of a very long tail. He showed it to Mary, swinging it to and fro to draw her attention to it, then to Ellen and Molly, and then sat down before Obadiah, placed the dead creature on the floor and carefully pinned it down with one paw, and looked the terrier firmly in the eye as he made a brief statement, apparently to the effect that this was *his* kitchen. The terrier extended his neck, dropped his ears sideways, and looked impressed, so Oliver scooped his mouse up in his paw, caught it in his mouth in mid-air, and took it out into the yard, his tail standing up behind him like a flag-pole.

'Where is he going with it?' Mary asked, looking out of the window to see where he went.

'He buries 'em under they old rose-bushes down alongside the track,' Obadiah replied. 'As neat as the sexton, but don't put up no headstones. That were nobbut a fieldmice. Ain't no housemices nor ratses here. He's had 'em all long since, him and his three missuses, not to mention the kits. All good micers, and never wanting for a home. Them three out there now is all spoken for, ain't they, Dog?' The dog did not disagree.

Sukey came in from the stableyard at that moment, two large milk-cans dragging down her thin arms and shoulders. She looked hot and tired, and her eyes were so big that they seemed to fill her small face.

'Cowman left these in the paddock,' she said, putting them down on the floor before lifting them one at a time on the table, then wearily wiped the back of her hand across her brow.

'D'you feel any better for a breath of air?' Ellen asked kindly, giving her an anxious look.

'Yes, thankee. A little, but—but . . .' The girl hesitated, biting her lip. 'I 'spects its jest that it's hot in here, and I didn't sleep too well . . .'

'What is it?' asked Mary, a sad foreboding in her mind, but kept carefully from her voice, for there were two flushed patches on the girl's cheek-bones. 'Does your head ache?'

'Yes, ma'am and my throat's all sore, like I'm starting a cold,' she replied in a low, nervous voice, as if she were still afraid of speaking to the gentry. 'Ellen kindly said to take a walk round the paddock for some air and see if the milk had come up from the dayhouse.'

Mary put one hand lightly on the girl's forehead, and found it burning hot. 'I think a dose of Miss Jemima's medicine might do you good,' she said gently. 'Will you come along to the sick-room and take some?'

'I got plague, ha'n't I?' Sukey asked, looking her straight in the face.

'I'm not sure, but I think we must assume that you have,' Mary replied honestly, relieved that the girl seemed quite calm. She looked understandably afraid, but there was no sign of hysteria or panic.

'Oh, well . . . Saves waiting about, getting worrit sick about it!' Sukey said with a little shrug. 'I'm sorry, Ellen.'

'Oh, you dear child!' Ellen exclaimed; her eyes filling. 'No need to say sorry, dear! I'm the one that's sorry, that you're feeling poorly.' She rubbed the tip of her nose with one knuckle, sniffing and blinking. 'Don't you worry none. You'll be fine, you see if you ain't, and we'll manage, wi' Obadiah to help.'

The tranter looked startled, and muttered, 'That ain't what she said when I scraped the first carrot too thick, were it, Dog?' He gave the dog another sliver.

Mary put her arm about Sukey's thin shoulders, took a firm grip of the heavy earthenware jug in her other hand, and propelled the girl gently out of the kitchen and along to the sick-room, where Jem was mopping up spilled water with one of Cook's soiled sheets, which she had somehow managed to replace. She looked up as they entered, gave a little sighing gasp, and said, 'Why, Sukey! Do you not feel well?'

'She has a headache and a sore throat,' Mary reported quietly. 'I think we should dose her, and let her lie down in the other room until she feels better, or . . . It's cleared in there, isn't it? It will be more peaceful, if she wants to sleep.'

'Yes,' Jem replied, nodding; then, to the girl, 'Sukey, I want you to drink this. It doesn't taste very good, but medicine doesn't usually, does it?'

'My mam says that the worser it tastes, the more good it does,' Sukey replied in a small, hoarse voice, took the proffered cup, closed her eyes, and manfully swallowed a good big dose of Jem's concoction. She pulled a face after it, but made no complaint, and Jem gave her an approving pat on the arm.

'Good girl! Now, go into the other room, take off your clothes, and get into one of the beds there. It doesn't matter which. I'll fetch you a nightshift.'

Sukey looked doubtful, as if she thought she ought to fetch it herself, but did as she was told. Mary finished wiping the floor, rolled the soiled sheet up in a small bundle, and tried to soothe Cook by talking in a quiet, monotonous voice, but without any appreciable effect.

When Jem returned, Sukey was already between the sheets and, by the time Mary and Jem had given her a swift examination and slipped the shift on her, she seemed drowsy, so they left her to sleep and returned to the next room, leaving the communicating door open.

'What do you think?' Jem asked.

'I could see no sign of buboes, but there's a mark on her arm. Did you see it?'

'Yes. It looks angry, but it could be an insect bite. We must watch her, and wait, I think. Mary, would you take that sheet to the wash-house—do you mind? You know where it is?' Mary nodded. 'And then perhaps you'd find Francis and tell him we think Sukey may have . . . may be ill? He'll be in the kitchen garden, I think, or perhaps helping the grooms weed the front terraces, now they've turned gardeners.'

'Is the kitchen garden behind the brick wall beyond the stableyard?' Mary asked, and, when Jem said that it was, went out with the sheet. The wash-house was next to the kitchen, and the copper there was already boiling in preparation for washing the other sheets from Cook's bed, so Mary dropped them all in, poked them under the water with the dolly-stick, and went on her way to the kitchen garden.

It was a quiet, orderly place, surrounded by warm red-brick walls against which apricot, plum and apple-trees were trained. The ground was planted with neat rows of vegetables, with not a weed in sight, but it was, of necessity, within Mr Hartwell's *cordon sanitaire*, so presumably the gardeners would not be able to tend it for some time. Mr Hartwell, however, was not going to let it get out of hand, for he was there, digging a piece of empty ground with his back to the gate, pushing the spade in with one foot, turning each spit with a practised, economic movement.

It was very warm in this sheltered place, and he had stripped to the waist, revealing that his broad, muscular back was laced with a crisscross network of fine white lines.

CHAPTER SEVEN

MARY STARED BLANKLY for a moment, then realised that the marks were scars, and caught her breath in a startled gasp, wincing in reaction as she thought how many lashings it must have taken to cut him about so much. He heard her and turned sharply, then walked unhurriedly across to the wall, where his shirt hung on a branch of a plum-tree, pulled it down, and slipped it over his head, looking thoughtfully at her as his head came through the neck opening, and continued to eye her steadily as he fastened the cuffs and tucked the tails into his breeches.

'Jem asked me to find you,' she said at length, unwilling to mention his back unless he chose to speak of it first. 'Sukey is unwell, and we think she may have the plague.'

'Unwell in what way?' His voice was quietly neutral, as if he thought she might turn hysterical if he showed any sign of alarm.

'A sore throat, very hot, flushed cheeks, headache. There are no buboes under her arms, or—or elsewhere, but an angry patch, about the size of a shilling, on her left arm.'

'Is that what Jem said?'

'No. It's what I saw,' Mary said irritably, feeling that he was implying that she was capable only of relaying someone else's observations, not of making her own.

'It sounds like the plague. Where is she?'

'We've put her to bed in the second store-room. Cook is very restless and noisy, and Sukey seems to wish to sleep.'

'Best let her do so, then.' He pulled his spade out of the soil and contemplated his half-dug patch. 'I'll finish this, and then come and see her. Jem doesn't want me there immediately, I take it?'

'No. We just thought you should know.'

'Yes. Thank you.'

He stood still, holding his spade, but not turning back to his digging, as if he might be considering saying something more, and there was a long pause.

Mary broke it at last by saying what she had not intended to say. 'I suppose your back was scarred like that in the galleys?'

'Yes. Galley slaves refrain from pulling as hard as their masters wish unless they're—encouraged,' he replied in a dry, sardonic voice. 'The Mediterranean's hot, and the work hard. It's worse in the Atlantic. Cooler, but the sea is rougher, and tends to fall away from the oar-blades.'

'That must make rowing very difficult,' Mary said in a careful tone of mild interest, not wishing any of the pity or sorrowful anger she felt to be apparent in her voice. 'How *did* you escape?'

'Do you really wish to know? Very well, then. We were patrolling in a thick mist one evening, aware that a Barbary corsair was somewhere nearby—another galley. They'd been capturing and sinking ships in the vicinity. The oar in front of mine caught in some floating wreckage from one, and couldn't be freed, so the two men who pulled it, and my partner and I—he was the physician I told you of—were unchained to give the crew room to get at it. One of the officers ordered me to go over the side to pull the wreckage away from it, for they were concerned that the corsair might come out of the mist and catch us motionless . . . I dived off the gunwale, but went straight down and under the hull . . .'

'Under!' Mary exclaimed.

'A galley has a shallow draught—it's not deep in the

water, like a sailing-ship. I swam under the hull and the oars on the other side, and went on swimming as long as I could under water, and when I surfaced, the galley was out of sight in the mist, and I was free. They'd not waste time looking for a mere convict, with a corsair in the offing! I found a part of a mast, perhaps from the same wreck, tied myself to it, and waited for morning. The water was quite warm, for it was summer.' He paused, looking across the garden, perhaps into the past, recalling that night.

'And in the morning?' Mary prompted.

'In the morning, the sun came up, the mist melted away, and there was a Portuguee merchantman coming straight towards me, every lookout with his eyes peeled for corsairs! They saw me as soon as I waved, and sent a boat to collect me. That's all.' He turned dismissively, and pushed his spade into the ground, conveying that he wished to go on digging.

'Thank you for telling me,' Mary said politely, and went away, back to the house, in a somewhat confused state of mind. Here was a man she could admire, a strong character, resolute, courageous, sensible, kind, modest—yet bigoted! Perhaps bigoted was too strong a term, yet he was certainly blinded by prejudice as far as she was concerned, for he had made up his mind that, as a Court lady, she must be immoral and stupid, and seemed incapable of realising that her conduct proved him wrong. It was really most provoking!

She passed through the kitchen on her way back into the house, and found work there suspended, for one of the housemaids was sitting on a stool by the table, crying and clutching her head. Molly and Ellen were trying to persuade her to go to the sick-room and see Miss Jemima.

'It might not be the sickness at all, Joan,' Ellen was saying. 'Please go and see her, and maybe she'll tell you it's just the headache, and give you something to help make it better.'

'First sign, that is,' Obadiah said unhelpfully from
his seat by the spit-jack, where he was now shucking
peas. 'Headachings and limb-achings and feeling poorly,
then the spotses and the fever, ther the gurt wens. Bin
sneezing, 'ave yer? That's another sign, some says. Allus
goes the same way, don't it, Dog?' Dog thumped his
tail on the floor.

'Be quiet, Obadiah!' Mary said sharply. 'You're
frightening Joan with your talk!'

'Yes, hush your noise, Obadiah!' Ellen echoed, turning
on him. 'I won't have you talking like that in my
kitchen, scaring poor bodies half to death!'

'*Yore* kitching now, is it?' asked Obadiah,
unimpressed. 'Well, if yer wants *yore* peases podded
and *yore* wortses fettled, don't yer goo telling me what
I can do and what I can't do in it! Yer ain't my mester,
nor Dog's! We'm here doin' yer a favour, seein' as how
yer can't be doing all yerself, and it ain't *yore* kitching
yet, miss! That's right, ain't it, Dog?' Dog wagged the
end of his tail, but also put his head and ears down and
rolled his eyes towards Ellen, no doubt knowing who
would be cooking his dinner.

Ellen opened her mouth, taking a deep breath, but
Mary cut in sharply, before battle could be joined,
'We're all very glad of your help, Obadiah, but if you're
going to frighten people with your talk, I expect Mr
Hartwell will tell you to pod your peas and fettle your
worts out in the yard, and I'm sure Dog would prefer
to be in here, where he can smell the meat roasting.'

Obadiah looked at her, frowning, for a moment, and
then a twinkle appeared in his pale blue eyes, his
weather-beaten face broke into a grin, and he said,
'That's a right clever argyment, that is! Awright—I'll
not fret silly gels wi' little bits of megrims in their empty
skulls, but only fer Dog's sake, mind!' And he gave
Dog an empty peapod to chew.

Joan was eventually persuaded along to the sick-
room and put to bed alongside Sukey, although she

had, as yet, no great fever on her, and no sign of plague-spots, and Mary went to confer with Jem in the next room.

She found her mixing some more of her concoction, for she had brought the ingredients along from the stillroom after breakfast. She looked worried, and, when Mary caught her eye and raised her eyebrows enquiringly, she glanced towards Cook and shook her head doubtfully.

'She's wandering in her mind,' she said quietly, 'and says she can't see—everything's misty. There are marks like bruises coming all over her. Was that Joan's voice I heard next door?'

'Yes. She has the headache, and a slight fever. Nothing more, so far.'

'It's going to be difficult to keep the household running, with three female servants out of action! I was hoping Joan and Bess, the other housemaid, would do the washing, for the washerwoman won't be able to come, of course. She lives in the town, and comes three days a week, usually. Perhaps Prue, the sewing-woman, would help, or Susan, my maid.'

'Oh, heavens! I put the soiled sheets in the copper to boil when I went out to your brother!' Mary exclaimed. 'They'll still be there.'

'If you'll stay here for a bit, I'll go and speak to Bess about them.'

Jem went out, Mary continued to pound the mixture of herbs in the mortar, and Cook moaned and cried, tossing about on her narrow bed, her voice rising to a crescendo when she jarred one or other of the buboes. Mary went to look at her, and caught sight of one of them as the woman flung her arm up above her head. It was completely black.

'Where's Jem?' Mr Hartwell asked abruptly as he came in.

'Gone to ask Bess to take the sheets out of the copper,' Mary replied, returning to her pounding. 'Sukey is next door, and now Joan's there too, although she has only the headache and a slight fever.'

'Did Jem see no marks on her? They may be anywhere on the body, not only the arms.'

'*I* saw no marks,' Mary replied coldly. 'I looked all over her. Jem hasn't had time to see her yet. I'm quite capable of seeing a red mark if there's one to be seen!' she added, glaring at him over her shoulder.

'Yes, I suppose you are,' he replied mildly, his mouth twitching at one corner. 'I'll go and talk to Joan—if I may?'

'Don't wake Sukey if she's asleep!' Mary admonished. He made her a slight, ironic bow and went through into the next room, and presently returned to his work in the garden from there, without passing through Cook's room on the way.

Obadiah turned up, without Dog, to keep watch while Jem and Mary had their dinner. He brought his meal with him on a tray, saying that he had no sense in his nose, so the smell didn't worry him. He shook his head over Cook, and said, 'Poor 'oman. Not a bad sort, she ain't, though given ter throwing things at Dog.'

The afternoon was long, hot, and very trying. Sukey woke up crying, and burning with fever, and Joan also became much more fevered. Cook's cries grew louder still, and sometimes she screamed. Her ramblings were disjointed, and some of the language she used and the things she said were quite shocking, coming from the lips of a respectable woman, and a spinster at that! At last, supper-time came, and Jem and Mary were freed for the night.

'I must have a breath of air before I eat anything!' Jem exclaimed. 'The spices in the masks become almost as bad as the smell they half-disguise, after a time! Will you come for a turn about the garden?'

Mary went willingly, and they strolled along the winding path of the terraced garden, amid the late flush of roses, down to the road and back again.

'Did Francis tell you about old Matthew Hartwell?' Jem asked. 'He made this garden for his Kate. It was just a rough pasture before. He called her his "briar rose", and I have a brooch which he had made for her. It's a wild rose, an eglantine, done in enamel, with gold briars caging it in, and a Latin phrase—something about passing through the thorns to reach the rose. It's very pretty.'

'Did she give him a thorny passage in his wooing, then?' Mary asked, smiling.

'I think so! It's hardly surprising, for he was one of the King's officers who came to close down the Abbey, and that meant Kate and her father losing their home, this house. Then the King gave the house to Matthew, so it was little wonder she thought him perfectly horrid and villainous! I don't know how he persuaded her that he wasn't what she assumed him to be!'

'No,' said Mary reflectively. 'It's very difficult, once someone has condemned one as guilty, to establish one's innocence. Prejudice is so blinding!'

Her thoughts were interrupted by a call from the top terrace, where Obadiah was waving his straw hat at them.

'Visitor at the parrock!' he shouted, using the old form of the word. 'Cen't find Mester!'

'Oh dear!' exclaimed Jem. 'I wonder where he is! We'd better go and see who's come, and what he wants.'

It turned out to be Polycarp Wharton with a large hamper, which he had humped through the paddock gate and left near the boundary marker, before retreating to the far fence and perching on the top rail again.

'Good avening, leddies!' he called. 'Ai hope, nay, Ai trust, you are wall? Good! Frencis quaite wall? Axcellent! Ai've brought a small awffering of things which may be halpful to you. Is there anything Ai can do to be of sarvice to you? Any arrends to run? You hev but to speak the word!'

'You're very kind,' Jem replied. 'Thank you for the

hamper. I do need some snake-root, if you can find any. Do you know what it's like? It's sometimes called bistort, and it grows in the water-meadows.'

'Ai axpect Ai cen find some. Thar's en old waise-woman lives in Wast Street—she'll know, Ai don't doubt.'

'It's the roots I need, not the stems or leaves.'

'Roots. Ai'll bring tham!'

'Thank you.'

'Is, ah, your cook . . .?'

'Cook's very ill, poor soul, and we have two more servants . . .'

Mr Wharton sighed, and said soberly, 'Ai shell prey for you all most arnestly. Ai wish Ai could do more. Thar er savarel more houses shut up in the town. Ai har the Greygoose femily is awl visited.'

The 'prentice bell began to ring across the meadows from the church tower, signalling the end of the working day, and Mary looked up towards the top of the ridge above the house. A solitary figure on a tall horse sat there, watching. She stepped forward to the boundary mark and waved. The figure waved back, waited a few moments, and then rode away.

As he disappeared, Mr Reeve emerged from some trees to their right, sitting very upright on Archimedes, with his black steeple-crowned hat worn tilted back on his head instead of in its usual straight position. He was followed by a mounted groom, who kept well back from the paddock fence. Polycarp Wharton jumped down from his perch and went to hold Archimedes' head in a solicitous fashion, which the horse seemed to resent, for he bared his teeth and flicked his ears irritably.

'Good evening!' Mr Reeve called, then, in an aside, 'I think perhaps Archimedes would—er—*prefer* not to be held, Mr Wharton, if you don't mind. It implies a lack of *trust*, I fear, and he may—er—*resent* it.' He continued more loudly, 'I trust things are going as well

Mills & Boon

Love, romance, intrigue...
all are captured for you
by Mills & Boon's top-selling authors.

Take four exciting books absolutely FREE

TURN OVER THE PAGE FOR DETAILS

Also FREE
— a digital quartz clock.

A sensational offer to readers of Mills & Boon, the world's largest publisher of romantic fiction.

As a special introduction we will send you 4 exciting Mills & Boon Romances and an exclusive Mills & Boon tote bag FREE when you complete and return this coupon.

At the same time we will reserve a subscription to Mills & Boon Reader Service for you. Every month you will receive six of the very latest novels by leading Romantic Fiction authors, delivered direct to your door. **POST & PACKING FREE.**

And you can enjoy many other advantages:

FREE CLOCK

This digital quartz clock is yours FREE – whatever you decide.

You have nothing to lose and a whole world of romance to gain.

- ● THE NEWEST ROMANCES — 6 books reserved at the printers for you each month and delivered to your door by Mills & Boon. **POSTAGE AND PACKING FREE**

- ● FREE MONTHLY NEWSLETTER — packed with exciting competitions, horoscopes, recipes and handicrafts PLUS information on top Mills & Boon authors.

- ● SPECIAL OFFERS — specially selected books and bargain gifts created just for Mills & Boon subscribers.

- ● HELPFUL FRIENDLY SERVICE from the girls at Mills & Boon. You can ring us any time on 01-684 2141.

- ● NO COMMITMENT — you may cancel your subscription at any time.

It's so easy! Send no money now — you don't ever need a stamp. Just fill in and detach the reply card and send it off today.

Mills & Boon Reader Service, P.O. Box 236, Thornton Road, Croydon, Surrey. CR9 3RU as may be expected?'

Jem called out the latest news, and by then those of the household who were not too busy elsewhere had come out, having heard the distant bell. They straggled over to the paddock, where Mr Hartwell joined them, once more dressed in more formal fashion, having changed for supper. He exchanged a few words with the visitors, and then Mr Reeve prayed aloud, hands uplifted, while Archimedes stood rock-still. After he had pronounced the Blessing, the Rector promised that they would all be remembered in church at Mattins the next morning, and rode away with the groom and Polycarp Wharton.

'Mikes yer fill better, like, being blessed,' said one of the grooms, picking up the hamper and carrying it into the kitchen at Jem's request. It contained two gallipots of apricots conserved in brandy, a quantity of expensive green figs, a dozen quails, and a bunch of grapes.

'Very kind of him,' observed Mr Hartwell. 'I suppose it makes him feel he's doing something to help.'

'I dunno how to cook them liddle birds!' Ellen said dubiously. 'Best put 'em in a pie, like squabs, I s'pose. What about them greeny-black things?'

'They're figs. We'll keep them a day or two, and then they'll be ripe to eat,' Mary told her. 'You won't need to cook them.'

'Will you be ready for supper now?' Ellen asked more cheerfully, now her problems in respect of Mr Wharton's gift were solved. ''Tes all ready.'

It was customary at Canons Grange for the footmen to bring in and serve each course, and then withdraw from the room until Mr Hartwell rang a small handbell to summon them to take out the remains and bring in the next course. Conversation remained general while they were in the room, but could become more private while they were out of it.

It was during the first of the footman-free intervals that evening, while they were eating mutton broth, that

Mr Hartwell said to Mary, 'I wish you would not encourage Polycarp Wharton to come to see you.'

'I don't encourage him!' Mary exclaimed indignantly. 'I can't imagine how you may have formed the opinion that I do!'

'It's obvious that he comes to see you.'

'That I doubt, but if he does, it's hardly my fault! A cat may look at a king, I believe!'

'He wouldn't continue to come if you didn't encourage him.'

'Then will you pray tell me in what way you consider me to be encouraging him?' Mary demanded. 'As far as I can recollect, beyond an initial greeting, I didn't speak a single word to him this evening! What conversation there was, I believe, was entirely between him and your sister.'

'That is true, Francis,' Jem put in quietly.

'But you can't deny that it's you he comes to see!' Mr Hartwell persisted, frowning at Mary.

'I've no idea why he comes,' she replied airily. 'Neither do I much care! It's kind of him to be concerned about the welfare of us all here, but I've no reason to think that his concern is for any one of us in particular. If it is, I think it may well be for Jem, as his remarks were mainly addressed to her! In any case, he's only come twice, so I don't know why you speak of him *continuing* to come.'

'I do have a reason for asking you not to encourage him,' Mr Hartwell persisted doggedly, with no sign of losing his temper.

'I'm well aware of your reason, and agree with you,' Mary retorted. 'Did I not make that clear yesterday evening, when you asked my father to keep away from the house? If you wish Mr Wharton to stop coming, you must tell him so yourself. It's nothing to do with me!'

'Do you really believe that?' He looked quite astonished, as if he had just made a surprising discovery.

'Have you really not observed the way the man looks at you?'

'Not particularly,' Mary replied with patent honesty. 'To tell truth, I'm a little short-sighted, and can't make out a person's face quite clearly at that distance.'

Mr Hartwell gave a little sigh, which to Mary sounded irritatingly patient and forbearing. She exclaimed in a flash of temper, 'I'm growing tired of your persistent and unfounded belief that I'm no better than a whore, and an empty-headed one at that! Just because I happen to serve my unhappy, *virtuous* Queen in a Court which considers virtue something extraordinary and laughable, why must you assume that I necessarily follow the scandalous majority? We're not all lewd and libertine at Whitehall, though I'll admit that those who are not are much in the minority, and sadly out of fashion!'

'Why do you remain at Court, if you find it distasteful?' he asked, apparently unmoved by her outburst.

'For two reasons,' she replied more calmly. 'One is affection for my dear little Queen, and the other is for my father's sake. When the King offered him a reward for his services, he could have chosen a greater title, or land, or some rich sinecure, but he chose a place at Court for me. He expects me to make good use of it to obtain a comfortable place in life through an excellent marriage. How can I say to him that I don't want what he chose as a reward for risking his life?'

'You could terminate the unpleasant experience by making the excellent marriage,' he pointed out, his tone very slightly sardonic. 'I don't imagine you lack offers.'

'Indeed no, but few of them are either honourable or concerned with matrimony!' Mary returned tartly. 'Were I what you think me, I could have a dozen establishments, more wealth than the Queen of Sheba, and titles for my bastard sons by now! As for the few more legitimate offers—I fear that my idea of an excellent marriage is not limited solely to wealth and title!'

Jem was listening to all this with an expression of shocked fascination, and Mary felt a twinge of conscience, fearing that her outspokenness might be upsetting her friend, but Mr Hartwell gave her no remission, for he asked, with every appearance of interest, 'What more do you require, then?'

'Not more,' she replied, 'but as well, or even instead. I want a husband worthy of my respect and affection. A man of honour, integrity, courage, resolution, and kindness. I've found but two men at Court with all those qualities. One is far above me in rank, and the other was killed off Lowestoft, in the recent battle.'

'Charles Berkeley,' Mr Hartwell said. It was a definite statement, not a question, as was its rider. 'And the other, Prince Rupert.'

'Precisely,' Mary replied, and applied herself to her mutton broth. Her lace sleeve fell back as she did so, and Mr Hartwell's attention seemed to be distracted by it, for he stared at it for a moment, and then turned his eyes away and did not look again.

After that, he appeared to retreat into his own thoughts, and maintained a brooding silence, apart from rousing himself to summon the footman, and, in due course, the roast chicken with Obadiah's vegetables, and the inevitable blackberry pie, which seemed to figure so largely in everyone's diet at this time of year. He excused himself and retreated to the library afterwards, while Jem and Mary sat in the parlour, watching the afterglow fading across the valley while they drank some coffee.

'I don't think Francis can really believe you're—what you said,' Jem ventured timidly. 'He wouldn't allow me to be your friend if he did.'

'Oh, he warned me not to lead you astray into Whitehall ways,' Mary replied in a bright, brittle voice, for it still rankled. 'He's glad that you have a friend of your own age and class, but would be happier were it someone else.'

'But I don't see how he can think that of you,' Jem persisted. 'I'm sure you're not a bit like that!'

Mary reached over and pressed her hand warmly, smiled, and said sincerely, 'Thank you for that, Jem. I value your friendship, and I hope, one day soon, we'll be sisters as well as friends.'

Jem blushed and hung her head, but she did not disagree, and, after a few moments, said more light-heartedly, 'I do hope it's not me whom Mr Wharton comes to see! I can barely keep a straight face when he talks in such a comical manner! Do all the gallants at Court speak in that strange fashion?'

'Only the more affected, but even then not usually as extremely as Polycarp!'

They both laughed, and then Jem said, 'He's such a kind, sensible man really, and manages his father's estate and Lady Dallance's so very well! Poor Lady Dallance had a villainous steward when she was first widowed—he mismanaged her estate and lost her a great deal of money, they say, and Mr Wharton found out, went to see Lady Dallance, and offered to manage her land for her, and now she's far better off and much happier. I believe he expects to marry a Miss Sherburne, if her father will give his consent.'

'I don't believe I know her,' Mary said after a moment's thought.

'She lives in the North somewhere, I believe. Her uncle is a Judge, and the marriage is being arranged by him and Mr Wharton's father. Her name is . . .' Jem started to laugh, and could hardly get it out, ' . . . Philadelphia!'

'Oh heavens!' Mary laughed too, and then said shame-facedly, 'Poor girl! She can't help her name, and we shouldn't be laughing at her, or at all really, with those poor souls in the sick-rooms. Oh, but Philadelphia and Polycarp! I wonder what they'll call their children!'

This light-hearted interlude was brought to an abrupt end by the arrival of Henry, who said in a hushed tone,

'Beg your pardon ma'am, Miss Hook, but Bess says she feels poorly. She's gone to the sick-room.'

Jem and Mary looked at one another, all merriment forgotten, and went soberly to see the new invalid, who was stoically resigned to the fact that she had the sickness, and was already undressed and in her night-shift, having brought it with her, together with her own wash-cloth and towel.

'I got the sheets and other things washed and out on the line, at any rate,' she said with a certain satisfaction. 'Me throat's bad, and me head, and I felt that dizzy, the yard were going round like whirligig all the while I was pegging 'em out.' She was obviously already light-headed with fever, and consequently to be forgiven for speaking with such a lack of deference to her superiors.

'Have you a sore place anywhere, a red spot, perhaps as big as a shilling?' Jem asked.

'Yes. Here, on me neck!' Bess pushed her hair back to show an angry scarlet disc just below her ear. 'I felt it 'smorning, when the neck of me frock rubbed it. Be it a plague-spot?'

'I think so. Have you another anywhere?'

'Nobbut the one.'

Jem looked at Cook, who was whimpering like a hurt puppy in a trying, monotonous way, as if she was aware only of hurting, but had not the strength to make any greater complaint.

'I think you'd best go in the other room with Joan and Sukey. We'll need to make up another bed. Where's Obadiah?'

'He went next door whiles I got me clothes orf. It weren't decent him staying.'

Jem went to the communicating doorway, and asked Obadiah if he would fetch another cot from the tack-room, where the grooms were keeping those they had made, until they were needed. He came through into Cook's room, looking sheepish, and with one hand clamped to his weathered cheek.

'What is it, Obadiah?' Mary asked sharply. 'Why are you holding your face?'

'Got a worm in me tooth, hevn't I, D——' He broke off, looking even more sheepish, for he was so used to calling on the terrier to confirm what he said that he had forgotten that Dog was waiting for him in the kitchen.

'Is it a hollow tooth?' Jem asked from the doorway.

'Ay. The worm must've burrowed well in.'

'Mary, would you mind going to the stillroom and bringing three or four water-pepper seeds? You'll find them in a little stone pot on the shelf to the right of the door,' Jem said, and added to Obadiah, 'You must put them into the hollow of the tooth, and keep them there until the pain stops.'

Obadiah nodded, but did not bother to reply, as he was already on his way to fetch the cot. He brought it in just as Mary returned with the seeds, which he took with a polite word of thanks, and worked them into this aching tooth with his tongue.

'Thanks, missus,' he said to Jem. 'I'll let you know if they does any good.'

Bess was put to bed, and Jem inspected the other two maids while Mary poured doses of medicine and brought them to the patients. Sukey was in a high fever, but still had no sign of a bubo, and Joan had a small plague-spot on one breast. She said she felt all the time as if she were falling, despite being in bed, and she was very tearful, although her fever seemed to have lessened rather than increased.

'I don't think we should sponge her,' Jem said to Mary in a low voice. 'She's not even sweating now, but Sukey would perhaps feel better for it.'

Mary nodded and went to fetch water for washing, taking Obadiah with her to bring more drinking-water, for both Joan and Sukey had sensibly been drinking at frequent intervals.

Obadiah's turn of duty was now over, so he retired,

and presently Prue, the sewing-woman, came to take the first of the night watches. By then, Sukey had been washed, and said she felt more comfortable, and Mary and Jem tried to wash Cook, but gave up when she started to scream when they touched her. She now had great marks, like bruises, all over her, and was quite unconscious of anything but the pain of the buboes, which showed no signs of coming to a head and bursting, but only grew larger.

Mary caught Jem's eye across the bed, over the poor woman's body, and raised her eyebrows questioningly. Jem shook her head slightly, and tried again to get the patient to take a little water, but she would not swallow, and it ran out of her mouth on to her pillow.

Mr Hartwell came in as they were putting the sheet and blankets back over her, and stood looking down at her suffused face. He lifted the covers, gave a brief, impersonal look, and lifted one arm to see the bubo. She screamed and twisted with apparent violence, but, in fact, had not enough strength to break even the light grip of his fingers on her wrist.

'A bread poultice might do it, but I don't think she would tolerate anything on them,' he said doubtfully. 'If she becomes more deeply insensible, we might try . . .'

He spoke to the sewing-woman, asking her to keep a careful watch, and, if Cook became silent, to call him, and to pass the instruction to the next watch after her. 'No matter what the time is, I'm to be woken and told. You understand?'

Mary waited while he went with Jem for a few words with the other three women, and then returned, saying to his sister that he thought they were not so badly infected as Cook. 'Although I may be wrong, of course, but she seemed to become more ill more quickly than they. Sukey has hardly changed since I saw her earlier, except for an increase in fever, but she's still perfectly lucid. You'd both better be off to bed now, and try to sleep well.'

He addressed his words to Jem, hardly glancing at Mary, as if he wished to avoid any further conversation with her, and she assumed, with a tinge of bitterness, that their exchange at supper had failed to convince him of her innocence. She raised her chin at a defiant angle, bade him 'Good night' and went up to her room, pausing at her door to call a more friendly greeting to Jem, who had followed her up the stairs.

Her room seemed too warm and airless, so she drew back the curtain and opened a window before turning to her mirror to unpin her hair and shake it down, noting as she did so that her cheeks were flushed, presumably still with anger at Mr Hartwell's obstinacy.

After the usual difficulty with her back lacing, she undressed, slipped on her shift and nightrobe, and picked up her hairbrush. As she raised her right arm to begin brushing her hair, the sleeve of her nightrobe fell back as that of her gown had done at supper, and she saw, reflected in the mirror, a bright scarlet spot, the size of a shilling, on the underside of her forearm.

For a moment she stared at it, the whole universe in suspense about her, and then the realisation dawned and she began to shiver with fear, turning her head from side to side, as if to evade the knowledge that she was visited. It took a major effort of will to still the trembling, to brush her hair as she had intended, to put on her slippers, and only then to go to the door, force her hand to stop shaking while she opened it, and step out into the corridor.

Her room was the last at that end of the house, near to the side wall of the house and the window in it which lit the corridor. Someone was standing at that window, looking out at the moonlit garden below. He turned as she came out of her room and looked at her. It was Mr Hartwell.

'Francis,' she said quietly, trying to stop her voice

from trembling. 'I have a plague-spot!'

'I know. I saw it at supper,' he said gently, and she moved blindly forward into his arms.

CHAPTER EIGHT

IT WAS IMMEASURABLY comforting to be held close to his warm, lithe body, to let her head rest against his shoulder and allow a few tears to run down her cheeks, without any need to explain herself, or, indeed, to say anything at all. He stood quite still for a long time, one arm round her waist and the other about her shoulders, relaxed and silent, his cheek brushing the top of her head, and then he gently stroked her hair and twined it about his fingers.

'Were you waiting for me?' she asked at last.

'Yes. I knew you'd find it before long. You already have a fever, I think.'

'Must I go down to the sick-rooms?' she shuddered.

'Not if you don't wish to.'

'But I can't stay up here . . . It would mean poor Jem trudging up and down stairs . . .'

'Stay in your own room for now, and we can move you later, if it becomes necessary.'

'When I'm too ill to care?'

He was silent for a moment, biting his lips, then he said, 'To be brutally plain-spoken—yes! What do you wish me to tell your father?'

'That I'm ill, but not seriously . . . I suppose that would be foolish—he won't believe it! No one could ever be said to have plague, but not seriously!'

'Do you wish your mother to come here and nurse you?'

'Oh, on no account!' Mary was horrified. 'She might catch it, and—and . . . No, you must make Father see that she mustn't come!'

'Very well. Don't agitate yourself—I'll convince him. Now, into bed with you, and I'll bring you some of Jem's mixture, and a jug of water for drinking. Do you wish for someone to sit with you?'

Mary hesitated, thinking of the long night ahead, and the unlikelihood that she would sleep, but, however reluctantly, she said, 'No, thank you. Best to let everyone sleep while they can.'

'I'll bring a chair and sit out here, then,' he said, as if it were nothing out of the ordinary. 'I can sleep like that as well as in my bed—something I learned to do in my seagoing career! I'll leave your door a little ajar, and you can call me if you want anything.'

Perhaps he mixed a little poppy-juice into the cup of medicine he brought her—it certainly tasted very bitter—or perhaps the sickness made her sleepy, as it had done with Sukey. Whatever the reason, she drifted into a deep sleep before she had time to become too terrified of the immediate future, and her last vague thought was one of comfort because Francis was within call, just outside the door.

In the morning she felt very strange indeed. Her head seemed to be locked in a tight cage, and moving her eyes made the room spin wildly round her. Her whole body ached and burned, as if she had been beaten, and then roasted. The furniture appeared distorted, and when Jem came to see how she did, her face was an extraordinary parody of itself, constantly changing in size and shape, so that one moment she had a huge nose and no chin, and the next, her nose had shrunk to a button and her forehead swelled out to a monstrous size.

Sounds were curiously changed, too. Voices seemed to echo from far away, and to repeat the same words over and over again, mixing together, as if several people were present, until she wanted to clap her hands over her ears and scream to them to be silent. It was almost impossible to identify the speakers, although she did think at one time that Francis said, 'You're not going to die, to die, to die, to die . . .' Perhaps it was only a memory of him saying it to—to whom? It was too hot to think, and there was the pain . . . Where was it? Somewhere, in a body which belonged to someone else, someone who had got into her bed with her and was moaning and crying, whose tears were scalding her own cheeks . . .

She was quite oblivious of the passing of time, and it seemed that it was only a few minutes since she woke with that dreadful headache. She wondered, confusedly, why someone would keep moving her about, wiping something cool over her burning body—or was it that other person's body? Was that cool liquid trickling down inside her throat, or outside, on her neck? Whose hands were those, touching her so gently? They were firm and safe, and sometimes she thought they lifted her out of the burning fire of a hot, wet chrysalis and held her up, where the cool air could flow about her and quell the flames, before lowering her into something cool and smooth.

'Clean sheets!' she heard someone say once, quite clearly, yet in such a strange, hoarse voice, which she could not identify. Another voice, familiar, gentle, but equally unidentifiable said, 'Yes, Mary, clean sheets! Do they feel better?'

'Better,' the first strange voice echoed, and then said urgently, 'Tell him I'm not! You must tell him—he wouldn't believe me!'

'He did believe you,' the familiar, unrecognised voice replied calmly. 'Go to sleep.'

'I wish they'd be quiet,' she thought. 'I want to sleep. Why won't she go away, and then I can . . .'

Later, she drifted up out of darkness and oblivion, and felt vaguely that time had passed, but she seemed to be shrouded in a thick mist, and could not be sure of anything. The pain in that other body was worse, and seemed to be centred on one particular place, which she eventually managed to locate somewhere on her right, near her arm—but where was her arm? Surely it should be by her side, so why was it somewhere else—over her head? Perhaps it wasn't her arm, but belonged to the other person, the hot, moaning creature who had usurped her bed.

'One more try,' said a voice. 'It's almost ripe.'

'I can see a white spot,' said another voice. Was it Jem? 'Just there, see?'

The pain was suddenly terrible, and she abruptly let go her contact with that other body, the one which was feeling the pain, and sank into a deep, dark well of nothingness.

'Fight, Mary! Fight!' Someone was urging her from a long way away. 'Come along—fight!'

Slowly she swam up through the darkness towards the voice, faltering, expecting that the pain would return, but there was nothing, no pain, just the sensation of linen against her body, a soft pillow under her head, and something thick and bulky in her right armpit . . . No need to sink back into the dark, no need to be afraid . . . Just to sleep . . . To sleep . . .

She opened her eyes on a shadowy room, strange and ghostly in the light of a single flickering candle, and the lean, austere features of Francis Hartwell were looking down on her. The lines from his nose to the corners of his mouth were deeply scored, and he looked unutterably weary.

'Did I call out?' she asked, her tongue feeling thick and clumsy, and her voice sounding rusty, which she supposed must be another symptom of the sickness.

'Sometimes. Last time, I was calling you.'

'Why, where was I?'

'A long way away, but you're back now.'

'Is it time to go down to the sick-room?'

'No. You've been ill, but you're better now.'

'*Been* ill? But I thought . . . How long?'

'Since you found the plague-spot? Eight days.'

'Eight . . .? But it can't be!'

'I assure you. That was the evening of Saturday, the second of September, and today is Sunday, the tenth, at about nine in the evening. Your family is well, and everyone else at Pinnacles—oh, and Polycarp Wharton!'

Mary digested the information slowly, for it seemed terribly difficult to think, and movement, she felt, would be quite impossible. Something was irritating her forehead, but she was quite incapable of lifting her hand to brush it away.

With a great effort, she made her eyes look upward, to see if she could make out what it was, and then Francis leant forward and gently brushed a strand of hair away, as if he had read her mind.

'What happened?' She made another great effort to get the words out.

'To you?'

'The others . . .'

'Sukey was ill for three days, then suddenly got better, and was up and about two days later. Bess was very ill, and a bubo came up on her neck, but it was quite small, and burst of its own accord yesterday, and she's much better today. Joan and Cook . . .' He hesitated.

'Died?' Mary whispered.

He nodded. 'Yesterday. Cook had it so very badly from the start, with a dozen plague-spots, and Joan seemed unable to fight it. She assumed she had no chance and simply . . . gave up, I think. No one else has been visited since you.'

'The town?' she whispered, feeling quite exhausted with the effort of speaking even so few words, but wanting desperately to know what had been happening, to re-establish contact with life.

'Mr Reeve reports eleven dead of plague this past week, and fourteen houses visited.'

She could not summon up the energy to say anything more, but managed to shift her right shoulder, wondering what was in her armpit.

'Is it uncomfortable? We persuaded your bubo to break with bread poultices, and it's drained and healing, but there's a dressing on it of one of Jem's mixtures. Balm, lovage and holy thistle boiled in wine and oil, I believe. Would you like a drink?'

She whispered 'Please', and he fetched a cup from somewhere out of her sight, slid an arm under her shoulders to lift her, and held the cup to her lips, tilting it just enough to allow the mixture of wine and water to enter her mouth sip by sip. She fell asleep before it was finished.

It appeared to be morning when she woke again, but she could not be sure, for she was still very weak and confused. The sight of Sukey sitting near her, sewing, reminded her of at least a part of her conversation with Francis—she was surprised to find that she now thought of him as Francis without hesitation or reluctance.

'I'm glad to see you better,' she whispered, her voice still thick and rusty.

'Oh, Miss Hook!' Sukey exclaimed, getting up and coming to her. She moved slowly, and looked weak and pale herself. 'We was all so worried about you, being so very ill, and poor Master up all hours and looking real bad hisself! He's sleeping now, and has bin fer hours 'n hours, but Miss Jemima said to let him rest. I'll go tell her you're awake . . .' She went out of the room, steadying herself with a hand on whatever piece of furniture was within reach as she passed, without waiting for Mary to reply.

Mary lay still, contemplating the canopy over her head and feeling her own body with her mind, as if reaccustoming herself to the sensation of moving her toes and fingers, making various muscles tense and relax. It felt strange. The lump in her armpit was still there, but she could remember what it was, and now discovered that there was also something round her right arm. With a tremendous effort, she lifted it and saw that there was a bandage, which, after some thought, she concluded must be covering the place where the plague-spot was.

Jem came in before she could make any more discoveries, greeted her with great pleasure, and put down a steaming bowl on the table by the bed, while she helped Mary to sit up, propped against a pile of pillows.

'Now, you've no strength, so you must eat,' she said briskly. 'I've brought a little meat broth, and Francis says you're to take all of it, but we'll go slowly—there's no hurry.'

'Francis says?' Mary queried. 'Sukey said he's asleep.'

'He gave his instructions last night, before he collapsed.' Jem busied herself spooning broth, a little at a time, into Mary's mouth, so that all she had to do was swallow. It took a long time, and was very tiring, but she managed the half-bowlful eventually.

'I'm sorry I've been so much trouble to you,' she whispered when she was lying down again.

'No trouble at all to me!' Jem assured her. 'In any case, it's not your fault you were visited! I dare say you'd not have chosen to have been ill, or, indeed, to have been here at all.'

Mary smiled, and admitted that she would have preferred not to have taken the sickness.

'We arranged with your father that we'd put a flag on the roof when we had news of you,' Jem said, straightening the bedclothes. 'Henry fixed a broomstick on one of the gable-ends, and he tied a bolster-case to it, first thing this morning, just at dawn, and your father was at the paddock fence scarce half an hour later, so your family knows you're better.'

Mary smiled her thanks and relief, and said, 'Francis told me some of the news last night. How's Obadiah's toothache?'

'It got worse, so he pulled the tooth out himself, with a little help from Dog. You'd scarcely credit it, but he tied one end of a length of pack-thread round the tooth, and the other end to Dog's collar, braced himself with

a hand on either side of the door to the yard, and got
Henry to throw a stick for Dog! The stick flew across
the yard, Dog went after it, and the tooth flew behind
him, caught him up, and struck the poor thing on his
rump! He was so surprised that he forgot the stick and
ran yelping back to Obadiah to be comforted, and now
he blames Henry for it, and hides behind Obadiah every
time he sees him!'

She laughed, and Mary managed a chuckle herself,
but her eyelids were drooping, and it was a relief to let
them close and go back to sleep.

In the evening, as the setting sun was filling the room
with warm red light, she opened them again, and Francis
was sitting there, with another bowl of broth, some
bread, an apple and an orange at the ready.

'Good,' he said. 'I was just about to wake you for
your supper. See if you can sit up.'

It was an enormous effort, but she managed to raise
herself a little, and he helped her to sit up completely
while he put the pillows behind her again. He fed her
with pieces of bread soaked in the broth, then with
small slices of the apple, cut with a silver knife, and,
finally, peeled and quartered the orange and gave her
it, piece by piece. The fruit was cool and refreshing, and
made her mouth feel less stale and unpleasant.

'Jem is worried that she didn't wash you this morning,
or brush your hair,' he said, 'but she thought she'd tired
you too much with talking to worry you any more.
Shall I brush your hair now?'

Mary thought it would be pleasant, but was surprised
that he had offered, and also that he had come to feed
her, rather than Jem or one of the maids.

'Everyone else is busy,' he said, as if guessing her
thoughts. 'There's a mountain of washing to be done,
and Bess's plague-spot has come to a head and is
weeping now, so Jem is occupied with her.' He brought
her brush from the table below the mirror, perched on
the edge of the bed, and started to brush her hair,

teasing out the tangles very gently and coaxing the curls round his fingers.

'That feels much better, thank you,' she said when he had finished.

'You'll be able to wash it in a day or two, and perhaps take a bath,' he said. 'You'll soon recover your strength, now you're eating again.'

This statement proved to be true, for by the next day, Mary could sit up without help, and two days later, ventured out of bed and tottered across to the window, leaning on Jem. By the end of the week, she could manage that small journey unassisted, and finished the day by taking a bath in the tub which two of the footmen carried upstairs, and Sukey and Ellen filled with jugs of warm water.

With her hair washed and dried, her body feeling fresh and clean, and the bandage removed from her arm, revealing a round, black scab, which was dried up and flaking already, she began to feel that she was really on the way back to full health, and ate her supper, unassisted and with good appetite, while the bath was being emptied and removed. The next day she ventured to walk the length of the corridor and back, and gradually increased this each day until she could go quite briskly from one end to the other and back a dozen times without a rest. She began to spend most of each day up and dressed, although still keeping to her room between forays along the corridor.

During these days of convalescence, Jem spent many hours with her, for Bess was now well on the way to recovery and could be left in the care of Prue and Susan, and no one else had fallen ill. Francis appeared once or twice each day for a few minutes, but always when Jem was present, and only to stand about, saying very little, except to ask how she did, and if she wanted for anything. Sometimes, after she had settled for the night and Jem had kissed her and left her, she would wonder if his presence during the first hours of her

recovery had been in her imagination, for she could not
reconcile his gentle attentiveness then with his present
rather formal manner, which was virtually indistinguish-
able from his attitude towards her before she was ill.
She had a confused recollection of thinking, at the time,
that he seemed somehow . . . different, but in what
respect, she could not remember.

'Four weeks without anyone being visited, and we
can return to the world!' Jem announced cheerfully one
afternoon while he was present, standing looking out of
the window at the declining sun.

'I trust you're not superstitious,' he replied, looking
over his shoulder at them. 'We end our six weeks'
incarceration on Friday, the thirteenth of October.
Hardly an auspicious date! Are you ready yet for news
of how the world has been wagging during our absence
from it?'

'If there's anything of great interest,' Mary replied,
smiling.

'Lord Sandwich captured nine Dutch Indiamen at the
end of last month. That was the best news. The rest is
less good. The King has been ill, but not, thank God!
of plague, only sheer anxiety and weariness. The sickness
reached Salisbury, and the Court had to move again,
into Dorset. Polycarp Wharton told me that nigh on
eight thousand died last week in London, according to
the bills, but he thinks it's more likely to have been ten
thousand in reality!'

'Merciful heavens!' Mary exclaimed, appalled. 'Can
there be anyone left?'

'They say that grass is growing in Cheapside . . .
However, it's best not to think too much about it, for
your spirits need to be raised, not lowered!'

'What of the poor folk in the forest?' Mary asked,
remembering how Mr Reeve had told them about the
group which had taken refuge there—it seemed so long
ago now!

'All is still well with them, despite the infection being

in all the towns round about. They thought of moving further away at one time, but found their way barred by sickness in every direction, so they thought best to stay where they are. Your father gave them a porker, and Polycarp sent two sheep, and Lady Dallance a calf, so they've not lacked meat. It seems they have a biscuit-maker with them, who's built himself an oven and made their flour into biscuit-cakes in place of bread. They found an old derelict keeper's cottage, and made it weatherly and snug for the winter, and the Rector managed to get them enough boards for the repairs, and other needs, from one place and another. Your brother John's been helping Mr Reeve with buying their food and selling the articles they make to pay for it.'

'I'm glad to hear it!' Mary exclaimed. 'John's a good, kind man, but he's always been overshadowed by Richard, who was the clever one . . .' She looked at Jem, hoping her friend would not think she was slighting John by implying he was not clever, but Jem only smiled to herself over her sewing.

Across the fields, the 'prentice bell began to ring from the church tower, and Francis swung round and said abruptly to Mary, 'Do you feel strong? If I carry you, would you like to come out to the paddock and see your father?'

'Oh, I should like it above all things!' she exclaimed.

'Come, then!' He picked her up with no more effort than if she had been a child.

'She should have a cloak . . .' Jem protested, but her brother was already out of the room and heading for the stairs, so she hastily found Mary's cloak and ran after them, leaving her sewing lying on the floor where it had fallen, and her thimble rolling away under the bed, where it was not found until the next spring-cleaning.

Mary's unorthodox arrival downstairs caused a great stir in the kitchen as Francis carried her through on the way to the paddock. Obadiah gave her a cheer, setting

Dog barking, Ellen and Sukey clapped their hands, and
they all followed behind, until Mary found herself
standing, unassisted, by the boundary marker in the
paddock, with Francis beside her and the servants
grouped behind. Jem came running after with her cloak,
and draped it round her shoulders.

Presently Sir Charles appeared on the top of the ridge
on his horse, stared at the group from the house for a
moment, saw Mary wave, and started down the steep
slope, arriving just as Mr Reeve came plodding up on
Archimedes, with the groom and Polycarp Wharton
close behind.

'Wall, Ai daclere!' Polycarp exclaimed. 'If it en't Miss
Mary! Ai'm varry gled to see you up end ebout egen,
dear me'em! Ai've brought you grepes end orenges from
Leddy Dellence's hothouse.' He dismounted, unloaded
the basket which was tied rather insecurely to his horse
behind his saddle, and heaved it on to the top of the
fence, climbed over, and lowered it to the ground. Then,
as usual, he perched on the top rail and beamed cheerfully at everyone.

'Now the Lord be praised who has spared his daughters Mary, Bess and Sukey!' Mr Reeve declaimed, raising
his hands and allowing his normally severe expression
to melt into a smile. 'Love is strong as death, and has
conquered it, for in love were the visited nursed and
brought to the healing of their sickness! Hallelujah!'

'*Amen*!' said Francis Hartwell firmly, and was echoed
in varying tones by everyone else, some of the servants
appearing unsure whether what the Rector had said was
a prayer or not. Obadiah muttered that he did not hold
with Independent utterings and hallelujahings, glaring
at the Rector under his bushy eyebrows. This was unfair
to Mr Reeve, who had never been a convinced Presby-
terian, let alone an Independent, and had welcomed the
re-establishment of the Church of England with great
relief.

Sir Charles merely said 'Mary' in a satisfied tone, and

blew his nose with a great trumpeting.

Mr Reeve, having come to give his Blessing, expanded it into a lengthy prayer of thanksgiving, not forgetting to add a few sentences of commendation for poor Cook and Joan. Mary began to fear that he might be about to develop it into a sermon addressed to the Lord, but he reached his final *Amen* before she was too weary from standing, and she was able to bid her father and the others a cheerful 'Good night', and watch them go out of sight, before she subsided with reasonable gracefulness on to the grass, her legs having simply given way under her.

'I think I'd better take you to the dining-room and feed you before I take you upstairs again!' Francis said, regarding her with some amusement.

'Oh, Francis! Can't you see she's tired out with all the excitement and standing!' Jem remonstrated.

But Mary said, 'I think I could manage to sit down to supper. I'm not really tired in myself, only in my legs.'

She smiled up at Francis, looking humorously rueful. He smiled back, and there was no longer any reserve in his expression, or in the dark eyes which surveyed her pale face. Silently, he bent to take her hands and raise her to her feet, and then picked her up, so easily, to carry her back into the house.

'You're a deal thinner than you were when you fell ill,' he remarked. 'We must feed you well, or your family'll think we starve our guests!'

'Did I eat anything while I was ill?' she asked.

'You lived on Jem's mixture, and some huge pills which Polycarp brought. He insisted they were a sovereign remedy for everything from gout to swine fever, but Sukey couldn't swallow them, and Bess spat them out, so you were the only one to benefit from them!'

'All of them?'

'All but the ones Bess rejected. I had to hold your nose to get them down you! I did think of using a blowpipe, like dosing a horse, but Jem wouldn't let me.'

Mary marvelled at the easy, half-joking exchange, which was so different from the awkward, stilted conversations they had shared before her illness, and she wondered what had brought about the change.

'I'm afraid it's going to be rabbit again for supper,' Jem said as they sat down in the dining-room. 'Joel Warrener brings a bunch of coneys every day and leaves them hanging on the paddock fence. I think he's courting Ellen with them, instead of flowers, but he'll not have much luck if Obadiah has any say in the matter! He has to skin them, and he curses poor Mr Warrener up hill and down dale while he's doing it, so if there's any truth in the matter of ill-wishing . . .!'

'I suspect that Obadiah's not the only one,' Francis said. 'There's a limit to the variety of ways of cooking coneys, and we're all like to grow long furry ears before mid-October! Dog must be the only one in the house who still likes the taste of them, and even he was heard to sigh last night, when he sniffed his supper-dish.'

'Has it been difficult to obtain food, with everyone confined to the house and garden?' Mary asked anxiously. 'I'm sure my father would help, if he knew . . .'

'No problem at all,' Jem assured her. 'We only feel obliged to eat the coneys because it would be wicked to waste good food. Mr Palmer took charge of the arrangements from the first, and we've been well supplied with all the necessities, and Mr Wharton has brought a succession of gifts of fruit and meat from various of our friends about the countryside. Fancy him persuading Lady Dallance to send some more of her oranges! This is the second time! She always claims that her trees bear so few, and all small ones, so I suppose there's something amiss with her orangery, or with the trees.'

'The former, I imagine,' said her brother. 'The building's the remains of the chapter-house of the Abbey, and I dare say the long-dead Abbots lying beneath their

roots stunt their growth and turn their fruit sour, out
of annoyance about the Dissolution!'

The oranges, which were served for dessert, along
with spicy russet apples and the grapes, proved to be
quite sweet, although they were small, and had a distinc-
tive flavour, unlike any Mary remembered tasting before.
When she remarked on this, Jem said that Lady
Dallance's cousin, Lord Peterborough, had sent her the
trees from Tangier when he first went there as Governor,
and she thought they might be a different variety, not
China oranges at all.

After supper, Mary thought she would try to walk
upstairs to her room. She managed the first flight, but
then found herself trembling with fatigue and weakness,
her knees feeling as if they could no longer support her,
and she almost fell. Jem caught her arm, and Francis,
who was watching from the foot of the stairs, came
flying up to put a secure arm about her, and then
carried her the rest of the way.

'So silly,' she said, feeling angry with herself for her
weakness.

'You've been very ill,' Jem pointed out. 'We hardly
thought you'd live through it, several times. It's little
wonder you've no strength yet.

Mary was too tired by then to do more than undress,
with Jem's help, and fall into her bed, to sleep soundly
all through the night, but Jem's words returned to her
often during the next few days, as her stamina gradually
increased, and she was able to do more and more before
exhaustion overcame her. By the end of another week,
she was walking down the stairs unassisted, and spending
much of the day belowstairs, although Jem insisted that
she rest on her bed for an hour or two each afternoon.
In the following week, she took to going to the kitchen
during the morning to help, for Molly had turned
housemaid in Joan's place, and Ellen and Sukey had to
do the work which had formerly occupied four women.

Obadiah still helped with the preparation of vegetables, for his beloved great horses were lodging down the valley with Polycarp Wharton, and there was no occupation for him in the stables. The grooms, once they had finished their day's stint of unaccustomed gardening, had cleaned and polished everything in the cart-shed and tack-room a dozen times over, and, according to Obadiah, had now resorted to tidying the hayloft for something to do.

'Tiddyvating every blade and stem straight and proper, they be,' he assured her. 'Upsetting the hens, what likes the hay tumblesome and dusty for their liddle nestses. All a-clucking and complaining, they be, wi' their eggses sliding off they smooth, tidy piles o' hay. Ain't they, Dog?'

Dog thumped his tail agreeably, not wishing to contradict, and Obadiah bent down to take his muzzle in one hand and shake it gently, which sent Dog into an ecstasy of squirming delight.

Mary smiled to herself, thinking that Obadiah seemed determined to set himself up as a Character, with his quaint ruralism growing ever more fantastical and eccentric. He grinned in return and winked, and they continued to string the last of the beans in amicable silence.

Mr Hartwell came into the kitchen soon after, with a flitch of bacon balanced on his shoulder and a basketful of big green apples, which he dumped on the kitchen table for Sukey to put away, although she had a struggle with the flitch, which was large and heavy.

'Be someone come home from Dunmow?' she asked, with a deal more boldness than she had ever shown in the past.

'No one in this house!' Francis assured her. 'Do you realise that there's not one person in this house who's married, let alone managed to be happily so and without a quarrel for a year! Apart from Oliver, that is, and I don't think having three wives and being a cat would recommend itself to the Dunmow Flitch judges!'

'But there's mebbe going to be some gets wedded afore long, ain't there, Dog?' Obadiah observed slyly from his place by the hearth, his eyes firmly fixed on the bean in his hands.

'Only ten days now, and we kin all go to Dunmow, if we've a mind to it!' said Ellen, up to her elbows in flour as she made a small mountain of pastry. 'Or anywhere else, for that matter!'

'I hope you're not thinking of going to the Hiring Fair, come the end of the month!' said Francis, half-jokingly. 'I'll have to go myself, unless any of you has a sister would come here to be second kitchen-maid, or scullery-girl? Molly's decided she'd prefer to continue as housemaid.'

'Scullery-girl?' Sukey said in a small, forlorn voice. 'But I'm scullery-girl!' She looked timidly at Mr Hartwell, and her eyes filled with tears.

'No,' he said gently. 'You're first kitchen-maid, and Ellen is Cook!'

Ellen gasped and dropped her rolling-pin with a crash on the floor. Dog gave a startled yelp and got under Obadiah's stool, and Oliver who was asleep on the settle, woke up and glared suspiciously about him.

'Me, Cook?' she exclaimed, her eyes shining. 'Oh, sir!'

'If you'd like to be, that is,' he said, smiling faintly.

'Like to be? Oh, would I like to be!' Ellen waved her hands about, unable to find words, and scattering flour in all directions. 'Oh, thank you, sir!'

'My mam won't believe it!' Sukey whispered, her eyes bigger than ever. 'Me, first kitchen-maid! And not fourteen yet! Oh, jest wait 'til I tells her! Oh, sir! Thank you, sir!'

'Well, that's all right then,' Francis said, backing hastily to the yard door and looking a little embarrassed.

There was a festive feeling in the kitchen after that, with little outbursts of laughter, but Ellen said, suddenly sober, I wonder what old Cook would say if'n she knew.

She learned me all I know, and I'll not forget her, nor cook worser nor she did, God willing, in cause of I'd not want to let her down, like!'

'There's allus two souls'll think yer better nor her,' said Obadiah. 'Yer never throw nowt at Dog, like she useter, and me and Dog thinks well of yer fer that!'

Mary finished her share of the vegetables, and slipped away, feeling she would like a little quiet time for a while, before dinner. She went through the house, out of the front door, and down the winding path of the terraced garden, which was so much less formal than that at Pinnacles with its balustrades and steps. She found a wooden bench and sat there in the autumn sunshine, watching the light playing on the leaves, which were just beginning to turn gold.

Presently Jem came down to join her, bringing a shawl. 'I saw you from the window,' she said. 'You should put this round your shoulders, I think. It's still quite warm, but it is October, and I'd not wish you to take a chill.'

'How kind you are!' Mary said, smiling, and patting the seat beside her to invite Jem to sit down. 'You've so much to do, yet you still find time to take care of me. I've not thanked you yet for nursing me while I was ill. I'm sure I'd have died if it hadn't been for you and all your caring!'

Jem flushed, shifted uncomfortably, opened her mouth, shut it again, then made up her mind and spoke up bravely. 'You'd better know the truth! It wasn't me—I had as much as I could manage with Cook and the three maids. It was Francis!'

'Francis? What do you mean?'

'It was my brother who nursed you while you were ill. It was Francis who saved your life!'

CHAPTER NINE

MARY STARED IN shocked silence, the implications of Jem's revelation running through her head in a disconnected series of thoughts, her memory jumping from one thing to another which she and Jem had done for the other sufferers from the sickness, all of which must have been done for her, but by a man!

'I—I didn't realise . . .' she said at last. It seemed a remarkably lame response, but she was quite unable to say more. After all, what could she say to Jem about it? That, somehow, the poor girl should have managed to nurse five desperately sick females, with no help but that of a few frightened servants, who must not be allowed to touch the visited in case they caught the sickness themselves? Clearly, if Jem had tried to do that, there was little chance that she or Bess would have survived, and perhaps not Sukey either.

'I'm sorry,' Jem said anxiously. 'I can guess how it must seem to you, but the maids were all too frightened to be much use, and Ellen had the cooking . . . There was no one else.'

'I quite understand,' Mary replied as reassuringly as she could. 'I should have realised for myself that—that someone else must have . . . Would you mind not telling Francis that you've told me?'

Jem looked a little doubtful, but agreed to do as Mary wished when she explained that she would find it less embarrassing if Francis were unaware that she knew he had nursed her.

It happened that the first time she encountered Francis after that was at dinner, and she felt the colour rise to her cheeks every time she looked at him, however much she tried not to think of him washing her body, changing her linen . . .

'You're not feverish, I hope?' he asked, frowning at her, the first time he noticed her flushed face. 'Your colour is a little high.'

'I've been sitting in the sun,' she replied a shade too quickly. 'It's quite warm, for all it's October.'

'Yes. I found it almost too hot to work in the kitchen garden. There's no *Zephyrus with his sweet breath* . . . Just as well, perhaps. The pigstye is next to the kitchen garden!' His teeth flashed in one of his brief smiles.

'Pigs!' Mary exclaimed. 'I didn't realise! Who's looking after them?'

'The swineherd. They're outside the quarantine boundary.'

Jem, who had a literal rather than a literary mind, had been looking a little puzzled since his quotation, and now said, 'But, Francis—Zephyrus is the *west* wind!'

'Yes?'

'The pigstye is *east* of the kitchen garden!'

He smiled again, and said, 'I hoped you wouldn't think of that—you've spoiled my joke, poor as it was!'

After dinner, Mary went upstairs to rest, thankful to have escaped the company of Francis without betraying that she knew he had nursed her, and unaware that she was followed by a silent, spotted shadow. It was, indeed, a very warm day, more like summer than autumn, so she propped her door open with a chair, and opened the casements to let in what little movement of air there was.

When she went to lie on her bed, she found Oliver already comfortably settled on it, blinking up at her with lazy golden eyes and an agreeable smile. She stroked his stomach, and he purred, a deep, throbbing rumble from the very core of his body, then obligingly shifted over a little to make room for her.

'You're a wicked cat!' she told him. 'I don't believe you're allowed upstairs, let alone on the beds!' He yawned, and purred all the more. As he seemed disinclined to leave, she stretched herself out beside him, closed her eyes, and tried to relax her mind as well as her body, gently kneading with the fingers of one hand in the cat's soft fur. The purring was soothing, and she felt quite drowsy, but her mind would not stop exclaiming to itself, 'He must have . . .! Oh, thank God the bubo was only under my arm! What if . . .? Did I talk as wildly as Cook? What could I have said?'

Another disturbing thought occurred to her before long, surprising her very much, for she found that the idea of the scarred hands of Francis Hartwell touching her body was not distasteful—not at all! In fact, if she were honest with herself, she had to admit that her reaction to the idea was one of pleasure and excitement!

'Do you love your man, Oliver?' she whispered to the cat, who rubbed his head against her and purred all the more. 'I'm beginning to think that I could love him. He's all that I admire and respect in a man, and I suppose he's quite handsome . . . I don't think he cares much for me, though, because he thinks I'm like most of the Court ladies. He's been more friendly since I was ill, so perhaps he's beginning to realise that I'm not what he assumed me to be!'

Oliver butted her firmly in the side with his head, probably in an excess of affection, but it seemed to Mary more like an irritable request that she be quiet and let a hard-working cat take his well-earned rest in peace, so she ceased to speculate aloud, and drifted into a doze for an hour or so.

She had just drifted out of it again when Jem came to see why she had not returned downstairs, and exclaimed, 'Why, what's Oliver doing here? I've never known him come abovestairs before, save when Francis was ill!'

'He must have followed me up, I suppose,' Mary

replied. 'I'm sure he wasn't in the room when I entered it, but when I came to lie on the bed, he was already in occupation!'

'He hasn't worried you?'

'Not at all.'

Jem was so surprised by the occurrence that she mentioned it to Francis at supper, but he, after a speculative look at Mary, which made her self-conscious, merely remarked somewhat obscurely that Oliver was an intelligent feline, who could see further than most into a millstone.

'Now, what do you mean by that?' Jem demanded. 'What has a millstone to do with anything?'

'Well, in this case, I'd say that some people attempt to set a solid barrier about their thoughts or emotions, in the hope that others won't suspect them,' he replied.

Jem looked puzzled. 'I thought the saying meant that the person who can see was exceptionally wise or knowledgeable.'

'Or perceptive. May I help you to a little more of this chicken?' was all the answer Francis seemed prepared to give to that, so the topic was abandoned.

For a few days Mary tried to avoid Francis, to speak as little as possible to him when she was, of necessity, in his company, and, as far as she could, not to look at him when he might be looking in her direction. He made no remark about it, and she hoped he might not have noticed, but one morning he appeared from behind a rose-bush, just as she had settled on the bench in the garden to sit in the sun, walked purposefully up to her, and sat down, uninvited.

'Well?' he said questioningly.

She felt her cheeks redden again, for she had, naturally, looked at him when he appeared, and his eyes held her gaze in a compelling, almost hypnotic fashion. She hastily looked away, down the slope towards the road and the copse beyond, and said, 'It's still so warm in the sun.'

'For the time of year,' he added sardonically.

'Yes. Although October is often a warm month. During the day, that is.'

'But it always becomes much cooler when the sun goes down, and one must beware of the sudden evening chill, and the frost which may strike before dawn. Why are we pursuing this extraordinarily trite conversation? Have I offended you in some way?'

She bit her lip and looked down at her hands, folded in her lap, but found no inspiration there, and could only reply, 'No. Why should you think so?'

'For three weeks after your return from the country of the plague-stricken, we seemed to be on easy terms of friendship, but now you avoid me, you hardly speak to me, save to answer any direct remark I may address to you . . . What have I done?'

She shook her head wretchedly. 'You haven't offended me.'

'Then what is it?'

She sighed, turned her head, and almost looked at him, her eyes falling away to his hands, which lay on his thighs, still and relaxed, and a strange thrill ran through her at the thought of their gentle touch . . .

'What is it, Mary?' he asked, his voice softer and more coaxing. 'Try to tell me.'

She was silent for a few more moments, still looking at his hands, and then she said abruptly, 'Jem told me about—about when I was ill . . .'

He let out a long breath, and murmured, 'Why did she not tell me you knew?'

'I asked her not to,' Mary replied baldly. 'I thought it would be less embarrassing if you didn't know that I knew that . . . I'm grateful to you, more grateful than I can ever put into words, for I'd have died if you hadn't . . .'

'But the thought of what I had to do to save you fills you with horror? Yet if it had been Jem washing you, and all the rest, you'd not have worried.'

'Another woman . . .' she began, then, in a bitter outburst of the half-forgotten resentment, 'If I were what you think me . . . I suppose you thought I'd be used to a man's hands about my body, and his eyes seeing me . . . Several men, no doubt . . .' Her voice became so unsteady that she broke off, clenched her hands together, and tried not to cry.

'Jem told you why I nursed you, I hope?'

'Yes.'

'Can you not accept that as a good enough reason?'

She made a helpless little gesture. 'Yes! I can see it was necessary! My mind, my reason, accept it, but my—my spirit, my emotions . . . I suppose I'm being foolish. If I'd been sent to a pesthouse, I'd have been glad of anyone, man or woman, to do so much for me!'

'If the situation had been reversed, if all the men had been visited, but none of the women, would you still have helped to nurse the sick?'

'Yes, of course.'

'Even me?'

'Of course I would! I couldn't leave someone to die rather than risk offending my own modesty!' she flashed at him indignantly.

'Or his? Or do you not believe that a man has any modesty?'

'I'd not thought about it.' Her surprise was apparent in her voice and the startled expression on her face.

'Either way, it's an embarrassing situation for both parties involved,' he pointed out calmly. 'But we must accept that both must put up with it, as the one has no wish to die, and the other must try to save him, or her. Given that, what now? Must we both decide never to set eyes on each other again, or may we agree that either would have done as much for the other, and it was mere fortune of war which made it you who was visited and I who nursed, and let the uneasiness about it slip into the past?'

She gave him a sidelong, uncertain look, but this time

her eyes reached his face, and dwelt there long enough
to see that he looked serious, concerned and sympathetic.

'I give you my word that I shall not be thinking of
your naked body every time I look at you,' he said,
then added more lightly, ' . . . which is more than may
be said for some of the gentlemen at Court, I suspect! I
accept, by the way, that all of them have to rely entirely
on imagination in their carnal thoughts of you!'

Mary managed a smile at that, and felt strangely
happy that his last remark implied that he no longer
believed her to be debauched.

'I'll try,' she said in reply to his earlier question. 'I
should have thought about the matter more carefully,
and realised that it couldn't have been easy for you,
either. It didn't occur to me, for you seemed so . . .'
She gestured with both hands, unable to think of a
suitable word.

'I've had more practice in dissimulation, having spent
half my life in situations where it's best not to show
one's embarrassment, or fear, or whatever. I'm going to
pull up the markers round the boundary. Will you come
and watch?'

'The markers?' Mary echoed, startled.

'Tomorrow is the thirteenth. We've had no fresh
visitation for forty days, so tomorrow, God willing,
we're free!'

'Free!' Mary laughed with the relief of it, and followed
him, lending her still-small strength to the uprooting of
the boundary markers. Presently Obadiah and Dog
joined them with a wheelbarrow, and soon all the
markers were gathered and carried to the paddock,
where Francis piled them in a cone-shaped heap.

'We'll burn them after supper,' he promised.

Something of a celebratory air had crept into the
household by the end of the day. It was cautious, for
nobody wanted to tempt Fate by being too beforehand
in assuming all was well, and restrained, for two
members of the household had left it during the forty

days for the last, night-time journey to the churchyard, and it would be unseemly to forget them. Nevertheless, Ellen and Sukey excelled themselves in the preparation of a supper which was considerably more elaborate than usual, and Henry was sent down to the cellar to fill some bottles from a cask which was very old and seldom used, instead of the usual canary and clarry.

Mr Reeve arrived as usual, as did Sir Charles, still conscientiously remaining on the top of the ridge to wave reassuringly to his daughter. Polycarp Wharton, who had, it seemed, come every evening of the quarantine, despite hints and polite but discouraging remarks, arrived before Mr Reeve had finished his preliminary greetings and enquiries, and perched, as usual, on the fence, beaming good-naturedly at everyone.

'So tomorrow you may move freely again,' Mr Reeve said, 'and Archimedes may return to his proper home. I cannot express to you, Mr Hartwell, my *gratitude* for your generous loan of this noble beast!' Archimedes looked modestly down his nose, pricked his ears, and poised one front hoof on its tip, looking, Mary thought, for all the world as if he were about to dance a coranto.

'I suggest that he remains with you, as you seem so much in accord,' Francis replied in such a matter-of-fact tone that Mr Reeve hardly understood him for a moment. 'He gets too little exercise here, and he can eat grass in your orchard and be fed his oats and hay just as well in the Rectory stable as here. As for his grooming—well, it's but a few minutes' walk from the dayhouse to your stable, and young Jack Plomer who works there can see to it. It'll cost you nothing but the orchard grass and the use of the stable, and save you a deal of time in going about the parish, which no doubt you'll be glad to have for preparing your sermons!' He managed this last remark with a completely straight face, but several others allowed sly grins to appear, and Polycarp Wharton had to clear his throat loudly. 'How are things

in the town?' Francis continued, almost in the same
breath.

'We've buried fourteen these past two weeks, but one
was a stranger, come from Shoreditch, and there was
Nathan Harris, the carter, and a woman in childbed.
Eight were infants with the whooping-cough, which is
bad this year. The folk in the Forest remain healthy,
they say.'

'And in London?'

Mr Reeve shook his head and looked at Polycarp,
whose face lost its cheerful grin as he replied, 'Mai
fether writes most dolefully. It eppears thet tha sickness
is daclining, at lest, end but two thousand end a half
died lest wake. Tha marchents ere et thar wits' end,
with trede quaite dropped. Ell tha warld rafuses our
ships antry to thar ports, elthough many throughout
Europe hev tha infaction elready. Thar is a great crowd
of shipping lies et tha Nore and balow Grevesand. They
say on 'Chenge thet many ere ruined!'

'But if they be still *alive* they have much to be
thankful for!' Mr Reeve remarked a trifle sharply,
obviously feeling that the merchants' losses were as
nothing against the vast loss of life in the City and the
country. He terminated his visit with his usual blessing,
and departed, after another abortive effort to thank
Francis for what was the virtual gift to him of
Archimedes, and a final, 'I hope to see you all about
your usual business after tomorrow, and in church on
Sunday, of course!'

Polycarp stayed a little longer, to unload his last
collection of gifts, which included a sucking-pig, medlars,
quinces and a fruit-cake, and then took his leave with
an elaborate speech made with even more excruciatingly
distorted pronunciation than usual, and rode off into
the gathering dusk.

'That'll roast real well fer Sunday dinner,' Ellen said
gloatingly, inspecting the piglet. 'I've allus wanted to
hev one o' they to roast! Will you be wanting supper

now, sir?' she added firmly.

'If you please,' Francis replied meekly, and the grand supper was duly served, followed, after an interval to allow the servants to eat and the dishes to be washed, by a bonfire of the boundary markers, with ale for everyone, and gingerbread men which Sukey had spent half the afternoon making.

'It seems a lifetime since I came over to help with the blackberries!' Mary said reflectively, as they all stood at last round the dying embers of the fire.

'I trust you'll not misunderstand if I say I'm sorry you came that day,' Francis's voice murmured just above her head.

She started, not having realised that he was so close, and automatically moved away a little. He did not follow, and she felt oddly disappointed.

The night passed peacefully, and the household assembled for morning prayers with all of them shooting anxious glances at one another, hardly daring to believe that they had reached the end of the forty days at last. Francis again read the ninety-first Psalm, as he had done that dreadful first morning, which seemed so long ago, and when he reached the words *A thousand shall fall at thy side, and ten thousand at thy right hand, but it shall not come nigh thee*, his voice was unsteady, and Ellen, Sukey and Bess unashamedly dissolved into tears, Obadiah sniffed and bent to fondle Dog's ears, and both Jem and Mary blinked hard and bit their lips. They all joined heartily in the prayer of thanksgiving, to which Francis added a simple prayer of his own for those who were still suffering, or had yet to endure their visitation, for they all knew that the plague had not yet run its course in Woodham, or anywhere else where the infection had spread.

After breakfast, there was an influx of visitors which entirely disrupted the household, for the families of the servants arrived to weep and laugh over their relations, several of the neighbouring gentry came to call on Jem and Francis, and Sir Charles arrived in his chariot to carry Mary home.

She had packed her trunk the night before, and while the footmen carried it downstairs and loaded it into the chariot, she went to the kitchen to speak to the servants, and then joined Jem and Francis in the parlour, where they were talking to her father.

It was easy enough to embrace Jem, the two friends clinging together and kissing like sisters, despite the half-dozen visitors sitting and standing about, who nodded and smiled approvingly at such a sweet and touching scene, but to approach Francis before so many interested eyes was another matter.

He was standing before the great fireplace, which was filled with autumn flowers and beech-leaves, very straight, his hands clasped behind his back, his face as austere as ever it had been, and his lips twisted in more of a grimace than a smile. Somehow, as she approached, his hands and hers moved forward at the same time and met in a warm double clasp, and he bent his head to kiss her just as she looked up at him with lips parted to say something. She could never remember afterwards what she had intended to say, but whatever it was remained unsaid, for his kiss, by accident or design, landed firmly on her mouth, albeit lightly, and with no sensation of lingering.

Some of the interested eyes looked knowing, or glanced at others with eyebrows raised in speculation, but Francis disappointed them by saying clearly, 'You'll be glad to go home, Cousin, after the poor hospitality we've shown you! Thank you for your help and your patience!'

'I have so much for which to thank you,' she replied in a low, strained voice, and could not go on with others, interlopers, listening.

'There'll be time to talk of everything later,' he said reassuringly. 'I trust you'll not be deterred from visiting us by what's happened? I think we may safely promise you that we'll not give you plague again, and Oliver would be most upset if you stayed away from us, as would we all!'

Mary smiled, and managed to depart lightly and easily, with both Francis and Jem excusing themselves to their visitors in order to walk with her to the chariot. As they stood talking for a few minutes more while Sir Charles checked that the trunk was safely strapped on and would not fall off on the road, Dog trotted round the side of the house with a carrot in his mouth, and came to lay it at her feet, his tail wagging and his eyes rolling up in a winsome manner which quite disarmed her, and she crouched beside him to give him a hug and have her cheek licked in farewell. The carrot had a scrap of blue ribbon tied round it, so she guessed the farewell gift was not only from Dog, and left Canons Grange on a small wave of amusement.

Her reception at home was very moving, with every female in the house, including Lady Hook and Mary, in tears of relief and joy over her preservation and safe return. By the time the family sat down to dinner, they were all quite worn out with emotion, yet still kept looking at one another, smiling and wiping their eyes, hardly making any coherent conversation at all.

'I shall love that dear girl as a daughter all her life!' exclaimed Lady Hook. 'That angel who preserved my own dearest Mary!'

'That's good,' said John rather prosaically, after swallowing a mouthful of roast goose. 'Because I intend to marry her as soon as I've finished my studies. If she'll have me.'

Nobody was particularly surprised by this announcement, but his parents and sister expressed their pleasure, and then the latter said, 'But John—I thought you would be one of the arrivals at Canons Grange this morning, yet you've not been near, nor while the quarantine was in force!'

'Oh, I'd knew she'd be safe, having been visited

before, and to tell truth, I couldn't bear just looking from a distance. I couldn't trust myself not to run down the hill and seize the pair of you, one under each arm! As for this morning—I'll wager all the world and his wife—especially his wife—was there, all Argus-eyed! What could I say to Jem in front of them all that wouldn't make her red as a Dutchvrow? I'll go down tomorrow, after church.'

Mary felt very tired by the end of the day, partly from emotion, but mainly because she was still far from having regained her full strength, and she passed the next two or three weeks very quietly, retiring early and rising late, strolling about the gardens, along the Selvedge path at the Forest's edge, or into the Forest itself, watching the leaves change colour and fall, the squirrels collecting their winter stores, and occasionally seeing the deer, which were said to be increasing again after their near-extinction during the Commonwealth. The weather gradually grew colder, and an occasional wet day confined her to the house, but whenever it was fine she was out in the air for a few hours, feeling herself improve in health and strength every day.

During this time, Jem frequently visited her, but Francis not at all, and she saw him only in church on Sunday mornings, where he paused for a few words of conversation after the service, but only of generalities. She felt increasingly that there was something important left undone, something she must somehow find an opportunity to say to him, but she was not sure what it was.

During one of Jem's visits, when the two friends were leaning on the balustrade at the foot of the terraced garden, looking out over the valley and the town, she said, 'We've seen hardly anything of Francis since I came home. I suppose he's very busy.'

'Yes,' Jem replied. 'Mr Palmer managed all the day-to-day work while we were shut up, but he left so many decisions for Francis to take, and now, of course, they're all six weeks more urgent, so he's very occupied. Obadiah's horses took a fit of sulks at being away from him and kicked down part of the dayhouse wall before they went to lodge with Polycarp Wharton, and he's been helping with the repairs all this week.'

Mary's surprise at the idea of a gentleman actually helping to repair a wall must have been apparent in her face, for Jem said ruefully, 'You may have noticed that Francis can turn his hand to most things in an emergency, but you may not have realised that it's not only in an emergency! If he sees something needing to be done, he'll start doing it himself, rather than direct someone else to the work! He says it's easier to get better work from the men by example. He always asks how you are when I go home from here. I expect he takes a proprietary interest in you, having brought you through the sickness!'

She spoke lightly and laughingly, and Mary also treated her words as a joke, but was secretly pleased to know that he thought of her sometimes, and was interested enough to ask how she did, but she found herself increasingly wishing to see him, to be with him. When she felt stronger, she took to going to Canons Grange with John again, but each time it seemed that Francis was either out in the fields somewhere, or preoccupied with other concerns than herself. By mid-November, she considered herself recovered from the sickness, but not from her longing for Francis, which seemed to increase as time passed. One misty morning, she was thinking of him as she walked along the Forest path to the pool, and by the time she reached the log seat, she had concluded that she must be in love with him, for nothing else could explain the constant ache for his voice, for the touch of his hands, for the rare smile which lit his face. She sighed, and sank on to the damp log, unmindful that the moss would stain her gown, the skirts of which were already damp and muddy from brushing against the bushes and plants along the narrow path.

The mist was heavy between the trees, turning the trunks of those on the far side of the pool into dark phantoms, spangling the spiders' webs with diamond drops, and deadening sound, so that the distant voices of woodcutters and the chunk of their axes were muffled and remote. A red stag materialised suddenly across the pool, bent to drink, and then looked up, tossing its head as it saw her still figure, and vanished as suddenly and silently as it had come. I'm sure he's avoiding me, she thought, not referring to the stag. I suppose he disliked me from the start, and nursing me while I was ill hasn't changed that. Why should it? If he'd nursed Sukey or Bess, I'd not have expected him to fall in love with either of them!

A sound from along the path made her look in that direction, just as a dark figure emerged ghostlike from the shrouded trees and came towards her. She knew it was Francis, even before she could see his face.

'Good morning,' he said prosaically.

She replied in a surprised, slightly defensive tone, absurdly afraid that he had appeared so pat because she had been thinking about him.

'May I?' he asked, looking at the log seat. She moved along a little to make room for him, and gestured an invitation to be seated.

He sat squarely, leaning forward, his arms on his thighs and his hands hanging loosely in unaccustomed idleness between his knees.

'It seems such a long time since we were all complaining of the heat and drought!' he remarked.

'Yes. At least the plague will die down as the weather grows colder.'

He was silent for a second or two, then said abruptly, 'I've been to see your father.'

'Yes?' She could think of nothing else to say, as the statement seemed so ordinary. Why else should he come to Pinnacles? Not to see her, she thought bitterly.

'I have his permission to ask you to marry me.'

She stared at him in shocked silence, quite deprived of speech or thought, and he straightened up and half-turned towards her.

'Is the idea so appalling that you're stricken dumb?' he enquired with a ghost of a smile.

'I thought you disliked me,' she heard herself say in a small, quavering voice.

'Disliked? No, why should I?' he asked, considering the matter. 'I disliked what I thought you were, but I was mistaken. I know it's not the grand marriage you once spoke about, but your father seems pleased with the idea.'

Mary replied absently, 'That doesn't matter—I mean the grandeur, not my father . . .' Her mind was furiously searching for an explanation, and found one only too easily. 'It wouldn't be a very good idea,' she said, sadly and reluctantly.

'Why not?'

'Because it would be based on the wrong things. I mean—I'd always think you offered because of—of what happened while I was ill, and you'd always think I accepted either because I felt compromised, or—or from gratitude to you for saving my life.'

She looked at him, longing for him to say that those were not the reasons, that he loved her and knew that she loved him, but he was gazing thoughtfully across the pool, considering her words, and eventually said only, 'I see. Yes, you're right, of course. You'd grow to feel guilty because you'd think that, in some way, you'd trapped me, and I'd grow to hate your gratitude . . . Gratitude can be a terrible burden to its recipient! Can you think of no other reasons why we might decide to marry?'

By now, she was too wretched to consider exactly what he meant by that question, and only shook her head miserably, saying 'No' in a subdued tone, clipping the word because she was afraid that she might begin to cry, but thereby making it sound decided and final.

'Ah, well . . .' He stood up. 'I hope we may continue to be friends, even if we may not be husband and wife?'

Mary nodded numbly, then forced herself to add, 'I hope so,' but did not look up, and so missed seeing the expression on his face, which was not as downcast as might have been expected in a rejected suitor, nor yet as relieved as that of a man who has offered out of a sense of duty, and been reprieved by a refusal.

'Well, I have to see Warrener about the accursed coneys, which still multiply like the seed of Abraham, so I'll bid you farewell for the moment.' He turned to go, but just before he disappeared along the path, called back, 'If you change your mind, let me know,' and then was gone.

Mary sat still for a long time, and then wept bitterly, her whole body, mind and spirit aching with loss.

CHAPTER TEN

MARY WAS ALMOST late for dinner by the time she felt able to return to the house, and had time only to slip upstairs, change her bedraggled gown and wash the traces of tears from her face before she went into the dining-room. Her mother remarked that she did not look quite so well today, but supposed there were bound to be ups and downs in recovering from so serious an illness. Her father gave her a few concerned looks, but resolutely avoided any mention of personal matters, and talked firmly about the scandal of Lord Sandwich's having broken into the cargoes of his Dutch prizes and distributed much of the goods to his officers and men, without waiting for the permission of the Lord High Admiral, and then of the reported doings of Parliament, which was in session at Oxford.

After the meal, he managed to draw Mary away to his cabinet on the pretext of showing her something in a book he was reading, and said quietly, 'So you refused Francis Hartwell? Is he not rich enough for you, or high enough in rank?'

There was only curiosity in the question, not sarcasm or condemnation, so Mary replied calmly, 'More than rich enough, no doubt, and far more worthy than many a duke—even a royal one!'

'Hmm. I gathered from your mother, some time ago, that you found him cold and reserved, but I hoped you might have come to know him better by now.'

'He is reserved, but I think not cold. I like him very well, but there's too much for which I must be grateful to him, and I think that's not a good foundation for a marriage.'

Sir Charles scratched the end of his nose thoughtfully, then said, 'As long as you don't think that I want a Croesus with a title for you, m'dear! I'd rather you married a man like Francis than a dozen earls and dukes. Still, I'll not tease you about it any more. It's your decision, and I'll abide by it.'

'Thank you, Father,' Mary said, managing a grateful smile. She was, indeed, very grateful, for almost any other father of their class of Society would have chosen a husband for his daughter, and not necessarily have granted her any say in the matter.

She had hoped that she might be left in peace during the afternoon to come to terms with what had happened in the morning, but a succession of visitors put paid to that. The first was Mr Reeve, who arrived on Archimedes with the news that the dwellers in the Forest were preparing to return to London soon, in the expectation that the plague would abate as the weather became colder, and he was hoping to collect clothing and money to help them on their way. He left Pinnacles gratefully, bearing a contribution of both, and a veal pie for his supper.

Soon after, Lady Dallance drove up in her chariot, attended by Polycarp Wharton. She was a lady of uncertain age, with sharp eyes and an even sharper tongue, giving to firing disconcerting questions at her victims, and she seemed this afternoon to be determined to discover the exact circumstances of Mary's stay at Canons Grange.

'So there were five females visited, including yourself, and but two people not in danger of taking the infection, having had it in the past—although I believe that is no guarantee, for a cousin of my sister's husband's stepfather had it a second time, and died of it not six weeks since! So how did Miss Hartwell manage to nurse so many? Surely Mr Hartwell was able to help her in some way?'

'Oh, yes,' Mary replied, watching her words carefully. 'I helped a little myself, until I was visited, and then I believe he was able to relieve her of some of the burden. In fact, everybody helped as best they could, for I think we were all resigned to the knowledge that we were likely to fall ill ourselves.'

'All? But two had already . . . Oh, you include the *servants* in your "all"!'

'Indeed.'

'And was Mr Hartwell able to do anything for you, personally, during your sickness?'

To judge by the way she screwed up her eyes and peered at her, the tip of her nose appearing to quiver a little, Mary deduced that she had either heard something, or suspected a scandal.

'I've almost no memory of what happened while I was ill,' she replied truthfully. 'There's high fever in the sickness, almost from the outset, and great confusion of the mind. It all seems like a strange, half-remembered nightmare, full of heat and pain and thirst. I can't say who gave me drink or medicine, or sat by me through the days and nights. I believe everyone took a turn at watching by the sick, but whether at any one time it was Miss Hartwell, her brother, the sewing-maid, the cook, or the tranter, I really have no idea. I'm very grateful to them all, for between them, they saved my life!' Enough of the earlier part of her speech was true to lend conviction to the latter part, which she suspected was not, but as it was quite true that she had only the most confused of memories of the period of her illness, she felt that there was no need to add anything she had been told afterwards.

'Most unpleasant!' Lady Dallance commented distastefully, but whether she referred to the sickness, or to the idea of having one's sickbed watched by a cook or a tranter, was not clear. However, she lost interest in the topic, and moved on to other scandalous tidbits, which she related to Lady Hook with considerable relish.

It was some time before Polycarp Wharton was able to seize the opportunity of a pause for coffee to take the centre of the stage and announce that his betrothal to Miss Philadelphia Sherburne had been formalised, and he expected to be married in the New Year.

'Philadelphia!' snorted Lady Dallance. 'The gel hasn't got any brothers, so why did they call her *brotherly love*? Plain as a pikestaff, they say! Couldn't you have caught a better fish, Polycarp?'

He gave Mary a rueful, languishing look, and replied, 'Ai could imegine a varitable selmon, a sturgeon, nay, a *whele*!—but Ai hev no doubt Miss Sharburne will prove en axcallent choice, es mai fethar assures me!'

Mary could not help but be amused that he had likened her to a whale, and intended it as a compliment, as the look which accompanied the statement implied, and she felt quite sorry for him when Lady Dallance continued remorselessly, 'Well enough, as she's heiress to a fine property, but not good breeding stock—too many gels and precious few boys, and those generally sickly! I suppose your father knows his business, though I always thought him a fool over the petticoats—and most else as well! The only sensible thing I can ever recall him doing was to leave you to manage his land in your own way. Pity he couldn't let you manage your marrying on the same basis! Come along, now—can't stay gossiping here all day about your affairs.'

With that, she heaved herself out of her chair and made her farewells, informed Mary that she'd best catch a husband before her looks faded entirely, told Lady Hook to send a housemaid to the Manor House for a copy of her own receipt for furniture polish, as that used at Pinnacles was obviously very inferior, and swept out, with Polycarp drooping resignedly in her wake.

'Damned canting, crop-eared bitch!' said Lady Hook

with mild indignation after they had passed out of
earshot, her small store of expletives having been
garnered during the Civil War. 'My polish is every bit
as good as hers, and my starch is a deal better. Her lace
is positively yellow! So old-fashioned!'

To round off a very trying day, a messenger arrived
towards evening with a letter for Mary from the Queen's
Chamberlain, bidding her return to her duties at Court
at the beginning of December, when the Queen would
be at Oxford. It included a kindly message from the
Queen, expressing the hope that she was well, and
saying that Her Majesty had missed her; but it was still
unwelcome, for Mary had hoped to spend Christmas at
home.

'Perhaps you could write and say that you've been
visited, and don't feel fit to travel,' Lady Hook said
dubiously, 'but I suppose it wouldn't do . . . What a
pity!'

During the next two days, Mary made the arrangements for her journey, and packed her trunk with
steadily increasing reluctance, and then rode over to
Canons Grange to bid farewell to her friends.

John had already told them that she had been recalled,
so Jem met her in the parlour with a brave face, trying
to conceal her own sadness at the impending departure
of her friend because she assumed Mary would be glad
to be returning to Court.

'You'll be in time for all the Christmas festivities!'
she said. 'It must be exciting!'

'To tell truth,' Mary said wryly, 'it's all rather dull.
Some of the courtiers will probably perform a masque,
badly danced and worse acted, all forgetting their words
and trying to attract attention away from whoever's
speaking or singing. There'll be a deal of gluttony and
drunkenness, and no real joy in any of it, for hardly
any of them remember what Christmas is really about!
I'd rather be at home.'

'But surely it would be dull here, as well?' Jem said

dubiously. 'With so many people having been sick and so many dead, very few will feel like merrymaking.'

'Which is how it should be,' Mary replied seriously. 'We expect everyone in Woodham to be subdued and thoughtful of those who've lost members of their families, so why should the Court be so careless of the suffering of a whole nation? Thousands have died in England, but I doubt if many at Court will spare them so much as a thought.'

'A few will,' said Francis quietly. He had entered the room in his usual silent and unobtrusive fashion, unnoticed by Jem and Mary. 'The King cares, and his few wise men—and fewer wiser women.'

Mary was so startled by this sudden interpolation that she swung round wide-eyed and looked him full in the face, which she had meant to avoid doing since that disastrous conversation in the Forest. He met her gaze, his face as closed and austere as ever, but with something in his eyes which made her catch her breath and put a hand to her throat, feeling that her heart had shifted painfully within her.

'Very few,' she said, still looking at him.

Oliver chose that moment to dash in through the still-open door with a chirrup of welcome, and rush to entangle himself in Mary's skirts, purring loudly and trying to rub against her legs, nearly oversetting her. By the time she had sorted him out from her voluminous riding-skirt, picked him up, and suffered his affectionate head-butting and rubbing against her cheek, what might have been an important moment had passed, and the conversation became ordinary as Mary and Jem tried to raise one another's spirits by promises of writing, and possibly of managing to meet somewhere when the Court returned to Whitehall.

'Oh, Francis!' Jem exclaimed. 'Surely you have to go to Court before long, to take the arrow?'

'The arrow?' Mary queried, mystified, and then remembered. 'Oh, your rent! Of course! Do you have to deliver it to the King personally?'

'That was the custom, until it became impossible because of the wars and the King's exile,' Francis replied, stroking Oliver, who had returned to him and was sitting across his lap. 'During that time, Grandfather sent it to the Exchequer when it fell due, but it would have been my first payment of it this year, as it's due only once every seven years. I wrote to enquire, but was told to defer it until next year, because of the sickness and the King being away from London. It appears he wishes to revive the personal receiving of it.'

'So when will you go?' Jem asked.

'It was due in September, so I suppose it will be next September.'

'So long! I hoped it might be sooner, and that I might go with you,' she said disconsolately.

Francis's expression became very bleak, and after a brief pause, he said, 'I'm sorry, Jem. I will not take you to Whitehall.'

The finality in his tone was so apparent that neither Jem nor Mary attempted protest or persuasion, but looked sadly at each other, and Mary said, 'Well . . . we'll think of something.'

She left them soon after, for she had a round of visits to make before she departed the next morning. Jem hugged and kissed her, shedding a few tears, and then she turned to Francis, hesitating, uncertain whether to offer him her hand, or what to say. He solved the problem for her by holding out both his own hands, took hers, and drew her to him, then bent and kissed her, apparently as he had done before, the day she left Canons Grange after the quarantine, but it was not at all the same sort of brotherly kiss, and yet it was so brief that she had no chance to respond, and was left achingly unsatisfied.

She wondered a great deal about it during the tedious and very trying journey to Oxford, which took her through towns and villages where guards armed with staves refused to allow her coach to stop, and along roads made miry by the autumn rain. It was impossible to buy food anywhere, and she was thankful that her mother had provided an enormous hamper, filled with enough provisions not only for Mary and Eleanor, but for the driver and the two escorting grooms as well, and her father had thought to have fodder for the horses put into sacks and piled under a tarpaulin on the roof.

They followed a roundabout route, avoiding St Albans, where the plague had been bad and was but now subsiding, and passing by Watford and Chesham to reach the old Roman road beyond Risborough, and so down it to Oxford. Because of the state of the roads, they had to spend three nights on the way, Mary and Eleanor sleeping in the coach and the driver and grooms under it, out of the drizzle which seemed to fall most of the time, reflecting and deepening Mary's general feeling of unhappiness.

Oxford was crowded, with Court and Parliament both there. The lack of servants and the carelessness of the courtiers had made all their lodgings in the college buildings squalid, and the university authorities were in a state of resentment at the occupation of their buildings by a crowd of dissolute hedonists, and were courteously uncooperative.

The Queen and Miss Bellamy were pleased to see Mary, and both exclaimed in horror when they heard that she had been visited, the Queen crossing herself repeatedly, and praying aloud in Latin and Portuguese in thanksgiving that she had survived the sickness, and Miss Bellamy weeping copiously. Harry Killigrew greeted her with, *'What! My dear Lady Disdain, are you yet living?'*, but smiled in a friendly fashion as well to soften the quotation.

Hardly anyone else even remarked that she had been absent for over four months, and, indeed, after a few days, she found it hard to believe herself, and those eventful, important weeks began to seem like a dream. Apart from the different location, nothing at Court seemed to have changed, save for a certain amount of serious discussion between the King and his chief advisors. As this took place mostly in private, however, the rest of the Court took no heed of it, or of the fact that nearly a hundred thousand people had died in London, and nobody knew how many in the rest of the country, that trade was at a standstill, both internally and overseas, and it was impossible to gather any taxes to carry on the government of the country or the war with the Dutch. Mary discovered these things from one conversation with Lord Craven, who had come down from London to report to the King on the state of affairs in the capital, but most of the Court seemed more interested in shocking the moral susceptibilities of Town and Gown alike, and she spent a great deal of her time in the room she shared once more with Miss Bellamy and Miss Webster, writing to her parents, or to Jem, who sent her frequent accounts of the humdrum but desirable life of Woodham.

In January, the King went to Hampton, and then back to Whitehall, and most of his Household accompanied him, but the Queen and her Household remained at Oxford a few weeks longer, partly to be certain that the cold weather had abated the plague, and partly because a violent storm and gale had washed out some parts of the road and brought down trees across it. They were still there when St Valentine's day brought its usual crop of gifts and verses, some sentimental, and possibly expressions of genuine feeling, but most obscene or insulting, and the young ladies amused themselves with the various traditional methods of identifying their future husbands, scattering hemp-seed by the bushel and robbing the bay-trees of leaves to put under their pillows.

Mary received several packages, mostly of verses ridiculing her obstinate adherence to virtue, but a few were kinder, and some were gifts, including two pairs of gloves. One pair was clearly very costly, embroidered with quatrefoils and stalks of wheat in gold thread, the stamens of the flowers and the ears of the wheat being small rubies and topazes respectively. As both these things figured in the coat-of-arms of Lord Sherford, she sent the gloves back to him by one of the couriers who travelled daily between Oxford and Whitehall.

The other pair puzzled her, for although they too had a little embroidery, it was a simple design of oak and beech-leaves worked in green and coppery silks on ribbon, and then applied to the gauntlets of a practical, well-made pair of riding-gloves, quite unromantic, but of far more use than the usual elegant kid trifles. She wondered if their arrival on that particular day were mere coincidence, but there was no indication of the sender, no message. She thought vaguely of Polycarp Wharton, for the leaves reminded her so much of her beloved Forest, but surely he would not send a Valentine gift to anyone but his newly-wed wife at this stage in their marriage? Even the means of arrival of the gloves was a mystery, for the porter at the college gate, ever surly towards any member of the Court, would only say that the packet had been left by 'a man, but not the royal courier'—more than that, he would or could not say.

Eventually the whole Court reassembled at Whitehall. Lord Sherford celebrated the event by proposing marriage to Mary again, managing to do it more graciously this time, but he received a firm and icy refusal, and went away with the baffled expression of a hound which has just been told that foxes were become extinct.

Life at Court went on as if there had been no plague. Only Mary herself seemed to have changed, or, rather, to have become even more heart-sick over her life there, and stronger in her desire to be at home. Not a day passed but she longed to be at Woodham, and wished most fervently that she had accepted Francis's proposal, becoming convinced that it would have been better to be married to the man she loved than not, whatever his reasons for offering. It was generally accepted that few couples were in love when they married, but, in most cases, affection increased through the years of shared life. She dreamed of him, awake and asleep, compared all the men she met with him, to their detriment, and grew gradually thinner, paler and quieter.

After a while the Queen noticed, and insisted that her doctors should examine her, thinking that she had perhaps not entirely recovered from the plague. They conferred solemnly together, took her pulse, looked at her eyes, held a phial of her water to the light, and concluded that she was of a melancholic disposition, and should take senna and polypody to purge her head, heart and lungs of the evil humours, promote mirth, and enliven the habit of the body. The mixture made her sick, and she poured her daily dose into the privy after the first week of it.

Quite apart from her personal problem, Mary realised that, as the year progressed, it was proving not a good one for anyone, save the hedonists. With the warmer weather, plague reappeared, although with less severity. Harry Killigrew said that it had killed so many the previous year that there were fewer left to take the sickness, and he was not entirely joking. The war went badly, for Lord Albemarle had joined Prince Rupert in command of the Fleet, and although the latter's cavalry strategy was reasonably effective at sea, the former's infantry tactics were not, and he caused stupefaction among the seamen by ordering his ships to right or left wheel. He seemed to know no battle tactics but a simple frontal charge, and well-nigh shattered his own fleet. The tarpauling captains evened matters a little by an attack on Schelling, where they burned two towns, a hundred and fifty ships, and a million pounds-worth of property. The summer was again hot and dry, and plagued by an east wind, which roused and maintained fears of a Dutch or a French invasion, and there was no money to pay the soldiers and sailors, or even to refit and provision the ships.

The one bright aspect of Mary's life during this time lay in her letters from home. Her father wrote monthly, as he had always done, and usually enclosed a sheet or two from Jem, who gave a lively account of affairs in the town and at Canons Grange, and, best of all, almost always included a brief message from Francis. It was usually no more than his regards, but once he said that the continued drought made him hope for a better foggy day, which gave Mary something to puzzle about, alternately hoping and fearing over his possible meaning.

Towards the end of August, she began to hope that she might see him when he came to bring his arrow, and prayed that Somerset House might not be ready for the Queen's occupation before he came. It was intended that the Palace should be her residence, now that the Queen Dowager had returned to France, but the difficulties of the year since Queen Mary's departure had delayed its refurbishment.

Despite Mary's hopes and expectations, she was caught unawares when the day came. It was a Saturday, the first day of September. She had been with the other maids on duty in the Queen's drawing-room for an hour or two, after accompanying Catherine on a gentle ride in the park, and had been subjected to another siege by the ever-persistent Lord Sherford, from which she emerged with relief when the Queen went to dinner. She had first to take a torn piece of the Queen's lace to the seamstress in her office, and came out from there into the Stone Gallery to go for her own meal just as the King and his gentlemen, with a squadron of small dogs, emerged from Lord Lauderdale's apartments, and stood talking in the gallery near by.

Several people were waiting to present petitions to the King, this being one of the few times when he might be walking slowly enough for them to catch him, and a few others were expecting, for various reasons, to be presented themselves. Among these was a tall, dark-periwigged man, very elegant in crimson silk and silver ribbons, even his silk hose and shoes crimson to match. It was not until he turned round that Mary realised that it was Francis.

She stood transfixed, hardly breathing, and he saw her immediately, came across the gallery and made her a courtly bow, sweeping back his white-plumed hat with one hand, and holding a plain clothyard arrow in the other.

'I hoped I might see you,' he said, his eyes smiling, then sobering as he looked at her. 'Have you been sick again? You look far from well.'

She could have wept, for she knew that her face was pinched and pale, her figure, never fashionably voluptuous, slimmer than ever, and her puce gown not one in which she looked her best. 'I miss the country,' she said, drinking in the sight of him, bronzed and healthy from harvesting, bright-eyed, firm-skinned, and so unlike the puffy-eyed, unhealthy-looking sybarites of the Court. 'I'm glad to see you.'

'You've not forgotten me, then?' He sounded serious.

She replied, 'How could I?' with a shade more feeling than she intended, and hastily added, 'Jem said nothing of your coming in her last letter. Have you anywhere to stay?'

'One of our neighbours at Woodham has a house in the City, in St Martin Orgars, near to the Bridge. I'm staying there while I deliver my rent and see to some other business. I was summoned by the Exchequer at fairly short notice—I think someone had discovered my rent was nearly a year in arrears!'

'St Martin Orgars,' Mary repeated, frowning a little, for she rarely went into the City, and knew the whereabouts of only a few of its hundred or so churches.

'It lies among the lanes in the angle between Canning

Street and Fish Street Hill. A tiny parish, and my friend's house is next to the church,' he replied, still studying her face in a direct manner which she found unnerving, fearing that he would see in it some indication that her heart was pounding, her stomach churning, and something was making it difficult for her to breathe properly.

'Mr Hartwell?' a voice called in a reproving tone. 'His Majesty awaits you!'

Francis flickered one eyelid at Mary in the ghost of a wink, said quietly, 'Don't disappear,' and went to make a most elegant bow to the King in the latest French fashion, and to drop on one knee, proffering his arrow balanced across his upturned left hand, his right being occupied with his hat. Two of the dogs approached cautiously to sniff him, and then wagged their tails, looking up at their master.

The King, his melancholy face looking genuinely amused, reached to take the arrow with both hands, commenting, 'A most unusual rent, but I've heard the history of it!' and then his eyes fell on the palm of the hand which was offering it, and his amusement vanished. He looked sharply at Francis's face.

'Hartwell,' he said thoughtfully. 'Are you the same Francis Hartwell who sailed to the West Indies with my Cousin Rupert?'

'Yes, Sire, the same,' Francis replied quietly.

'Had I the power then that I have now, you would not have come by those,' Charles said, touching the scarred palm. 'I owe more than I can ever repay to men like you. Why have you never come to claim your reward?'

'I have no need,' Francis replied simply, letting his hand fall to his side. 'I lost nothing but a few years of my life and a little skin, and I learned a great deal.'

The King considered him with close interest, and then said, 'But there must be something you desire, something you lack, which is close to your heart?'

'Only one thing, Sire, and even you can't give me that,' he replied with his wry smile. Charles made a slight gesture with the arrow, and Francis rose to his feet, standing only a couple of inches shorter than the King's six feet. Charles continued to look at him, obviously considering his odd reply, and then turned his head slightly and looked across at Mary, who was still standing by the door to the seamstress's room. It was only a glance, and, although Mary had heard the King's side of the conversation clearly enough, Francis had spoken so quietly that she had not caught his replies, so she thought nothing of it.

The King said, 'It appears you're acquainted with Miss Hook?'

'Her parents are my neighbours at home.'

'Then she shall see that you have your dinner before you go,' Charles said, smiling a little. 'And if you think of something which I may be able to give you, pray let me know.'

With that, he nodded in a friendly fashion and passed on along the gallery, his pace quickening so that his waiting petitioners had to get smartly off their marks and dodge among the small dogs to catch him before he disappeared through the doors at the end, still absent-mindedly carrying the arrow, on his way to dine in state with the Queen in the Banqueting Hall.

Francis watched him go, almost everyone else following, and then turned back to Mary. 'So, you're to bear-lead me, by Royal command,' he said lightly.

'It's a little early to go to dinner,' Mary replied. 'Is there anything you would like to see on the way to the hall? The pictures, perhaps?' She gestured towards the late King's collection of paintings, which hung on both long walls of the gallery, retrieved from the various people who had bought them during the Commonwealth by the present King after his restoration.

'Could we perhaps take a turn in the garden?' he

asked. 'I've seen the pictures. This isn't my first visit to
Whitehall.'

'Oh?'

'I've been here once or twice to see Prince Rupert.'
He gestured towards the door of the Prince's apartments
at the Westminster end of the gallery. 'He showed me
the pictures. He's a fine artist himself.'

'The gardens, then,' Mary replied, not averse to going
with him somewhere away from the ever-watching eyes.
There was still a score of people about, and the guards
on either side of the doors to the King's apartments
watched everyone with sharp interest.

Even out in the garden, she was aware that there
might still be curious eyes watching, for the windows of
Lord Lauderdale's and Lord Arlington's rooms looked
out on it from either side of the doorway, so she walked,
not too hurriedly, away from the building and out
among the square beds of flowers, the bushes and
occasional trees, to the sundial where the King set his
watch right every morning, and then more slowly across
towards the far side, where the high wall of the Bowling
Green, with a row of trees before it, afforded a little
privacy.

'It will be cooler under the trees,' she said, having
come so far in silence, acutely conscious that *he* was
beside her, looking about him at the garden with a
lively interest, apparently not noticing that she was not
speaking.

Once in the shade of the trees, he came to a halt and
said, 'Can you not get leave to come home for a while?'

'I think not,' she replied with a sigh. 'I had four
months' leave last year, and there are several who've
not had any for a longer time . . . How are you,
Francis?' She clasped her hands tightly together and bit
her lip, trying to still the tremulous, half-frightened
feeling within her at being alone with him again, after
so long.

'In good health, praise God! And you? Not well, I

think. Have you found that ideal man yet?'

'Not at Whitehall,' she replied, evasively but truthfully, looking away across the garden, and so did not see the sudden sharpness of his eyes on her half-averted face.

'If I'm keeping you from something, don't concern yourself about me—I can shift for myself for my dinner,' he said.

She turned back to him, startled, and exclaimed, 'Oh, no! I mean, I'm free for an hour or so, to have my own dinner, and it's so good to see someone from home!' She had so nearly said 'you' and betrayed herself, she felt, that she rattled on, asking after Jem, Obadiah and Dog, Mr Reeve, and Archimedes, the Canons Grange servants, Oliver, and whoever else came to mind, in no sort of logical order, until he smilingly put up a hand to stop her.

'They are all well and send their remembrances to you! Oliver is saving you one of his sons, Dog has an old bone hidden away for you, and everyone is flourishing, including Warrener and his infernal coneys, the deer by our pool in the Forest, and Gabriel and all his brothers.'

'Sisters,' she corrected. 'All bells are she.' She hardly attended to what she was saying, the two words *our pool* echoing in her mind. Why had he said that?

'But their names are nearly all male!' he objected.

'Nevertheless, all bells are she.'

At that moment, Great Tom struck the hour at Westminster, just beyond the Bowling Green, and was echoed by Great Peter, and Mary laughed nervously and said, 'Shall we go in to dinner?'

They joined a throng of off-duty courtiers hurrying to the Great Hall to secure places at the long tables. To the uninitiated, there appeared a great many expecting to be fed, but to Mary's eyes there were fewer than in normal times, for many of the more adventurous young gentlemen were at sea with the Fleet, and the more prudent among those who had no duties to tie them to the Royal Presence had remained in the country until the plague should be entirely abated. She found good places for her guest and herself, and they waited for the servitors to reach them with dishes of food.

'So Lady Disdain has a lover after all!' exclaimed the teasing voice of Harry Killigrew behind them. 'My commiserations, Sherford. The hopelessness of your case appears proven!'

Mary stiffened, and kept her eyes on the table before her, hoping that Francis would not realise whom *Lady Disdain* might be, but Killigrew climbed over the table and took a seat opposite her, his merry face alight with mischief. 'There's room here, Sherford!' he called.

Lord Sherford mumbled something vaguely disagreeable and went elsewhere, but a couple of Killigrew's friends joined him, and the three sat looking at Mary and Francis with happy expectation.

'Why, it's the archer!' Killigrew exclaimed. 'That was an odd gift you brought the King, friend.'

Francis accepted the last word in the spirit in which it was offered, and replied pleasantly, 'It was my rent. King Hal gave my ancestor an estate for one arrow every seven years. I'm Francis Hartwell, of Woodham in Essex.'

'Harry Killigrew of His Majesty's Backstairs,' was the reply, followed by an introduction of the other two, one of whom was Sir Toby Ward, who had escorted Mary and her companions on the night of the celebrations after the Battle of Lowestoft more than a year before. 'So you know our ice-hearted Miss Hook?'

'Ice-hearted?' queried Francis, leaning back to allow a harassed servitor to put a silver platter of roast beef before him and deposit a dish of worts in the middle of the table.

'Ah,' said Killigrew soulfully, eyes twinkling. 'You'd not credit how many gallants have sighed for her favours, and not received so much as a smile. Virtue personified!

The archetypal Vestal Virgin! Perhaps you know her better?' The underlying meaning of this last was embarrassingly clear to Mary.

'I've known her since childhood,' Francis replied smoothly, and not entirely truthfully. 'Are you by any chance related to Tom Killigrew?'

'My father,' Killigrew admitted. 'You know him?'

'I knew him a little in Paris, in the fifties. Is he well?'

'In a state of irritation that the theatres are still not reopened after the sickness, but otherwise flourishing like the proverbial green bay-tree, and in high favour with His Majesty, although his tongue is more acid than mine, and his jests more pointed! I gather that our Miss Hook was visited by the sickness while she was at home last year. Was it much prevalent in your part of the world?'

'There too many smitten for anyone's peace of mind, but other places were worse.'

'You were fortunate yourself?'

'In that I survived an earlier visitation in my childhood. Four of my servants were visited this time, and two succumbed.'

Killigrew nodded sympathetically, his face sober for once, and then his eyes sparkled again, and he looked at Mary in such a knowing, speculative fashion that she dreaded what was coming next. Fortunately, Killigrew's valet came hurrying along, looking for him to tell him that the King was asking for him, and he had to go, abandoning his dinner with a grimace, and bidding Francis a friendly farewell.

Of his two companions, one was but a nondescript hanger-on who ate his food in silence, and Sir Toby, the other, had a certain underlying kindness which prevented him from adding to Mary's embarrassment, which his observant eye had noted, and the meal continued amid innocuous conversation.

Meanwhile, in Pudding Lane, not a half-mile from St Martin Orgars church, a baker was drawing his fifth batch of loaves for the day, and wishing the weather were less hot, as he wiped his sweaty face with his apron.

CHAPTER ELEVEN

FRANCIS HAD BUSINESS to see about in the afternoon, but he enquired if Mary would be free in the evening. She hesitated, torn between her desire to be with him and her fear that she might betray her eagerness for his company, and the former won, for she was, indeed, not required to be on duty once the Queen had gone to supper.

They were standing on the pier at the Privy Stairs, waiting for a wherry to come alongside in response to Francis's shout of 'Oars!' and convey him back to the City, so he said, 'Then meet me here, as soon as you're free, and we'll go to Vauxhall for supper. If you would like it?'

'Very much,' Mary replied, but with a shade of doubt in her mind. She had heard of the pleasures of Vauxhall Gardens, with its pleasant avenues and secluded bowers, and she was aware that large numbers of people went there—anyone who could afford the admission and was respectably dressed—but the presence of City tradesmen and Court gentry, respectable women and prostitutes, often led to unpleasant scenes, as quarrels broke out remarkably easily, particularly when one sort of woman was mistaken, genuinely or pretendedly, for the other. On the other hand, it was pleasant, green and away from Whitehall.

The afternoon passed very slowly. The Queen chose to stroll in St James's Park, by the canal, to feed the wildfowl (particularly the crane with the wooden leg), then to eat cakes at the little building set up by a cavalier widow nearby, and drink milk from the cows pastured amid the deer and elk. It was still hot, and a stiff breeze blew the dust about and disarranged the ladies' curls, making them irritable and causing long-standing quarrels between some of them to break out in childish poking and pushing behind the Queen's back.

Mary endured it stoically, waiting impatiently for each quarter-hour to chime from the various steeple-clocks within earshot, and feeling a little lift of her spirits as they mounted to each hour, bringing supper-time that much nearer.

By three o'clock, Her Majesty had tired of the Park, and they all trailed back to the Palace, to play inexpert games in the Bowling Green for another hour, and then to the Drawing Room for music, under cover of which various new flirtations began, or old ones continued.

Between two pieces of music, Lord Sherford sidled cautiously up to Mary and enquired, 'Pray, who was that country bumpkin with you at dinner?'

'Country bumpkin?' Mary replied coolly. 'You must be mistaken, my lord! I saw no country bumpkin at dinner. I sat with Sir Toby, Mr Killigrew and an old friend of my family from home. Perhaps you mean the silent gentleman with Mr Killigrew? I don't recollect his name, but he had not the appearance of a bumpkin!' She did, in fact, know the man's name perfectly well, and also his reputation as a quarrelsome bully, but continued her pretence with a certain relish, as she resented his discourteous allusion to Francis, and meant to pay him back.

The interval was continuing while the musicians conferred among themselves about what to play next, so she beckoned to Harry Killigrew, who came over with the nondescript but quarrelsome gentleman at his heels, and Mary said to him, 'Pray introduce your friend to Lord Sherford. He was asking just now who he is.'

'I was not!' snapped Sherford irritably. 'I know who he is, perfectly well! I meant the other fellow with you, the one in crimson.'

'But you described him as a country bumpkin!' Mary exclaimed in wide-eyed indignation. 'Really, my lord! If you wish me to identify someone for you, you must try to give a more accurate description.' With that, she walked away, leaving Killigrew grinning sardonically, Sherford fuming, and the quarrelsome gentleman trying to work out whether or not Sherford had insulted him.

The Queen at last dismissed the ladies whose turn of duty was finished, and went away to dress for supper with her brother-in-law and his wife. Mary hastened to her own room to change her gown, brush and rearrange her hair, and stare into the mirror, wondering how to make herself look more attractive without actually painting. She tried pinching her cheeks and biting her lips, decided it made no difference, seized her hooded cloak, and put it on as she hastened towards the Privy Stair and the little pier jutting out into the river. She found that the wind had increased and was whipping up the water into choppy waves, and there was far less traffic passing than was usual on a Saturday evening. She wondered if perhaps Francis would not come, or, at least, not on the river. He might take a hackney and come by road, but that would take much longer. All she could do was wait here, where he would expect to find her, and hope that no drunken party of gallants would come out on their way to take their pleasure up- or down-river.

The wind pulled at her skirts and blew her hood back, ruffling her carefully-arranged curls, as she looked downstream towards the City, crouching in the dusk about the enormous bulk of St Paul's, which soared so high above every other building that it looked quite out of scale. The pall of smoke which always hung over the massed houses was streaming like a grey banner across the sky behind the Palace, lit eerily by the declining sun.

A fair-sized wherry with two oarsmen and one passenger was coming along at a good speed, despite the rough water. It started to slope its course in towards the pier from a distance, and arrived safely, turning neatly into the lee of the pier, and Francis stood up to make the leap from boat to step in one swift movement, then came up to her, smiling far more broadly than usual.

'It's good to be on the water again,' he said, 'and quite exhilarating in this breeze! Will you come, or shall we take a hackney?'

Mary knew quite well that if she elected for a hackney, they must either go back to the City, over the Bridge, and back along the far bank, some four miles round at least, or along this bank for half a mile, and then over the river on the ferry. The first seemed a waste of time, and the latter had little to offer that was better than the same half-mile on the river.

'If the watermen are willing, so am I,' she said.

'You're sure? You've a right to be nervous, with the water so choppy.'

Mary smiled bravely, for she was nervous, but went gingerly down the wet, slippery steps, waited while Francis went into the boat, then gave him one hand and the nearer waterman the other, and was safely transferred. She settled beside Francis in the stern and had a piece of tarpaulin tucked over her skirts by the waterman, who grinned encouragingly at her and observed, 'It ain't fer ter Foxhall, lady. Me and Will'll get yer there, reasonable dryish, never fear!'

It was not a particularly comfortable journey, with the wind cutting across the river in this reach, and several cupfuls of water splashed her, one of them hitting her in the face, which made her turn her head away with a gasp of surprise. Francis stopped her turning back again with one finger on her cheek, and wiped her face gently with a fine cambric handkerchief, which made her thankful that she had not given way to the temptation to use paint.

'I wasn't expecting it!' she said by way of explanation, then nervously grabbed at the gunwale as another boat, going downstream, passed too close and just missed catching its oars in their own. The exchange of insults between the watermen was amazingly inventive, and did nothing for her composure, as most of it was obscene. Francis, she saw when she gave him a sidelong glance, looked quite amused, and remarkably lively.

'Do you like being in a boat?' she asked.

'Very much, as long as I'm not expected to row,' he replied, laughing as another cupful of water missed Mary and hit him. He wiped his face, and said, 'Though I don't mind rowing when it's by choice, and not compulsion!'

' 'Is Grishus Majisty loikes rowing,' volunteered the forward waterman. 'We orfen sees 'im, of a morning, rowing 'isself up ter Putney, wiv the Dook or by 'isself. They goes swimming, right early, afore anyone else is abaht—any o' them layabouts at White'all, thet is—there's plenty working folk arahnd! Yer row much, mister?'

'I used to,' Francis replied. 'But in something bigger than this, at sea.'

'Bigger, and at sea?' pondered the nearer man. ' 'Ere, d'yer mean one o' them galleys?'

'Yes. A Spanish one.'

'Yer don' sahnd Spenish!'

'I'm not. I was a prisoner. They send their prisoners to the galleys, instead of keeping them snug in gaol!'

The watermen regarded him with interest, and the nearer one with a shade of doubt.

'Show's yer 'ands!' he said.

Francis good-humouredly held out his hands, and the man looked at the scars and callouses with respect. 'Yer didn't get them playing wiv yer lapdog!' he admitted, and began counting a faster stroke, which the other man picked up without demur, and they pulled in to Vauxhall pier as if they were winning a race. Francis was out on the steps in a trice, and turned to take Mary about the waist, swinging her ashore with the greatest of ease. He then pulled out his purse and asked the fare.

The two men conferred in a confidential mutter, and then one of them said, ' 'Alf-price ter you, seeing as yore a waterman o' sorts yerself.'

Francis accepted the compliment with a bow, paid him what he asked, and added the balance as a *pourboire*, and the watermen wished him a pleasant evening and a better night, with much jocular winking and nodding, before they looked about for a passenger wishing to return down-river.

Mary and Francis entered the gardens, and strolled along a gravelled walk under the fine trees, where little candle-lanterns twinkled amid the branches, winking through the leaves in the gathering dusk. Behind them, the last of the sunset was sending a shimmering red light like flames across the broken surface of the river, but neither remarked it, for they were looking at the pleasure-seekers around them. Not so many of them tonight, in this sharp wind, but a good representation of City merchants and their wives or mistresses, young folk enjoying a rare evening out, a sprinkling of courtiers, and a number of single women, alone or in pairs, promenading slowly to display their rouged and patched faces, bare bosoms and shoulders, elaborate gowns and improbably luxuriant hair.

Francis spared these latter a glance, and remarked to Mary that they must find the wind blow cold, and thereafter ignored them, giving his attention to a troop of monkeys, dressed in fine clothes and performing a continual string of acrobatic feats, apparently of their own volition, although occasionally a man, dressed as they were, gave one or other of them a tidbit, or clapped his hands and handed one a plate of little cakes or a lighted candle. If the former, the monkey balanced it on his head and climbed a tree, then dropped the cakes one by one into the mouth of another on the ground, popping each alternate one into his own mouth. If it was a candle, the monkey held it either in his teeth and turned somersaults, or with his foot and walked on his hands.

After watching for a while, Mary and Francis walked on, pausing to listen to a talking parrot, and a man doing imitations of birds and animals, but going on towards the sound of music in the heart of the gardens, where a string orchestra was playing on a flower-surrounded platform under a canopy, in an area where several leafy bowers had been contrived, in which people could eat their supper in reasonable privacy. Francis gestured invitingly towards one of these, near to the music, and Mary sat down, wondering if perhaps she should have worn a mask, like many of the females present.

A remarkably fast-moving waiter brought a bill of fare, took their order, moved off, collecting more orders on his way, and returned with their anchovies, scallops, neat's tongue and gherkins, and a blue and white stoneware bottle of Rhenish, asking Francis to be so good as to ring the small brass bell on the table when they were ready for their pigeon and ham pie, syllabub and Canaries.

'This is a pleasant way of spending an evening,' Francis observed, obviously enjoying the well cooked and served food. 'I suppose you must often come here?'

'I've never been here before,' she admitted. 'It's not easy for a female to come . . . I mean, she must take care not to . . .' She floundered, not sure how best to express her meaning.

'You mean, it depends who invites her? I suppose some of the Court gallants assume that a visit here leads, as a matter of course, to bed?'

'Something of the sort.'

He thoughtfully unrolled an anchovy and contemplated it before eating it, then enquired, 'And who is Sherford?'

'The Earl of Sherford,' she replied, keeping her eyes

on her plate and her voice expressionless.

'And what hopes did he entertain, which my presence at dinner was supposed to terminate?'

'Illusory ones,' she said soberly. 'He's pursued me, intermittently, for the past two years, and seems unable to accept a blank refusal. A dozen blank refusals, in fact!'

'What does he offer? An establishment, or a ring?'

'Usually the former, occasionally the latter, but in a somewhat ungracious manner, and only when he feels desperate,' Mary managed a wry smile, but did not look at Francis's face. 'Apparently his mother expects his wife to equal him in rank, at least!'

'He's persistent?'

'Less so, recently. I think he's at last accepting that I won't have him.'

'I suppose there are others?'

'From time to time.'

'And no one appeals to you?'

She shook her head. 'I wish I could go home, and be rid of them all!'

Francis laid down his knife, and, apparently absent-mindedly, tapped with the nail of his little finger on the table, following the rhythm which the musicians were playing, their bows sawing away at their various stringed instruments in the latest English imitation of the works of Monsieur Lully.

'But then,' he said, with apparent inconsequence, 'you would refuse for fear I should think it was only to escape from Whitehall. A convoluted problem! Is the supper to your liking?'

'Very much, thank you,' she replied, longing to cry out to him to ask her again, knowing that now she would take him, whatever he might think of her reasons. Was it really less than a year ago that she had thought she could not bear to be his wife, loving him so much, yet knowing that he had married her only out of concern for her reputation? Now, she knew only too well that it was better to be with him, loving, but unloved, than without him! Could she, dare she, say to him, straight out, that she had changed her mind?

Before she could come to any conclusion, there was a wild, discordant sound of piping of some sort from the far side of the band's platform, voices uplifted in raucous, unmelodious song, and female shrieks of either excitement or outrage. Half a dozen young men came prancing and capering out from among the shady bowers and into the area lit by the many candles about the musicians' platform. They were stark naked save for some precariously-girded garlands about their loins and on their heads, and they were bawling a cacophony of which only the occasional 'Hail, Bacchus!' was comprehensible. Their appearance was rendered singularly startling, as well as lewd, by the fact that they were all wearing elaborately-curled periwigs, and fashionable velvet patches adorned their flushed faces.

Francis watched them with the expression of a Fellow of the Royal Society witnessing some curious natural phenomenon, and said, 'What do you imagine they think they are?'

'The leader is Sir Charles Sedley,' Mary replied, sounding more than a trifle exasperated. 'He has a penchant for this kind of behaviour—and worse. The pity is, he's really an accomplished poet and wit, and could make much of himself if he were less of a fool. As it is, he spends most of his time drunk, and is forever in trouble with the magistrates!'

The bacchanals danced wildly round the platform, some of them staggering in a fashion more ungainly than graceful, and the musicians stopped playing to wait, with resigned expressions, until the rout had pranced away, back into the darkness, before resuming their playing, more or less where they had left off.

'I assume that the King isn't over-pleased with this behaviour,' Francis remarked, returning to his supper.

'He exiles one or other of the crew from Court when

they become too scandalous, but a well-turned set of verses, or a suitably contrite petition usually earns a remission. Lord Rochester was sent to the Tower last year for attempting an abduction, but offered to serve with the Fleet if the King would release him, and did so. Oddly enough, he distinguished himself by his courage and good sense on several occasions, as did some of the other rakehells!'

'There seems to be a need in some young men for excitement, preferably with an element of danger, and if they can't find it legitimately, they'll manufacture some kind of a substitute,' Francis said reflectively. 'Often, they turn out to be intelligent, influential men when once they've worked it out of their systems. They're rather like horses in that respect—fractious colts often make the best and most reliable working or riding horses, once they've matured. Take Archimedes. As virtuous an equine as you'd hope to meet in a month of Sundays these days, and he even chooses to trot when necessary! In fact, not a month ago, when Mr Reeve was called to a death-bed with little chance of arriving in time, Archimedes *broke into a gallop* for the first time in his life, and got him there with five minutes to spare!'

Having neatly turned the conversation to light-hearted matters likely to cheer Mary's obviously depressed spirits, he firmly kept it at that level and in those regions for the rest of the evening, which passed very pleasantly, and she was laughing and talking in an easier manner by the time they returned to Whitehall as they had come.

It was now dark on the river, save for the little horn lanterns carried by the wherries, and the easterly wind had not dropped in the least, so they had a wet passage downstream, but arrived safely at the Privy Stairs. There Francis swung Mary ashore as he had done before, and held her for a moment to steady her on the wet steps, looking down into her spray-wet face, which was framed in her hood and dimly illumined by the lamps at the end of the pier.

'Do you go to the Queen's Chapel in St James's in the morning?' he asked.

'No. The service is Roman there, so we're not required to attend, unless we wish. I go to the King's Chapel here.'

'Then may I hope to see you there?'

'You'll not go to St Martin Orgars, then?'

'It's not often I have a chance to hear Mattins with my Sovereign—unless you would rather I stayed away? I'd not wish to be the cause of any teasing from Killigrew and his like!'

'Please come,' Mary replied, sufficiently at ease, after the past hour or so, to make the request without hesitation.

He nodded, thanked her for her company, and silenced her protest that she should, rather, thank him, by dropping a light kiss on her parted lips. Then he stepped surefootedly out and down into the wherry and was rowed away down-river, back to the stairs above the Bridge, not far from where the baker in Pudding Lane was raking out his ovens before retiring wearily to his bed, thankful that the morrow was Sunday, and he would have only the dinners of church-goers to bake.

Mary watched the bobbing lantern go down the river until she could no longer see it, then turned and hastened along the short pier and into the Palace. She was shivering a little, for their passage on the river had given her a soaking, right through her cloak and her bodice.

She found Miss Bellamy and Miss Webster already abed, but sitting up in the candle-light, arguing in furious whispers about something. All she heard of it was an angry 'And I say he's nothing but a friend, and she's not a hypocrite!' from Miss Bellamy as she opened the door, for the young ladies broke off and turned their heads towards her, scowling and with their mouths open. They both closed their mouths and hastily composed their features to greet Mary. Miss Webster did so frostily, and Miss Bellamy a little too fulsomely.

'And what were you arguing about this time?' Mary enquired in a resigned tone. 'Who is no hypocrite?'

Miss Webster was apparently overcome by fatigue, for she promptly lay down and pulled her sheet over her head, but Miss Bellamy replied sheepishly, 'We were talking about your friend—the dark gentleman. Webster seems to think he's . . . Oh, she's got hold of some silly rumour about him, but I was just explaining that he's a friend of your family, from the country.'

'Huh!' came a jeering grunt of disbelief from under the bedclothes.

'Just because he's handsome and new you're jealous!' Miss Bellamy flared at the mound on the other bed. 'My family has any number of friends, and a good many of them are handsome and agreeable, so *I* don't find anything amazing about it! I suppose the poor, benighted place from which *you* come is populated by nothing but rough, monkey-faced farmers with clumsy boots and great red hands, so you can't imagine that anyone in the country may have elegant, gentlemanly acquaintances. As for hypocrisy—you're the hypocrite, for you sneer at Hook only because she's beautiful and good, and you're silly and plain!'

'I'm not!' said Miss Webster indignantly, sitting up and scowling.

'Yes, you are! Your eyes cross when you're sewing, and your nose is too long, and you've spots on your chin!' Miss Bellamy exclaimed triumphantly.

'Well, your teeth are crooked!' retaliated her dear friend petulantly. 'And I don't care if Hook has a lover, or a dozen of them, so long as she don't pretend to be so saintly and virtuous when she's no better than the rest of us!'

'Oh, for Heaven's sake be quiet!' said Mary wearily.

'My friendships are my own business, not yours! I don't pry into your affairs, and I'll thank you both to keep your noses out of mine. If you must know, Mr Hartwell is our neighbour at home, his sister is betrothed to my brother John, and they'll be married when he finishes his studies at Lincoln's Inn. If I may not sup with my good-brother without setting up a hue and cry of speculation and scandal, you must be very hard pressed to find anything to talk about! Why do you not occupy your minds with something more important?'

'What is there more important?' asked Miss Webster blankly.

'There's the progress of the war, or the plans for repairing St Paul's, or the iniquities of Lord Sandwich . . .' Mary said at random, hanging up her damp cloak and unpinning her hair. It was wet, so she brushed it briskly.

'Who cares about the dull old war, or ugly old Sandwich?' said Miss Webster crossly. 'I hope St Paul's falls down! Ugly old monstrosity! Mercy on us—you're all wet! What have you been doing?'

'Crossing the river in a wherry in a stiff easterly wind,' Mary replied curtly. 'Now I'm going to undress, dry myself, and go to sleep. I trust you will do the same, in the last respect!'

The two young ladies subsided, and Mary was able to finish her toilet and climb into bed in silence, pinching out her candle with mingled feelings of contentment that the evening had gone so well, and regret that . . . That what? That Francis had not renewed his proposal of marriage? She could hardly expect him to do so, after what she had said on that misty morning in the Forest! After all, nothing had changed, except her own opinion, and he had no way of knowing that. Probably he had accepted her refusal with relief, knowing that he had done his duty in offering, and need not concern himself any more about it, for he had given her the chance to marry him, and she had refused. He had even given her a slight opportunity to say she had changed her mind during supper, but she had not had the courage to take it, and that was nobody's fault but her own! She shed a few silent tears, and lay awake in the darkness, filled with vain regrets and listening to Miss Bellamy's gentle snoring.

At least she would see him in the morning, in Chapel! She wondered if she should keep a seat beside her for him, but if he were late, he would then have to draw attention to them both by coming forward to join her . . . unless she sat right at the back, and not in her usual place . . . If she did not keep him a place, he might think she preferred not to be seen with him. In any case, the only reason he had given for coming was to hear Mattins with the King, not to see her! She dithered, in an unaccustomed fashion, most unlike her usual decisiveness, and eventually decided to keep a seat for him, but at the back, near the door.

That settled, she allowed herself to think about the past evening, remembering the touch of his hands as he helped her in and out of the boat, and that kiss, so light, so casual, so much desired, yet so disappointing! If ever anything conveyed the lack of any passion or desire in his feelings for her, it was that. It had been no more than a cold peck, not even brotherly, for he would probably and quite properly have kissed Jem with more feeling! Oh, why did Life have to be so very difficult?

She slept eventually, and woke with a resigned acceptance that all she might hope for was a little more time in his company during and, with any luck, after Mattins, which must not be spoiled by longing for more while she had it, for it would be many months before she saw him again. She dressed with care, putting on a becoming blue gown, not too low cut, with a pretty lace cap pinned over her curls for the head-covering necessary for church. A cloak and hood to match her gown seemed a desirable addition, for the wind had increased during the night and was now both strong and gusty, still blowing from the east. Perhaps it was a good thing that it was almost a gale, or it might bring the Dutch or the French fleets across to attack the coastal towns and shipping.

After a hurried breakfast of bread and ale, she went to the Queen's lodging to help prepare her Majesty to go to her Chapel, noticing, but not particularly heeding, as she passed through an open courtyard, that the air seemed even more smoky than it usually was when London's canopy of sea-coal fumes was blown across Westminster. The sky had a curious coppery tinge to it, a phenomenon which she vaguely recalled seeing once before, when there was a bad fire in the City, but her mind was too busy to take note, calculating how much longer it would be before she saw Francis, and what chance there might be of an hour or two with him after Mattins.

At last, the Queen and her few Catholic ladies were despatched in a cumbersome coach to St James's Palace, and Mary was free to walk across to the King's Chapel, which was sandwiched awkwardly between the Great Hall and the Privy Kitchen. It was long, too narrow, and wrongly orientated, but gorgeously fitted with crimson velvet hangings, cushions and hassocks, an altar-covering of cloth-of-gold, and some fine Italian paintings of religious subjects, which Lord Albemarle had been heard to complain were Romish. The choir of men and boys were cassocked in crimson to match the hangings, and the orchestra of twenty-four violins wore uniforms of the same colour. They accompanied the choir, supplementing the great pair of organs, in anthems which attracted music-lovers from all over England to come and hear services which gave the impression that Puritanism had never existed. The body of the Chapel was usually well filled, for anyone might come to worship with the King, provided only that he was respectably dressed and behaved in a seemly fashion, so City tradesmen, farmers up from the country and foreign sightseers mingled with the lords and ladies in the high-backed pews, while the King and his attendants sat high above their heads in a side-gallery called the King's Closet.

Mary took a seat near the door, and spread her skirts over enough space for two, then tried to abstain from looking round every few moments to see if Francis had come. Surely he would see her here, where he must pass on his way in?

Gradually the pews filled, the orchestra and the organ played a voluntary, and there was a curious but discreet turning of heads as the King took his place above, but Francis did not come. Mary assumed that somehow she had missed seeing him, for she was sure that, having said he would come, he would do so, and it was not difficult to miss seeing even a tall man among so many, and with such high-backed pews. She would see him after the service.

The sermon was not over-long this morning—not quite the full hour—but just after it, there was a disturbance at the back of the King's Closet, and looking up, Mary caught sight of Mr Pepys from the Navy Office, waving his arms about and looking agitated. She saw the King turn in his seat, then leave it and go out with Mr Pepys. He came back presently, but his melancholy face looked more troubled than usual, and Mary, putting two and two together, assumed that there had been some urgent news from the Fleet, perhaps of another battle begun, but not yet concluded.

She stayed in her seat at the end of the service until almost everyone else had gone out, but there was no sign of Francis, so she went out herself, puzzled, hurt and disappointed, to stand on the steps outside, looking about her, still hoping to see him among the gossiping groups in the forecourt. It was several moments before she realised that the gossips were excited, and that something out of the ordinary had occurred, so she moved towards one group, curious to know what they were discussing, and collided with Sir Toby Ward.

'What a to-do!' he exclaimed. 'God knows, they've been warned often enough! The King wrote only last year to the Lord Mayor, to remind him that all new building in the City must be of brick, and that filling every space with wooden sheds and outhouses increases the risk, but they wouldn't take any notice, and see the result!'

'Why, what's happened?' asked Mary.

'There's a great fire in the City, running quite out of control. Didn't you see the King go out to hear Mr Pepys? He's been out and about all round it, and reports it quite the worst he's ever seen, and he's not one to exaggerate!'

'Whereabouts is it?' Mary asked, a cold finger of fear in her heart, for Francis was not a man to say he would come, and then not arrive, without good reason.

'It seems it started somewhere near the foot of the Bridge, not long after midnight, but it's spread all along Thames Street, and up and down Fish Street Hill. St Magnus is burned, and the waterwheels on the Bridge, so there's no water for the fire-hoses! The wind's carried it along the river-front all the way to the Steelyard and beyond, and up to St Lawrence Pountney and on to Canning Street . . .'

'Canning Street!' exclaimed Mary. 'Oh, but . . . Do you know St Martin Orgars?'

Sir Toby thought for a moment, then said 'Yes—it's a little church next St Michael, the Fishmongers' Church. It'll be right in the heart of the fire now . . .' He gave Mary a sudden stricken look. 'Lord! Do you know someone who lives there?'

Mary nodded. 'My friend—he dined with us yesterday—Francis Hartwell . . . He's staying in a house next door to St Martin Orgars church. He said he would come to the Chapel here for Mattins this morning, but he didn't come.'

Sir Toby, like his friend Harry Killigrew, was a kindly

and sensible man at heart, despite their racketing about with their cronies. He chewed one end of his fashionable moustache reflectively. 'Would you like me to go and make some enquiries about him?' he offered.

'I'd rather go myself,' Mary replied. 'Would you come with me? I can't stay here, waiting and worrying, or go into the City alone . . .'

The expressions which crossed Sir Toby's face revealed his thought processes as they changed from surprise to realisation, to comprehension, and then to sympathy. 'We'd best go in my coach as far as we may,' he said, making no mention of what he had just guessed. 'It's by the gate, waiting for me. I was going out, but nowhere important . . .'

He took Mary's arm and propelled her rapidly between the various groups of people, still standing about talking, through a succession of courts and arches to the wide courtyard before the Banqueting Hall, where the King was already gone in to dinner. They crossed over to the far corner, and emerged beside the main gatehouse of the Palace, where a number of coaches and riding-horses with their attendant grooms awaited their various owners. Sir Toby raised a hand to signal to the driver of one splendid vehicle, which jerked into motion and came over to them.

'M'new coach!' he said proudly. 'Velvet seats and cushions, leather-covered panels, silk curtains . . . all the best available! God send me able to pay for it!' He handed Mary into its luxurious interior with a satisfied smile, but quickly adopted a more serious expression when he saw how white and strained she looked.

'Canning Street!' he instructed his coachman. 'And hurry!'

CHAPTER TWELVE

MARY LEANED FORWARD, strained and tense, staring out of the window at the vast cloud of ochre, flame-tinged smoke over the City, and hardly seeing the crowds of people streaming towards them along the Strand, some on wagons, some pushing handcarts, some laden with great bundles, others carrying children or invalids on their backs, all smoke-grimed, afraid, desperate only to get as far away from the flames as they could.

Why was I such a fool? she thought. I could have been married to him all this time, but for my stupid pride! I love him, he was willing to wed me, so what did it really matter what his reasons were? And now it may be too late! Please, Dear Lord, if he's dead, let it have been suddenly, in his sleep! Let him not have suffered! Please, please, Lord, let me find him alive! Common sense told her that there was little chance that he could still be alive, for surely he would have come to Whitehall hours ago if he had escaped.

'Do you know when the fire reached St Martin Orgars?' she asked Sir Toby, her eyes still fixed on that great mass of smoke which covered the whole of the heavens.

'Little Pepys said that St Lawrence Pountney was burning as he left to come up-river, and Fish Street Hill was burnt almost up to Canning Street, but there were two arms of the fire between, and they were only then moving together, taking in St Martin and St Michael, so it would have been past ten o'clock, I should think. Your friend would have had time to get away . . . I mean, if he meant to come to Whitehall for Mattins, he'd not still have been abed at that hour! There must have been a vast amount of noise going on all about. The Lord Mayor's had the Trained Bands out, pulling down houses in the path of the fire, and there'll have been people screaming and shouting, apart from the noise of the fire itself . . .' He was trying to reassure her, but he realised that she was hardly able to take in what he was saying, for her whole mind and heart were a mile ahead, in the narrow lanes at the centre of the city.

The progress of the coach was painfully slow, for the streets were full of people fleeing from the fire, laden with whatever they had been able to save. It was bad enough in the Strand and Fleet Street, which were wide, but Ludgate's arch was a narrow bottle-neck, and the hill beyond only half the width of the streets outside the gate. There, it became so difficult for the coach to move against the tide of humanity, wagons and carts that Mary felt she would go mad long before they reached Canning Street.

As they crawled up Ludgate Hill, Sir Toby leaned out of the window and craned his neck to see the weather-vane on St Martin Ludgate tower. 'The wind's changed a point or two more southerly,' he said gloomily. 'That's going to bring it into the heart of the City!' He did not need to specify what he meant by *it*, for *it* was making its presence obtrusive in a miasma of yellow smoke and a silent rain of ashes.

At St Paul's, the coach stopped, for the horses were becoming well-nigh unmanageable, frightened by the smoke and the hordes of people, so Mary and Sir Toby left it there in the care of the coachman, and set out along Watling Street on foot.

By the time they reached St Antholin's in Budge Row, they could see the flames roaring up in a great wall above the intervening buildings, with one peak, the spire of St Lawrence Pountney, still piercing the smoke

pall above like a flaming sword. The noise was terri-
fying, the smoke suffocating, and the air so hot and dry
that Mary felt that her skin must be scorching from the
touch of it, and her lungs shrivelling within her. She
pulled her hood well forward to shield her face and
eyes, and hurried on as best she could, for the road
here was littered with carts and piles of furniture and
household chattels, and people were still throwing or
lowering things from windows, anxious to save what
they could before the fire reached them.

As she edged past each group of toilers, she called
out to them, asking if anyone had seen Francis Hartwell,
a tall man with dark hair, but few bothered to reply,
being too busy and panic-stricken. Those who did
mostly shook their heads or stared blankly at her, and
one man said, 'Half the men in London are tall and
dark! How do I know if I've seen him?' in an irritated
tone, and pushed past her with a great roll of feather-
bed.

Somehow she picked her way through the crowded
street, edging round or climbing over the obstacles when
she had to, Sir Toby close behind, swearing under his
breath and baring his teeth like a dog at anyone who
tried to stop Mary or himself. Eventually, they reached
St Swithun's church, Lamb's Conduit, and the inn
which stood beside it. Normally, at this hour on a
Sunday, it would have been busy serving dinner, but
today it was deserted, its door standing open on a silent,
empty taproom.

Here, suddenly, there were no more frantic figures
removing possessions, but only three men in breeches
and shirts, hauling with all their strength on a rope
which was tied to the bressemer of the third storey of a
tall building. They were obviously trying to pull it down,
to collapse the timber building in the path of the fire,
and perhaps slow its progress by creating a break in its
continuous supply of fuel. They kept glancing to their
left along Canning Street, where the fire was only three

buildings short of where they stood, and then hauling all the harder.

A great flake of fire floated slowly down, only a foot or so in front of Mary, making her stop and recoil, suddenly realising that she was in a dangerous place, for it would have set fire to her clothes if it had touched them. She had hardly recovered enough from the shock to look again at the three men, when the scene changed with dramatic suddenness.

The fire, having crept along at the back of the row of houses, erupted without warning from the one they were trying to demolish, bursting through the windows and the roof, flinging tiles and pieces of burning wreckage in all directions. The three men dropped the rope, which was already burning, and two of them ran towards Mary and Sir Toby, calling to them to go back.

The third man would have been with them, but he glanced back over his shoulder and tripped on a baulk of burning timber that had been flung out of the house in its explosion. He fell full length on the cobbles, hitting his head, and lay still for a moment, stunned, and then got on his hands and knees, struggling to rise, but still dazed from the blow on his head. He put out a hand towards his erstwhile companions, croaking hoarsely for help, and Mary saw his dirt-streaked face. It was Francis.

She started forward to help him, crying out his name, and the other two men stopped and turned, just in time to see another great fire-flake float down and settle on the left sleeve of Francis's shirt, which immediately burst into flames.

Mary pulled the strings of her cloak undone, swung it off her shoulders, still running forward, and flung it over Francis, beating at his arm with both hands through its thickness, knocking him down again, but smothering the flames before they could spread to the rest of his clothes, or to his hair. 'Oh, my dear love!' she exclaimed, clinging to him.

'Well done!' said Sir Toby, arriving beside them, brushing Mary aside and heaving Francis bodily to his feet. Seeing that he was still dazed, he hauled his right arm up round his own broad shoulders and half-carried, half-dragged him away towards comparative safety. One of the other men came to give a hand on his left side, and Francis fainted with the pain as his burnt arm was seized and put over this fellow's shoulders, but, between them, the man and Sir Toby hauled him away along the street, well past St Antholin's, to a safe distance, where they could stop and reorganise. Mary trotted beside them, protecting her hair from fire-flakes by pulling her heavy skirt up over her head, thankful that she had on a velvet petticoat which was thick enough to be both decent and reasonably fire-resistant. She could feel hot sparks speckling her arms with burns as the next house burst into flames and spat wreckage after them, and the lace fall on one of her sleeves caught fire and was gone in a spider's-web of grey ash before she even noticed.

Once they were clear of the fire for a while, Sir Toby propped Francis against the front of a shop, pulled off his own broad-brimmed hat, and beat out the smouldering ostrich-plumes against the cobbles, swearing in a mixture of French and very Low German. Francis, who was still dazed, but had recovered consciousness, managed a faint grin at him, and then looked at Mary, and croaked, 'Are you all right?'

'I think so,' she replied uncertainly, but did not ask him how he was, for there was blood trickling down the side of his face from a cut on his head where it had struck the roadway, and it was obvious from the way he was holding his left shoulder hunched and the arm away from his body under the cloak that he was in pain. The expression on his face was unreadable, hidden by streaks and patches of soot and his overnight growth of beard.

'We'd best get you back to Whitehall and some skilled

attention!' said Sir Toby, clapping his ruined hat back on his head and putting Francis's uninjured arm about his shoulders again. The other two men had gone to join a group of the Royal Guardsmen who were just starting to demolish a house further back along the street, but Sir Toby was a fine, strapping fellow, and seemed to have no difficulty in supporting Francis, who leaned against him gratefully as they made their halting way along Watling Street, stumbling past the goods which were still coming out of houses on either side, to be loaded into carts and handbarrows. The activity was even more frenzied, for the fire was approaching steadily, and people were crying out that the French, the Dutch, the Papists, the Fifth Monarchy men were firing the buildings and meant to burn the whole City.

'Can't be *all* of them!' commented Sir Toby in a puzzled tone. 'I mean—Papists and Fifth Monarchy—how could it be? Nonsense, I say! The fire's spreading itself. It don't need any more help than bone-dry wooden buildings, which the fools should never have put in their yards in the first place, and a strong wind, not to mention stores of flammables of every sort! Come on, Hartwell! Bear up! We're nearly at my coach. A fine fright you've given us this day, I can tell you!'

'Fright?' asked Francis vaguely, his attention concentrating on putting one foot before the other without falling over anything, for he was near to fainting again.

'Not turning up at the Chapel. Miss Hook thought you'd been burned in your bed when she heard the fire had taken St Martin Orgars!'

'I'm sorry.' Francis turned his head towards Mary on his left side with a great effort. 'Meant to come, but there were things needed doing here, and nobody doing them . . .'

'Should have left it to the Lord Mayor!' grumbled Sir Toby. 'Much use he is! Told Pepys a woman could piss it out, when he first came to see, and then went back to his bed! Couldn't even enforce the building laws! Said nobody would pay attention to him when he tried, and what's the result? Three months' drought, everything bone dry, someone sets his own house afire, and the whole City goes up in smoke! No need of Dutch or French or Papists—the worthy citizens are quite capable of managing it for themselves!'

'Oh, Sir Toby!' Mary gasped, for the smoke was still thick and choking. 'Not a tenth of it!'

'So far!' said Sir Toby grimly. 'But can you see anything short of a cloud-burst stopping it now? Only the Guard and the Trained Bands are doing anything, and that too little and too slow! They need gunpowder to blow up a few streets and make fire-breaks big enough to be of some use, not piddling little one-house gaps piled with wreckage for fuel. Unless the King takes it in hand himself, there'll be nothing achieved, and the whole City will go, you see if it don't!'

He was almost carrying Francis by now, so he gave up any pretence that the injured man was walking, stopped, and heaved him bodily over his shoulder, so that he hung, head down, like a sack of coals. He clapped his hat more firmly on his head and strode on towards St Paul's, praying that the coach was still waiting there, and the horses had not bolted for a more congenial place.

They found the coach on the far side of the Cathedral, for the driver had taken the horses as far from the noise and smoke as he could without actually disobeying orders, and he was still having difficulty with them, standing between their heads and holding them with all his strength, talking incessantly to them to soothe them while they rolled up the whites of their eyes, and stamped and shied in their desire to leave.

'Best get in quick!' he exclaimed when he saw Sir Toby. 'I can't hold 'em much longer!'

Sir Toby nodded, pulled open the door, and tipped Francis in with scant ceremony, climbing in after him to arrange him on one seat, then gave Mary a hand to

get in, slammed the door, and put his head out to call
'Whitehall!'

The coachman nodded, dodged round the horses and
scrambled on his box just in time, as the horses took
off down Ludgate Hill, unable to go as fast as they
wished because of the press of people, but sufficiently
frightened to trample a way through if they were not
held in hard. Fortunately, they calmed down gradually
once they realised that they were going away from the
frightening things behind them, and were quite reasonable by the time they reached Temple Bar.

'Perhaps we should go to my brother's lodging at
Lincoln's Inn,' said Mary dubiously. She was wedged
in a corner of the coach, with Francis lying against her,
and was trying to pillow his head on her shoulder and
protect his arm from being knocked, for he seemed to
be too dazed to do anything for himself.

'He needs a good doctor,' said Sir Toby judiciously.
'He'd be better in my lodging by the Cockpit. Dr
Gumble lodges next to me.'

'Dr Gumble? The Duke of Albemarle's physician?
But surely he's at sea with the Duke?'

'Not him! He wouldn't go—says he can't stand ships
and the sea—make him sick! He's a good doctor
—hardly ever loses a patient for anything less than
smallpox or plague, and he's even managed to save a
few from those! He'll be able to do something for
Hartwell's burns, and maybe save his arm. If not, he
can take if off—he's a skilled surgeon, as well as a
physician, and much experienced with amputations, for
he entered Albemarle's service during the Wars, when
he was plain General George Monck.'

Mary was too upset to take in much of this, for it
had not occurred to her that Francis might have been
so badly burned in those few seconds that his arm, or
even his life, could be in danger. She sat there with a
feeling of choking helplessness, unable to do anything
but hold him and pray that Dr Gumble might be about

when they reached Whitehall, and able to do something before it was too late.

'Could be wrong, of course,' Sir Toby offered, seeing that he had upset her. 'Haven't seen how the arm looks, with that cloak over it—or what's left of a cloak! You won't be wearing that again! Maybe you put the flames out in time. You were very quick.'

Mary looked dubiously at the charred remains of her cloak, and then realised that most of the burning was from the outside, so had been caused by sparks and fire-flakes falling on it after she had smothered Francis's burning shirt. She was afraid to lift the cloak, for she might see that the arm was as bad as she feared it might be.

The coach seemed to move so slowly. Would they never reach Whitehall? Biting her lips, she resolved she would not give way to tears until either Francis was safe, or . . . But she dared not think of the alternative.

Francis stirred, moving his head against her shoulder, murmuring something, but she could not make out what it was, for he had been in the smoke for hours, and his voice was almost gone. She stroked his hair, gently feeling about the great bump where he had struck his head. There was no softness there, nothing to suggest that there might be a fracture. His hair was singed in many places, and his skin felt cold and clammy, but a pulse beat strongly beside his closed eye, and she thought he might have fainted from the pain of his arm.

The coach reached the top of King Street and turned down towards the Palace, moving more quickly now, for the refugees were streaming straight on westwards, towards Kensington. Within minutes they reached the great gatehouse, and Sir Toby leaned out of the window to tell the coachman to go on to the Cockpit Lane, where it stopped. In a trice, Sir Toby was out of the coach, had commandeered the services of two porters, and, with their help, got Francis out of the vehicle and along the narrow lane to his lodging.

Mary followed, watching to see that the arm was not knocked, or his head, and could breathe freely again only when he was safely up the stairs, through the door, and gently deposited on Sir Toby's bed. Its owner dismissed the porters, sent his valet for Dr Gumble, and then poured two bumpers of brandy, handed one to Mary, and downed the other in a single gulp.

'There's a fine entertainment for a Sunday!' he said, ruefully inspecting the remains of his hat. 'I won't say it beats cockfighting, but it certainly adds a little excitement to a dull life! Shall I pull off his shoes and make him more comfortable?'

Mary nodded dumbly, sank on to a chair as her knees gave way, and sipped the brandy doubtfully, wondering what effect it would have on a stomach which had not had food since breakfast. It burned its way down, and then went to her head, making her feel remarkably detached and calm, although she doubted if she could stand up unaided, and she certainly dare not try to speak, for if she did, she would dissolve into tears.

Sir Toby took Francis's shoes off and put them neatly side by side by the door, then gently eased the cloak away from him, little by little, for it was well wrapped round him. It was so scorched and charred that it was in several separate pieces by the time he had it free, and he dropped them on the floor and kicked them under the bed while he stood contemplating the scorched wreck of Francis's black silk breeches and white lawn shirt, apparently wondering what to do next.

Before he had decided on anything, the valet returned, flinging open the door and announcing 'Dr Gumble' in a hushed and reverent tone. He then shrank back to afford plenty of room for the physician's entrance, giving the impression that he must be a bulky and imposing figure.

In fact, he was small and thin, clad in severe black, with no ribbons, no trimming at all, save a puritanical white linen collar. He had a long nose, which twitched as if he were seeking to smell out his patient, and he wore his own iron-grey hair, straight and lank, cut off sharply below the tips of his ears. He was followed by a boy with wide brown eyes, a freckled snub nose, and a broad grin.

'Burning!' exclaimed the doctor accusingly. 'Which is my patient?' He looked at Mary, frowning, and she was suddenly conscious that she must look thoroughly dishevelled and disreputable.

'On the bed,' she said.

Dr Gumble was there before she spoke, swivelling his eyes past Sir Toby and fixing them on Francis, who lay quite still, with his eyes closed.

'Well, then? Tell me what's to do, or am I supposed to guess?' he asked disagreeably.

'He was helping to fight the fire in the City,' Sir Toby volunteered, sounding a trifle nervous. 'He fell and hit his head on the cobbles, and his shirt-sleeve caught fire.'

The doctor sniffed, twitching his nose busily, and bent over Francis, peering into his eyes, then carefully felt round the handsome bump on his temple. The cut which crowned it had stopped bleeding, but the area was bruised black. 'Hmm,' said the doctor, and turned his attention to the arm.

'Scissors!'

The valet and Sir Toby were both jerked into movement in the same direction, colliding before a table under the window, where the valet succeeded in picking up a pair of scissors from beside the comb and hairbrush before his master could locate them. He carried them quickly to Dr Gumble, and presented them with a bow.

Dr Gumble delicately snipped at the remains of the shirt and pulled the rags away, holding them out between finger and thumb for the valet to take, and then lifted the injured arm by the wrist and peered at it from various angles.

'Not as bad as it might have been,' he announced, sounding disappointed. 'Someone smothered the flames with promptitude. You, Sir Toby?'

'No. Miss Hook.' Sir Toby gestured towards Mary.

Dr Gumble looked at her thoughtfully, then nodded and said, 'Good. Come here, miss, if you please.'

Mary went to stand beside him, finding that the effects of the brandy had suddenly disappeared. She forced herself to look at the burnt arm, compressing her lips and remaining calm and sensible by sheer will-power.

'You see,' he said conversationally, 'the burning is superficial. Very painful, of course, so the body is defending itself by increasing the occlusion of the faculties occasioned by the blow on the head. The best treatment will be to apply soothing and healing medicaments, then to exclude the ambient air, so that the loss of fluid and the irritation caused by the passage of air currents across the damaged surfaces may be minimised. Boy!'

The boy sprang to attention, fixed his eyes on Dr Gumble, his grin broadening nervously, and exclaimed, 'Yessir!'

'*Mel saponis, ceratum refigerans Galeni populeon, ungentium album, triapharmacon, axungia porcina,* and oil of roses, together with a mixing bowl, paddle, measures and spatulas. Also linen towels, and the black box from the third shelf on the left! You have that in mind?'

The boy repeated the list, running the whole together into one word, save for two breaks for the intake of breath, then departed at a smart trot. His master meanwhile began picking out odd fragments of cloth that still adhered to the burn, instructing Mary to take hold of Francis's wrist and hold his arm steady and clear of the surface of the bed. She managed this by kneeling beside the bed and propping her elbow on it, so that her arm was braced.

'A sensible man wears silk or fine lawn if he's to be burned or wounded,' the doctor remarked conversationally. 'If threads be trapped within the wound, they cause less harm than thicker stuffs, and are, on the whole, easy to remove.'

The boy returned before he had finished, bearing a loaded tray, which he held in a long-suffering manner, staring at the valet until that worthy realised what was wanted, and hastily cleared a table and brought it to the foot of the bed. The boy put down the tray and set out the doctor's requirements, muttering the list through to himself and ending with a sudden loud 'and the black box from the third shelf on the left!', as if to signal that all was ready.

Dr Gumble nodded, took off his coat and handed it to the valet, who reached it just in time to stop it falling on the floor, rolled up his shirt-sleeves with finicky precision, and then proceeded to measure out varying quantities from the pots which the boy had brought, tipping them into the bowl, and then beating them energetically with the paddle.

His salve mixed to his satisfaction, Dr Gumble spread a clean towel on the bed below the injured arm, which Mary was still holding, and applied the salve liberally all over the burned area with his spatula.

'Will he be all right?' Mary asked anxiously.

'He appears healthy. The burns are extensive, but fairly superficial. There is no depression about the contusion on the head. Personally, I am not in favour of bleeding, but may take a pint or so later, if he becomes fevered. The arm will take a time to heal, and more time to overcome the resulting stiffness. Good diet will be essential, and he must be discouraged from attempting to use the arm until new skin has formed over the burned areas. I assume you are not his wife?'

'No,' Mary replied, and then added, 'Not yet, that is,' for fear he should send her away as having no business to be there.

'Ah well, I expect he will be fit to go to the altar before Christmas, given a sensible régime and a careful nurse. I would advise you to pay some attention to your appearance before he recovers consciousness, or you may frighten him into an apoplexy!'

This last was spoken so drily, and so much in the same tone as everything else he had said, that Mary was quite shocked for a moment, until she realised that he was joking, but as soon as the arm had been swathed in bandages from the mysterious black box, and the cocooned arm placed on a soft pillow, she edged over to the ornately-framed mirror and looked at her reflection.

The sight was enough to frighten anyone into a fit, in her estimation. Her hair was liberally sprinkled with ash, and some of her curls were frizzled and broken off, her face was streaked with soot like a Morris-man's, and the broad lace fichu about her shoulders was fretted with scorch-edged holes. Further investigation showed that her gown had burnt holes of various sizes scattered all over it, the lace fall of one sleeve was missing altogether, save for some blackened fragments, and the other was burnt ragged. She looked like an effigy left over from last Gunpowder Treason Day.

Sir Toby, who was contemplating her with rueful humour, was in no better case. His flowing periwig was quite ruined, and his clothes as disreputable as her own. 'You'd better go change your gown before he wakes!' he said.

'Indeed,' said Dr Gumble, wiping his hands on a towel. 'There's nothing to be done for the moment. I expect the patient will rouse in an hour or so, and he should then be fed a little meat broth with sops. Further sops in a good red wine might follow that, in moderation. He should not be moved overmuch, but perhaps you, Sir Toby, or your man, might contrive to remove the rest of his clothing, wash him, and get him under covers, save for the injured arm. I'll leave the remains of the salve in this pot, so that you may anoint any small burns you may find about his person—or your

own, for that matter! Miss Hook has some on her arms,
I see. The unguent will soothe the soreness and promote
healing. I'll call later this evening, after supper, unless
the patient finds difficulty in focusing his eyes, in which
case, summon me at once.' With that, he went out,
followed by the boy with the once more laden tray,
leaving a pot of salve on the table.

'You'd best take this with you,' Sir Toby said, holding
it out to Mary. 'Or, better still, I'll scoop some into . . .
Where's that silver box—the little one for patches?'

The valet brought the box, and Sir Toby filled it with
salve and gave it to Mary, who remarked that it smelled
quite pleasant, due, no doubt, to the oil of roses. She
hesitated for a moment, looking down at Francis, who
seemed to have a better colour and be less clammy-
skinned. Then she hastened away, hoping she might
reach her own room without being seen by anyone of
any importance.

A thick murk hung over the Palace, despite the Dutch
wind, which was blowing as hard as ever, swirling the
smoke about in great eddies, and most of the scurrying
figures who seemed always to populate King's Street
and the courts opening from it were coughing, or
holding handkerchiefs over their mouths and noses. She
slipped through them, virtually unnoticed, apart from a
few surprised glances from folk in less of a hurry than
the rest.

She entered the Privy Garden, hoping to get across it
and enter the riverside wing by way of the small door
into Prince Rupert's apartments, which were untenanted
at present, and thence across the Stone Gallery. It
should be fairly empty at this time of the day, she
thought, and she might be able to cross it and reach the
Maids of Honour quarters almost unseen. Unfortunately she came face to face with the Queen and some
of her ladies strolling along the gravelled walks, and
was seen before she could escape. She drew back almost
into some bushes, and sank in a deep curtsy, hoping

they would pass by without taking much notice.

But, for some reason, the smoke was less troublesome here, and the little Queen's sharp black eyes had seen her. She stopped, exclaiming, 'Why, 'Ook! Where 'ave you been? We 'ave missed you, and you couldn't be found. What's 'appened to you? Ah, dear Lord! Your face is all sooty, and your gown is—is *burned* ! 'Ave you been to ze fire?'

'Yes,' Mary replied, feeling a complete fool as the other ladies stared at her, and Miss Webster tittered and made some remark about a sweep's doxy. 'I'm very sorry, Ma'am, to have been absent from my duty, but I have a friend who was to join me in the Chapel for Mattins, and he didn't come, and he was staying in a part of the City which was burned this morning, so I went to look for him . . .'

She stopped, biting her lips to stop any more pouring out, for there were raised eyebrows and more titters behind the Queen, and she could feel hysteria rising inside her.

'And did you find 'im?' asked Catherine anxiously, wringing her hands in concern, her soft heart sharing something of Mary's anxiety and distress.

'Yes, Ma'am. He was helping to fight the fire, but he was injured, so we brought him back with us. Sir Toby Ward went with me, and has him safe in his lodgings now.'

'But 'e is 'urt? 'E must 'ave a *medico*—a physi —phys—a doctor, no?'

'Dr Gumble has treated him,' Mary assured her. 'Fortunately, he was close at hand, in the Duke of Albermarle's lodging.'

Catherine looked at Mary's ruined gown, and said, 'I zink you 'ave been very close to ze fire yourself, dear 'Ook! You must go to my bath-'ouse and tell the woman that I say you may use it. You will feel better clean and in a fresh gown. Zen you may go back to your friend, for you will wish to nurse 'im. You are excused duty, and you must send to me for anyzing you need.'

Mary stammered her thanks, and stood back to allow the Queen and her attendants to go on their way. Among them was Lady Castlemaine, the King's chief mistress, whose appointment as a Lady in Waiting had so hurt poor Catherine when she was first married to the King. She was well-known to be a hard, grasping woman with a calculating mind, and Mary was astonished to hear her say carelessly, pausing beside her for a moment, 'My lodging is near Sir Toby's. Pray, use my closet and my kitchen as you please, and my maid will give you a bed there when you wish to sleep. You can't watch by your invalid all the time!' She had passed on with a not-unfriendly nod before Mary could find her voice to thank her.

After that, Mary succeeded in reaching her room without exciting more than a startled glance from the sentries on duty in the Stone Gallery, and summoned Eleanor, who was obviously relieved to see her, but uttered a small shriek when she had taken in her appearance. Half an hour in the Queen's bath-house, a little skilled trimming of the burnt ends of her hair, a change of linen and a fresh gown worked wonders, however, and Dr Gumble's salve eased the soreness of the burns on her hands and arms. Eleanor persuaded her to take either a belated dinner or an early supper of bread, cold beef, an apple and some spiced ale, and then she hurried back to Sir Toby's lodging, wondering if Francis were still unconscious, Eleanor following with a valise of toilet necessaries.

They encountered Harry Killigrew in the Cockpit Lane, and he stopped to tell Mary that he had arranged for a bed for Sir Toby in his own quarters, which were close by. 'I have to make Toby's excuses to the King now, before he—the King, that is—goes down to the City.'

'The King? But is it safe for him to go?' Mary exclaimed, horrified at the thought of Charles going anywhere near that inferno.

'He's going on the river, if we can get through the press of boats and lighters! All the folk along Thames Street and the little lanes behind are loading their possessions into whatever craft they can get, for the streets are well nigh impassable now, with people fleeing. The watermen are so busy that they didn't have time to save their own hall—it burned down this afternoon! The King will be safe enough, although when did His Majesty ever put his own safety before his duty?'

'Watermen's Hall!' exclaimed Mary. 'But isn't that near the Steelyard?'

'It was, but the Steelyard's gone too! The fire's past Dowgate, and burning up the hill into the heart of the City. Nothing Lord Mayor, Trained Bands or Guards can do will stop it, it seems. As fast as they pull down the houses, the fire overleaps them and great flakes of it fly on the wind to set light to a house two streets further on. Unless the wind changes, or drops, or it rains cats and dogs, most of the City will be lost! But I'm keeping you from Francis Hartwell!' He broke into his own account, noting the expression of sick horror on Mary's face. 'He's a brave man! I couldn't have done what he was doing—or what you did, for that matter! I'll come and see you both when I return from the City, and report what's happening. Perhaps it will be better news!'

'I pray it might be!' Mary replied, a little embarrassed by his words about what she had done. It appeared that Sir Toby had been talking, and she had no wish to be made out a heroine, when all she had done was to follow her instincts, without paying any heed to duty or courtesy, abandoning her attendance on the Queen without a word to anyone, and commandeering Sir Toby and his fine new coach . . . Her cheeks flamed at the recollection of her behaviour as she almost ran along Cockpit Lane and up the stairs to Sir Toby's room.

Three heads turned to look at her as she entered. The valet, who was packing a variety of things which his master might need, Sir Toby, sitting on the edge of the bed with a bowl in one hand and a spoon poised in the other, and Francis, pale but clean, freshly shaved, and sitting up, propped by pillows.

Mary gave a gasp of relief, and went to stand beside him, her heart in her eyes as she looked searchingly into his face, and he reached across with his uninjured arm to take her hand in a firm grip, obviously having no difficulty in focusing his eyes.

'I think we may call quittance in the matter of saving lives!' he said, with his lop-sided smile.

CHAPTER THIRTEEN

SIR TOBY SURRENDERED his bowl of meat broth and sops to Mary with some relief, and hurried away to attend the King and the Duke of York on their visit to the City, while Mary took over the spooning of food into Francis's mouth, which was easier for him than trying to balance the bowl and feed himself one-handed. It reminded her of a bird feeding its nestlings, for he opened his mouth obediently as each spoonful approached, and managed, little by little, to swallow the whole bowlful, followed by sops in wine, and then settled back on his pillows with a comfortable sigh.

'I thought my last hour had come when I fell! Did something hit me?' he asked, quite calmly.

'The building you were trying to pull down exploded, and you tripped over a great piece of timber, and hit your head on the cobbles.' Mary shuddered.

'I don't remember very much about it, only falling and finding it so hard to get up. Then there was the pain in my arm, and you suddenly appeared from nowhere and flung yourself on me—or flung your cloak. Both, I suppose. Ward says I'd have gone up in flames if you hadn't moved so quickly!'

'Don't talk about it,' Mary said, her teeth digging into her bottom lip. 'I don't want to remember.'

'You came to look for me?'

'I was worried when you didn't come to the Chapel Royal, for it's not like you not to come when you said you would, and then Sir Toby told me about the fire, and that St Martin Orgars was burned . . . I couldn't sit here, waiting for news . . . I had to go and try to find you. Were you caught in the fire when the house burned? The one where you were staying?'

'No. I'd been up for some hours, helping people save their goods and chattels. I saw it come up St Martin's Lane from Thames Street, and across the back from Fish Street, both at the same time, until the two arms met at St Martin's. I wonder where my mare is? I let her out, of course, long before the fire reached the stable, but she wasn't harnessed, and I couldn't hold her, for she was panic-stricken, poor thing, and ran off.'

Mary shook her head, and said hopefully that perhaps she had run home, and then sat silent for a long time, not looking at his face, but only at his hands, one bandaged and the other smeared with salve on a few small burns. It was that one which again reached out to take her own hand and hold it in a warm, comforting clasp.

They sat for a long time, Francis dozing, and occasionally opening his eyes to smile before nodding off again. Eleanor lit the candles as dusk fell, and sat close by the light, sewing. It was very quiet, but even here there was a smell of smoke, and a strange red glow filled the window.

The King arrived unannounced and informally, opening the door with his own hand and striding purposefully into the room, like any ordinary man, with Sir Toby and Harry Killigrew behind him. All three looked tired and had sooty streaks on their faces and linen, and Sir Toby had another singed periwig, to judge by the uneven frizzle across his brow.

'How are you?' asked the King, standing by the bed and looking down at Francis, his normally sardonic, melancholy face looking younger, despite his weariness, and more alert than usual. Francis attempted to get up, but was gently pushed back by one long-fingered white hand.

'Well, Sire, thanks to Sir Toby and Dr Gumble.'

'And Miss Hook?' Charles's pleasant voice sounded

relieved and a trifle amused. 'Surely she had something
to do with it, if what I hear is true?'

'But for her, I'd not be feeling anything, well or
otherwise!' Francis replied with a smile.

'I'm sensible of your efforts to slow the progress of
the fire.' Charles pulled up a chair and sat down by the
bed. 'Some of the Trained Bands men told me you
directed the pulling down of eight houses, to their
knowledge, giving others time to escape, as well as
helping some of the elderly and infirm to leave their
homes with at least some of their possessions. I'm
grateful to you!'

'I hope I'll not be required to pay for the rebuilding
of the houses I pulled down!' Francis said ruefully. 'I
believe that's the law on the matter—that he who
destroys a house must meet the cost of replacing it.'

'No fear of that!' said the King, laughing. 'I've called
a meeting of the Privy Council for early in the morning,
to give me powers to overturn such laws in this
emergency! We'll set up fire-posts to control and direct
the fire-fighting by the Trained Bands and the Guards,
with powers to do what's needed in the way of demoli-
tion, preventing looting, and anything else required. I've
been to Queenhithe this evening, and consulted with Sir
Thomas Browne who's taken control of the Trained
Bands, and has them pulling down buildings ahead of
the fire as fast as they can, but it's too slow—the fire is
on them before they have the work half-done, as you
will realise only too well! Mr Secretary Pepys of the
Navy Board has sent to Deptford for seamen from the
Navy, who know how to handle gunpowder, which will
demolish houses more effectively and quickly, and we
hope they'll make wide enough fire-breaks to stop the
fire, if the wind will allow. The Lord Mayor is . . .
well, a good businessman, no doubt! But what of you?
What may I do for you?'

Francis looked a little bemused by the question, but
replied slowly, as if feeling his way, 'If I may borrow

Sir Toby's room for a day or two, until Dr Gumble
thinks I may travel, and beg some food for my
sustenance, for I've no money on me . . . All I had
with me was burned in my lodging.'

'Of course,' said Sir Toby with a sweeping gesture.
'As long as you like, and I'll see you're fed!'

' . . . And perhaps you would lend me a coach to
go home after that? I came to London on horseback,
but my mare ran off in the confusion and is likely to be
halfway to Edinburgh by now, judging by the way she
ran! I don't think I could ride, in any case, with this.'
He lifted his injured arm slightly, and winced before he
could stop himself.

'With all my heart!' said the King. He paused, waiting,
and then added, 'Nothing more? You're a moderate
man in your requests, Mr Hartwell!'

'I'd be glad if Miss Hook might go with me,' Francis
said, glancing uneasily at the two Gentlemen in Waiting,
who carefully avoided showing any sign of suggestive
looks or knowing grins. 'She was not in good health
when I saw her yesterday, and today's events must have
been a great ordeal and shock.'

'Consider permission granted,' Charles replied kindly.
'I'm sure the Queen will make no objection when I
explain matters to her. Have you been fed?'

'Yes, thank you, Sire.'

'Which I have not, so I must go to supper before I
faint!' Charles rose, and gently touched the plaster
which covered the bump and cut on Francis's head. 'I
wish I could heal your hurts by touching you, but it
only works for the King's Evil, unfortunately, and that
you don't have!' He nodded a friendly Good Night to
Francis and Mary, and even included Eleanor, who was
standing in the background with her mouth open and
her sewing clutched to her bosom. Then he left, followed
by his companions.

Sir Toby turned in the doorway, and said, 'There's a
bell-pull by the fireplace—pull it if you need anything.

My valet will be listening for it.' He closed the door gently behind him.

Dr Gumble arrived a few minutes later, while Mary was still trying to find the words to thank Francis for obtaining what appeared to be indefinite leave for her. The Doctor talked learnedly, mainly in Latin, and apparently to himself, although Francis did make some comment to him, also in Latin, on what he was saying, at which he looked considerably taken aback, and did not reply. Then, in English, he told Francis to eat well, rest, preferably asleep, to refrain from exerting himself, move his fingers but not his arm, and avoid excitement (this with a stern glare at Mary), and expect another visit in the morning. He gave Mary a small pillbox containing half a dozen large pills, and told her to give the patient one—and only one—if he complained of overmuch pain, followed by another not sooner than four hours after.

'He's not given to complaining,' she said anxiously.

'Then use your common sense, miss!' the Doctor replied sharply, with an unspoken 'if you have any' left hanging, only too clearly, in the air. 'And four hours after that, *etcetera, etcetera.* But not just for the sake of giving them, mind! Better none at all than too many. A good beefsteak pudding would not come amiss, at present, for both of you! I shall have one sent in.' And with that, he left.

Beefsteak pudding, complete with oysters and a thick suet crust, seemed an unlikely diet for an injured man, but it arrived, hot and savoury, and Francis ate it with good appetite, insisting that Mary eat her own serving, turn and turn about, as she fed him. There was a third dish for Eleanor, a kindness which surprised and pleased her enormously.

Francis slept fairly well, but woke at some time in the small hours and seemed restless, so Eleanor called Mary, who had been persuaded to take advantage of Lady Castlemaine's kind offer and snatch a few hours' sleep, fully dressed, on a truckle bed in the lady's lodging. She gave Francis one of the pills, which he said drowsily was probably meant for a horse, and was suspiciously like one of Polycarp Wharton's panaceas, and fell asleep again. Mary waited a good half-hour, then, as he had not stirred, crept back to her truckle bed and slept until sunrise.

She found Francis awake, and looking surprisingly well, and he ate his breakfast, when it arrived, almost entirely unaided, apart from having his bread and meat cut up so that he could take a mouthful at a time. Dr Gumble came again and twitched his long nose close against the bandages, pronounced himself pleased, asked how the patient had slept, felt his forehead, said cupping was unnecessary, and advised Francis to get out of bed and sit in a chair. He stayed to supervise the getting out of bed, helping Francis to put on the handsome brocade nightgown which Sir Toby had left for his use, and watched as he walked to and fro across the room.

'No vertigo? Feelings of dizziness, in lay terms? Good! Get back into bed when you feel tired,' Dr Gumble admonished, and departed in his usual rapid fashion, as if he had a score of other patients to visit before dinner.

A succession of visitors came during the morning, arriving in ones and twos and not staying too long, but they could all talk of nothing but the fire. Lords Craven, Ashley, Belasyse, Manchester and Harrison were now organising the fire-fighting under the capable direction of the Duke of York, and posts had been set up, provisioned and allocated soldiers, civilian volunteers, constables and Justices of the Peace, called in from all over Middlesex. Sailors and shipwrights had arrived from Deptford and Woolwich, and were blowing up houses on the eastern side of the fire with gunpowder from the Tower, but still the flames were advancing, creeping against the wind down towards Billingsgate, and marching rapidly down-wind across Eastcheap and onwards to Lombard Street, Poultry and Cheapside, and the whole river-front was afire almost to Baynard's Castle.

The halls of half the City Companies had gone, and also the Post Office, but one of the postmasters had set up a temporary office at Cripplegate, and Mary wondered if she should try to send a letter to Woodham, for surely Jem would be worried about her brother, who had been expected home today. They must know in Woodham about the fire by now, for one of the visitors said that the smoke and glow in the sky had been visible fifty miles away during the night!

Mary was persuaded by Sir Toby and Francis to go to Hall for her dinner, while Sir Toby sat with Francis, for he had been sent back from the fire-fighting with a burnt hand and another scorched periwig. She went, resolved not to be gone above half an hour, and saw the boys of Westminster School, with the Dean of Westminster at their head, march past on their way to help fight the fire, all carrying leather buckets or firehooks. She heard later that their work was invaluable, and carried out with great courage and devotion.

She was a little early for dinner, so she went through the rain of ash to the Privy Stairs and looked down-river towards the City, but then wished she had not done so, for the sight was terrible. A great arc of fire stretched across the sky, reflected luridly in the water, with ochreous smoke filling all the heaven above. Even from here, she could hear the dreadful roar of the flames. The river was thronged with craft of every description, all the wherries loaded to the gunwales with as much and as many people as the watermen dared carry as they pulled them upstream, and even one of the King's yachts went by, its deck piled high with furniture and bundles and people. The wherries returned empty as fast as the watermen could row, to fetch more away as the fire advanced. Even as Mary watched, her hand pressed against her mouth in horror, another church tower flared up like a great torch, to join the others already burning or collapsed in ruins, and the flames took another leap along the river-front, and ran back, uphill, towards the vast bulk of St Paul's, towering over a lake of fire, black against the gold and red, like a great beast waiting to be struck down.

She could bear no more, but ran, sobbing, back into the Palace, colliding with Will Chiffinch, the King's Page of the Backstairs. He steadied her and wiped her eyes with a clean handkerchief, which he kept for the purpose, for he had a great deal to do with the admission of young women—actresses and such—to the Palace, and often had a tearful female to comfort.

'That's better,' he said encouragingly, brushing ash off her shoulders. 'You can't weep the fire out, unfortunately!' guessing that the reason for these particular tears was not the usual one. 'Go and get your dinner, and then you could go into the Chapel and pray, if you want to help. It's been left open for anyone who wants it.'

Mary thanked him, blinking and biting her lips, and was surprised that so cynical a man, who knew the worst about everyone at Whitehall, should be so kind, and should advise her to pray—she would have thought that was something which rarely entered his mind! She managed to get her dinner and eat it without being engaged in conversation with anyone, for many of the gentlemen had gone to the fire, either to help or as sightseers, leaving the Hall half empty, and afterwards she did, indeed, go to the Chapel to pray, and found a surprising number of others there, doing the same. After a few minutes, she hurried away to go back to Cockpit Lane, and was startled to encounter her father, accompanied by one of his grooms leading two horses, standing in King Street and looking a little at a loss.

He greeted her with a blunt, 'Have you seen aught of Francis? He was staying in the City, but the street where he was lodging was burnt yesterday, it seems, and his horse came home by itself in the night. Jem is sick with worry!'

'He's well and safe,' Mary said quickly. 'I'm going to him now.' Then, to the groom, 'Mark, if you take the horses through there, you'll find stabling for them. Tell the ostlers I sent you, and they'll tell you where you can get food for yourself, and fodder for the horses. Then stay with them, and we'll send for you when you're wanted.'

Mark went off, talking soothingly to the horses, which were not used to the noise and bustle of White-hall, nor to the smoke which filled the air. Neither was Sir Charles. He glanced about him, keeping a firm hand on the pocket which contained his purse, and looked quite bewildered as he walked along with Mary. She told him what had happened the previous day, making very little of her own part in it, and assured him that Dr Gumble had attended to Francis's hurts, and was well pleased with him.

'Gumble?' Sir Charles muttered. 'Crop-eared rogue of George Monck's, ain't he?'

'Physician to the Duke of Albemarle,' Mary corrected, 'and has both his ears firmly affixed to his head!' Her prim expression was denied by the sparkle in her eyes, for her spirits had risen amazingly with the arrival of her father. 'I was wondering if I should try to send a letter to you, but the Post Office is burned down, and I've been so busy attending to Francis . . . I think I may be able to bring him home quite soon.'

They found Francis and Sir Toby playing chess, and the former got to his feet to greet Sir Charles with no trouble at all. Apart from his bandaged arm and the plaster on his forehead, he seemed quite well again, and was delighted to hear that his mare had made her own way home without injury.

Sir Toby, murmuring something about billeting the troops, went off to arrange a lodging and some dinner for Sir Charles, who sat talking to Francis all afternoon,

sending Mary off to walk in the Park with Eleanor,
who confessed to an inordinate desire to feed the
colourful residents in Birdcage Walk, which Mary was
happy to allow her to do, buying a paper poke of the
necessary assortment of seeds and pieces of apple from
the old soldier who had the licence to provide that
service. Everywhere was covered with ashes and bits of
half-burnt paper and cloth, and the smoke was as thick
as a fog, so there was little pleasure in being out, and
no fresh air to be had. Even the birds sat silent, with
ruffled feathers, looking thoroughly out of humour.

Dr Gumble called again in the evening, and, after
talking to Sir Charles for a few minutes, said that
Francis might be taken home the next day, provided
that he travelled in a coach, and promised to rest the
arm and not allow any country sawbones to interfere
with the bandages, or so much as look at it from a
distance, for at least two weeks.

'Best leave it in peace and undisturbed,' he said. 'By
then, provided there are no raw areas or signs of
suppuration when the dressing is removed, a gentle
washing with plantain water may be given, to remove
the residue of the salve and any dead matter. Don't try
to hurry the process by scrubbing, mind, or you'll
damage the new skin!'

This was the plainest speech he had made so far in
their acquaintance, so Mary was emboldened to ask
what to do about the plaster on Francis's forehead.
'Oh, that!' said the Doctor, and ripped it off with one
quick movement, fetching a yelp of mingled surprise
and pain from his patient, for a small tuft of his hair
came away with it.

Supper was served to the Hooks and Francis in the
sick-room, while Eleanor was given leave to go back to
her usual occupations. Shortly after the meal, Mary was
amazed when Lord Sherford walked into the room,
showing the same signs of having been fire-fighting as
many of the other courtiers.

He looked tired, and sucked a burned finger from time to time as he made a short speech, which began abruptly, 'I've just come to say that I bear nobody here any ill-will. I've been much impressed by what I've heard of the exploits of—of certain people in the City yesterday, and know something of what courage and—er—affection must have been involved, having seen the fire for myself—from close quarters, that is! Also, I'm happy to say' (this with a singularly gloomy expression), 'that my dear mother has arranged a most advantageous marriage for me, to an heiress.' He stopped, having apparently said all that he came to say, and not knowing quite what to do next.

'I hope she's truly beautiful, and that you'll both be very happy,' Mary said kindly.

He looked doubtful, and muttered 'Hobson's choice' (being a Cambridge man), but accepted the good wishes with a bow. Francis offered his hand, and Lord Sherford shook it gingerly, as if he feared it might fall off. Sir Charles, who did not know him from Adam, offered him formal felicitations, and he left as abruptly as he had arrived, saying inconsequentially, 'The Royal Exchange is burned down,' as he went out.

'What an odd fellow!' said Sir Charles. 'Ain't he right in the head?'

'A disappointed suitor, I fear,' Francis replied, giving Mary one of his inscrutable looks. 'Any man in love is not quite right in the head, and entitled to be so, the female of the species being as she is!'

Sir Charles looked from Francis to Mary and back again, and blew his nose loudly on a large pocket-handkerchief, then said he had better go out in the morning and buy Francis some clothes, as he could hardly, in all decency, travel home in a borrowed nightgown. He then asserted a little parental authority and sent Mary to spend the whole night in her own bed, saying that he was quite capable of looking after an invalid for one night, having cultivated the art of

being one himself for long enough, and, besides, it was
not proper for a young lady to sit by a man's bed all
night, if there was anyone else available. There was no
particular inflection in his voice, but the last phrase
made Mary wonder if he knew that Francis had nursed
her through the plague.

She spent the rest of the evening with Eleanor, packing
her trunk, finding a certain withered carrot, ornamented
with a scrap of blue ribbon, in the bottom of it, and
refusing for sentimental reasons to let Eleanor throw it
out. Miss Bellamy, who seemed to regard her with some
awe, offered to see the trunk safely despatched by carter
during the next day. Both she and Mary went to bed
quite early, and lay in silence, unable to tear their eyes
from the window, which looked across the great curve
in the course of the Thames towards the City, and
glowed with lurid red light. From time to time,
explosions rattled the window-frames, which frightened
Miss Bellamy very much until Mary told her it was
only the sailors blowing up buildings to make fire-
breaks.

'Why don't they just pull them down quietly?' she
asked tearfully.

'Because the wreckage falls across the street, and the
fire uses it to reach the other side,' Mary told her,
having gleaned that information from one of Francis's
visitors. 'With gunpowder, they can make it fold up
within itself, and keep the street clear.'

Miss Webster came in very late, a little drunk and
very maudlin, convinced that Whitehall itself would be
burned before the fire was put out, but she subsided
into injured silence after Miss Bellamy rose up and
slapped her face, calling her a hysterical ninny, and
Mary managed to sleep quite well after that.

In the morning she took leave of the Queen, who
kissed her and gave her a sapphire brooch, saying that
it matched her beautiful eyes. Sir Charles went out into
Westminster and obtained a handsome dark blue camlet

suit for Francis, together with body linen and a shirt, and managed to get him into them without jarring his arm, assisted by Sir Toby's valet, who complained that the suit was not a perfect fit, and had to be dissuaded from setting to work with scissors and thread to alter it, on the grounds that there was no time for such niceties, and Francis's own valet would be offended.

Various gentlemen, who considered Francis a hero after hearing Sir Toby's slightly imaginative account of his exploits, rallied round with cushions, a huge hamper of food for the journey and wine to go with it, offers of more shirts, periwigs, a cloak in case the warm weather suddenly turned cold, and a number of useless articles, but all meant very kindly. The King sent a message of good wishes, but was himself in the City, riding about from one party of fire-fighters to another, with a bag of gold guineas tied to his saddle, rewarding their efforts on the spot, and occasionally lending a hand himself, passing buckets of water, shifting timbers, and being alternately scorched and soaked in the process.

One of the more comfortable royal coaches was backed up Cockpit Lane with considerable difficulty, and stuck fast between two doorsteps which happened to be opposite one another in the narrowest part of the lane. It was freed after some time by the simple expedient of levering up one of the doorsteps, and replacing it in a wobbly fashion after the coach had drawn forward a couple of feet.

What with one thing and another, it was past noon before all was ready, and then Dr Gumble appeared and insisted that they all eat a good dinner before they left, so the coach eventually departed at one o'clock, carrying Mary, Francis and Eleanor, and accompanied by Sir Charles and his groom on horseback, with Mary's two grooms and two armed troopers of the King's Horse Guard for escort.

It was impossible to take the shortest route, for that lay through the City, so the small party was forced to join one of the rivers of refugees flowing along the roads out of London, intending to work their way round the northern outskirts, but they were trapped in the crowds at St Giles-in-the-Fields, and had to go, willy-nilly, up the road to Hampstead, crawling along in the moving roadblock of carts, wagons, barrows and people.

It was a little past eight o'clock when they eventually broke clear on Hampstead Heath, where many of the refugees spread out over the open common to camp for the night. Sir Charles suggested that they might take the opportunity to stop and investigate the contents of the hamper, which proved to contain a more than adequate supper for all of them. They found a space where the coach could pull off the road, and all settled on the grass to eat. Although it was long past sunset, there was plenty of light, a red, sinister glow, from the burning City spread out in a great panorama before them, with the black bulk of St Paul's silhouetted against it, like a great whale stranded on a burning beach.

They all turned their backs on the fearful sight while they ate, feeling that they could not bear to look—all but the coachman, that is. He stared at it in horrified fascination, and it was he who suddenly made them all turn to look, for he uttered a strangled cry, leapt to his feet, and pointed speechlessly.

The others were just in time to see the wind-carried flames run from end to end of the six-hundred-feet-long roof of the Cathedral, and, as they watched, mesmerised, the great windows all along its sides suddenly flared with brilliant light as the lead melted and rained down inside, setting fire to everything within. The windows burst out, spewing flame, and a great fountain of fire jetted out of the top of the tower, hundreds of feet into the air.

'That is the most aweful sight I have ever seen,' said Sir Charles soberly, 'and I hope I never live to see such another!'

Mary sobbed and tried not to cry, but Francis put his good arm about her and drew her head against his shoulder, and she shed a few quiet tears into the blue camlet, glad of the comfort of his warm body. He seemed to be breathing rather quickly, but replied that he felt very well when she asked him how he did.

After eating and resting the horses, the group went on, and reached Woodham, after a tedious passage across much the same route which Mary had taken—was it only fifteen months before?—some time after midnight. They first delivered Francis to a thankful Jem, who stoically refrained from weeping over him, and an ecstatic Oliver, who wound himself to and fro round his man's ankles until he seemed a continuous fetter of spotted fur, and well-nigh tripped him over.

From Canons Grange they went on to Pinnacles, where Sir Charles had already offered the coachman and guards lodging for what remained of the night, and until they and their horses were rested enough to return to Whitehall.

Lady Hook had gone to bed, worn out with watching the glow in the south-west which lit most of the sky, and the great yellow-grey cloud which obscured the moon, but she came running downstairs in her hastily-donned nightgown, her hair, still almost as golden as Mary's, loose about her shoulders, and embraced her daughter fondly, asking for news of Francis at the same time.

Mary promptly burst into tears, her stoutly-maintained pretence of calm giving way at last, and caused her mother considerable alarm until Sir Charles turned from giving orders for the reception of his guests to assure her that Francis was safely home and not much injured, and that Mary was only worn down by the fears and strains of the past few days.

With that reassurance, Lady Hook took Mary to the stillroom, extracted a disjointed account of what had happened to her, carefully refraining from any expression of horror or alarm, although she certainly felt both, especially when Mary described the scene in Canning Street and the rain of fire-flakes which had scorched her clothes and hair. The telling of it was interrupted by fresh outbreaks of sobbing, for Mary's control had snapped now it was all over, but she had to pour it out, as if to rid herself of her fears. Eventually she stopped talking and simply sobbed, so Lady Hook dosed her with valerian to quiet her hysteria, and poppy-syrup for a soporific, and put her to bed, where she presently lay still and quiet, deeply asleep.

She slept all through the day and the next night, so that her mother wondered if perhaps a half-measure of poppy-syrup had been too much, but the sleep seemed quite natural. She dozed through another day, then woke at the usual time the following morning, and went down to household prayers quite calmly, if a little pale and shaken, and assured her parents, with a wan smile, that she was much better.

This was, up to a point, true, but she still had fits of trembling, and the inclination at times to find herself near to tears, all of which she kept to herself. Meanwhile, she busied herself with the usual occupations about the house and garden.

Jem had come twice to ask after her while she was asleep, and came again in the afternoon of her coming downstairs, finding her sitting with her sewing in the garden, for the weather continued fine and the wind had at last dropped away to a breath of a breeze. She kissed her, and asked anxiously if she felt better, and looked greatly relieved to hear that she was.

'Francis seems almost himself again now,' she said, sinking on to the bench beside Mary. 'He was restless early in the night—a bad dream, I think—but he slept well after that, and is up and about today, and using his left hand, although I wish he would not! He—He told me what happened—at least, all your part in it—but it's still not clear to me what exactly he was doing so near the fire.'

'He was trying to pull down a house,' Mary said briefly. 'To make a fire-break,' she added, almost as an afterthought.

Jem looked puzzled. 'But surely, to do that he would need to be some way ahead of the fire . . .?'

Mary swallowed a sigh, and explained, 'The fire crept along behind the houses, and burst out suddenly in the one he . . .' She shuddered, and said no more, and Jem was silent for a while.

Then, very diffidently, she tried another subject. 'I wonder, Mary . . . Have you ever considered . . . Do you ever think that you and Francis . . . Perhaps I speak out of turn, but it seems that you and he would . . .' Then, in a rush, 'Would it not be pleasant if you were married?'

She looked so apprehensive that Mary, who could hardly think what to reply, managed to ask, 'What made you think of that?'

Jem gave a little shrug. 'He speaks so warmly of you! I've never heard him speak so of any female before —you know how reserved he is. I thought that . . . Perhaps you don't care for the idea. I'm sorry.'

'Have you said anything to him about it?' Mary heard herself ask, and wondered if the sound of her heart beating were audible to Jem, for it seemed to her to be very loud, and it was difficult to breathe properly.

'I mentioned it. Just had he thought of it . . .' Jem paused, looking perplexed.

'What did he say?' Mary asked, almost choking, yet sounding amazingly cool and collected.

'He said, "I think about it from time to time", in a rather crisp voice, and went out to talk to Mr Palmer about hedges and ditches!' Jem gave a rueful smile. 'Perhaps I'm just imagining something is so because I wish it might be! I'd so dearly like to see Francis happy, and I'd love to have you for my sister both ways—I mean, by my own marriage and by yours. I'm sorry if

I've embarrassed you.'

'I'm very touched that you should wish it,' Mary replied truthfully. 'I know how much your brother means to you. When do you and John plan to be married?'

'We thought perhaps at Christmas. He stayed at Lincoln's Inn all through the summer to work at his studies, and plans to be through the greater part of them by December. Mr Reeve suggests Christmas Day itself, for he thinks it the best day in the year for a wedding!'

Having successfully diverted Jem from talk about Francis and herself, Mary was content to listen to Jem's plans and offer advice about her wedding gown and trousseau for an hour or so, then returned to the house to give her some refreshment before she went home.

She was hardly out of sight when Polycarp Wharton arrived, with a basketful of cinnamon-flavoured russet apples and some ripe quinces, all agog to see Mary safe and well.

'And you actually saw the fire close to, with your own eyes!' he marvelled. 'I considered riding to London, but thought perhaps they would hardly welcome sight-seers. Besides, my wife wouldn't like it!'

It took Mary a few seconds to pin down what it was about him that had changed, but her father commented, 'You'll notice that he's dropped that peculiar mode of speech, the Lord be praised!'

'Yes,' Polycarp said, unruffled. 'Philadelphia thought it effacted—affected, I mean, and it made her—er —laugh.' He looked bemused, and was obviously already much under the thumb of his new bride.

No sooner had he gone than Mr Reeve arrived on the redoubtable Archimedes, who, to judge from his expression and general demeanour, might well have been seeking to become the first canonised equine, had Mr Reeve been of the Romish persuasion. However, the Rector remained firmly Anglican, and pronounced a good English benediction and a prayer of thanksgiving over Mary with heartfelt fervour, and announced that a day of fasting and penitence had been decreed for the tenth of October, then accepted an invitation to supper with his usual grateful alacrity.

If Mary was abstracted and silent during supper, her parents assumed she was still not feeling quite well, and did not worry her, but she was going over and over what Jem had said, and pondering Francis's reply.

She was still thinking about it in the morning, and went away by herself as soon as she could to the pool in the Forest, where she sat on the log, staring unseeingly at the dark water and thinking about Francis. She wanted very much to go to see him, yet was afraid that, if she did, she would make a complete fool of herself by running into his arms.

The sound of a step on the path by which she had come broke into her reverie, and she looked up to see Francis himself emerge from the trees. Startled, she stood up and took two steps towards him, then stopped, petrified.

He came on, put both hands on her shoulders, looking down into her face, and said, 'How are you?'

She opened her lips, staring up at him, but could only say, 'Your arm!'

'Is healing well, and I can use it, if I'm careful. Jem thought you looked a little unwell.'

'I was tired, I suppose, and upset.' She moved slightly, looking away, and his hands fell to his sides. She sank down on the log again, and, after a momentary hesitation, he sat beside her, and they both stared at the pool.

'The fire is out,' he said at length.

'Out?' Mary looked at him, then looked away again, and said, 'Is anything left?'

'Not much within the walls. It burned from a street or two short of the Tower across to the walls of the Temple, and from the river almost to Smithfield. There are still cellars and warehouses burning, but it's no longer moving on.'

'Were—Were many people lost?'

'Amazingly, only a dozen, it's said. Thank God!'

'Indeed, thank God!' Mary echoed, and they fell silent again.

Francis crossed one leg over the other, then uncrossed it again, and said, 'Last time we sat here, I omitted to say something which perhaps I should have said.'

'What was that?' Mary asked, feeling very wretched at the awkwardness between them.

'That I love you.'

It took a full second to penetrate her misery, and then she turned to look at him incredulously. '*What* did you say?'

'That I'm in love with you.' He looked amazingly uncertain and anxious.

A smile broke over her face, like the sun emerging from behind a cloud. 'Oh, why did you not say so?' she breathed.

'Would it have made a difference?'

'All the difference in the world!'

'I often think I must be a fool, in some ways,' he said reflectively, then proved that in other respects he was nothing of the kind by taking her in his arms and kissing her, and there was no opportunity for either to say anything for some time, although Mary did find room to wonder why she had ever thought him cold, for he was showing himself to be quite otherwise.

At last, he removed his lips from hers for the distance of an inch or so, and said, 'I take it we've achieved parity in the matter of nursing and saving lives?'

Mary nodded. 'Mr Reeve thinks Christmas Day a good day for a wedding,' she said inconsequentially.

Francis considered. 'Wouldn't Michaelmas be better?'

'But it's only three weeks away, and the banns take three weeks!'

'Oh, well—Christmas Day, then, and if you tell me that it might have been *last* Christmas if I'd not been so remiss, I'll set Oliver on you!'

Mary smilingly opened her lips to say something, but was effectively silenced by another long, heart-stirring kiss, and the only words spoken during the next half-hour were a brief and breathless 'But it does seem an *unconscionable* long time to Christmas!' from Francis between one kiss and the next.

A TALE OF ILLICIT LOVE

'Defy the Eagle' is a stirring romance set in
Roman Britain at the time of Boadicea's rebellion.
Caddaric is an Iceni warrior loyal to his Queen. The lovely
Jilana is a daughter of Rome and his sworn enemy.
Will their passion survive the hatred of war,
or is the cost too great?
A powerful new novel from Lynn Bartlett.

WORLDWIDE

Price: £3.50   Available: August 1987

Available from Boots, Martins, John Menzies, W.H. Smith,
Woolworths and other paperback stockists.

BETTY NEELS' 75th ROMANCE

"OFF WITH THE OLD LOVE"

Betty Neels has been delighting readers for the last 17 years with her romances. This 75th anniversary title is our tribute to a highly successful and outstandingly popular author.

'Off with the Old Love' is a love triangle set amongst the rigours of hospital life, something Betty Neels knows all about, as a former staff nurse. Undoubtedly a romance to touch any woman's heart.

Mills & Boon

Price: £1.50   Available: July 1987

Available from Boots, Martins, John Menzies, W. H. Smith, Woolworths, and other paperback stockists.

AS A MASQUERADE SUBSCRIBER YOU'LL ENJOY ...

★ **FOUR WONDERFUL NEW NOVELS** – every two months, reserved at the printers and delivered direct to your door by Reader Service.

★ **NO COMMITMENT** – you are under no obligation and may cancel your subscription at any time.

★ **FREE POSTAGE AND PACKING** – unlike many other book clubs we pay all the extras.

★ **FREE REGULAR NEWSLETTER** – packed with exciting competitions, horoscopes, recipes and handicrafts... plus information on some of the top romance authors.

★ **SPECIAL OFFERS** – specially selected books and offers, exclusively for Reader Service subscribers.

★ **HELPFUL, FRIENDLY SERVICE** – from the ladies at Reader Service. You can call us any time on 01-684 2141.

With personal service like this, and wonderful stories like the one you've just read, is it any wonder that thousands of women rely on Masquerade to bring them the very best in Historical Romance.

This beautiful heart shaped, diamond zirconia necklace is yours absolutely FREE!

Just fill in the coupon today and post to:
READER SERVICE, FREEPOST, PO BOX 236, CROYDON, SURREY CR9 9EL.

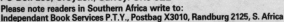

FREE BOOKS CERTIFICATE

**To: Reader Service, FREEPOST,
PO Box 236, Croydon, Surrey. CR9 9EL**
Please note readers in Southern Africa write to:
Independant Book Services P.T.Y., Postbag X3010, Randburg 2125, S. Africa

Please send me, free and without obligation, two Masquerade Historical Romances together with my free diamond zirconia necklace and reserve a Reader Service Subscription for me. If I decide to subscribe I shall receive four new Masquerade Historical Romances every two months for £6.00 post and packing free. If I decide not to subscribe, I shall write to you within 10 days. The free books and necklace are mine to keep in any case. I understand that I may cancel or suspend my subscription at any time simply by writing to you. I am over 18 years of age. Please write in BLOCK CAPITALS

Name _____

Address _____

_____ Postcode _____

Signature _____

Please don't forget to include your postcode.

SEND NO MONEY NOW – TAKE NO RISKS

The right is reserved to refuse an application and change the terms of this offer. Offer expires September 30th 1987 and is limited to one per household. You may be mailed with other offers as a result of this application.
Offer applies in UK and Eire only. Overseas send for details.

EP36M